Awakening Arorus

Book One: The Clan Destayy Chronicles

K. M. Lapointe

Awakening Arorus
Book One Of The Clan Destayy Chronicles

Tellwell Talent
www.tellwell.ca

ISBN
978-1-77370-851-5 (Hardcover)
978-1-77370-850-8 (Paperback)
978-1-77370-852-2 (eBook)

Table of Contents

Acknowledgements vii

Prologue 1

Chapter One 3

Chapter Two 11

Chapter Three 21

Chapter Four 31

Chapter Five 47

Chapter Six 61

Chapter Seven 71

Chapter Eight 87

Chapter Nine 97

Chapter Ten 115

Chapter Eleven 127

Chapter Twelve 135

Chapter Thirteen 147

Chapter Fourteen 157

Chapter Fifteen 167

Chapter Sixteen 175

Chapter Seventeen 185
Chapter Eighteen 197
Chapter Nineteen 209
Chapter Twenty 223
Chapter Twenty-One 233
Chapter Twenty-Two 243
Chapter Twenty-Three 253
Chapter Twenty-Four 265
Chapter Twenty-Five. 273
Chapter Twenty-Six. 283
Epilogue 293

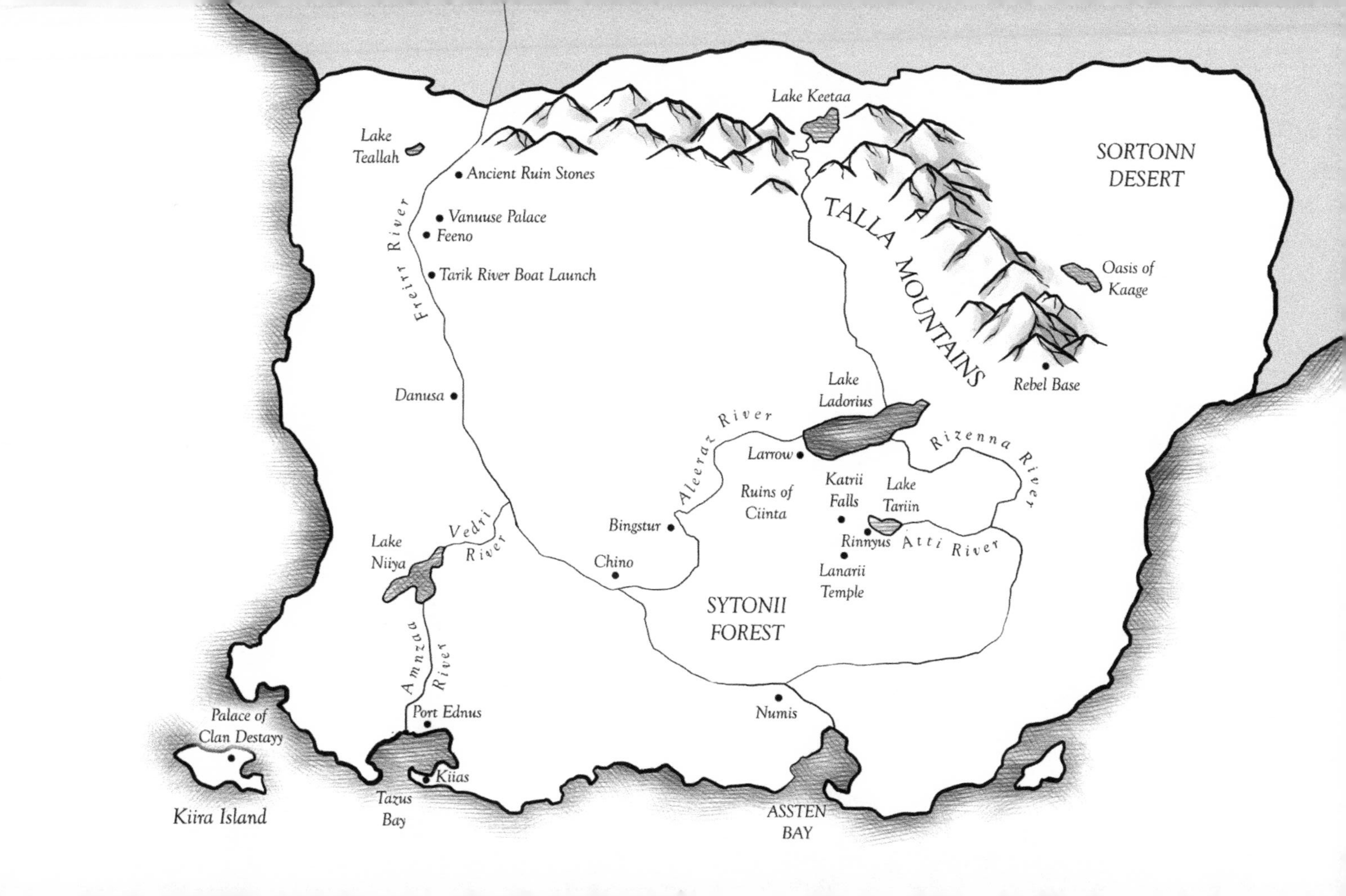

Lake Keetaa
SORTONN DESERT
Lake Teallah
Ancient Ruin Stones
Vanuuse Palace
Feeno
Tarik River Boat Launch
Freirr River
TALLA MOUNTAINS
Oasis of Kaage
Rebel Base
Danusa
Lake Ladorius
Aleeraz River
Rizenna River
Larrow
Ruins of Ciinta
Katrii Falls
Lake Tariin
Rinnyus
Atti River
Lanarii Temple
Bingstur
Chino
Vedri River
Lake Niiya
SYTONII FOREST
Amnzaa River
Port Ednus
Numis
Palace of Clan Destayy
Kiias
Kiira Island
Tazus Bay
ASSTEN BAY

A special thank you to my beta readers

Gene Lapointe
Nicole G. Ashcroft
Patrick Samuel John Lyttle
Lori-Lee Levi
Tarryn Gene Lapointe

Thank you to my dad, Ronald O'Neill. You put me onto the path of writing and have been here from the very beginning. My mother, Christine Lyttle for always asking how my book was coming along, even when it took me forever to get another chapter done. My mother-in-law, Kathy Hermance, for your support and telling me what I needed to hear to keep me focused and going. My Father-in-law, Gene Lapointe for your unwavering belief that I would one day be writing this acknowledgment page. Thank you to all my friends and family that supported me through these past few crazy years. And a special thank you to my Grandmother, Edna O'Neill. You were always encouraging me to be the best person I could be and you told me anything worth doing could be achieved with perseverance and hard work.

For my Husband Tarryn, for all your support, encouragement and being the rock I needed to see this through.

And for my daughter Trinette, my truly inspiring little Princess.

Prologue

Fire raged around the stone throne room, consuming anything its flames could reach. People screamed while running for safety as a battalion of men stormed the area, armor shining in the firelight as they cut down anyone not quick enough to get out of their way. In their midst, a man with armor stained the colour of blood strode forward, madness shining in his eyes as his gaze searched the area for something. He smirked deviously as he went after another man, this one dressed in fine robes with a golden circlet in his chestnut locks and a deadly blade resting at his side. Their swords clashed as the two men battled for their lives. All the while the fire raged on, surrounding them in a halo of hazy smoke. A woman stood across the room watching the battle with apprehension. The warrior's blade slashed at the King's shoulder, the blade striking true as the King was knocked to his knees from the crippling blow. The woman screamed. She also wore a golden crown, her blonde tresses bound in a corded braid halfway down her back. As the King fell to the floor, blood flowing from his chest, he gave her a haunting look, fear in his eyes as he yelled a single word before darkness claimed him.

"Run!"

His voice echoed as the woman was up and gone from the room like a shot. She raced down a long stone corridor and opened a large door at the end, racing down narrow spiral steps, the heat of fire bearing down on her and making her breathing ragged. She opened another door and blackness consumed all light, the overwhelming sensation of falling and then nothing....

Chapter One

Sunshine filtered in through the white blinds as a girl lay snuggled under her warm comforter, refusing to rise and greet the beautiful day. Neko Norston eyed the bright light with disdain, a headache pounding behind her eyes refused to let her return to slumber. Neko gave an audible groan and glanced at her alarm clock. It read 8:52 am. She dressed in a pair of blue jeans and a black V-neck t-shirt. Feeling a chill, she decided to put on her favorite violet zip up hoodie as well. Grabbing a brush from her dresser, she stood before her full-length mirror, taking in her reflection as she removed the tangles from her hair. The image before her was of a teenage girl. She stood at five feet five with a medium build. Straight golden-brown hair cascaded just past her shoulder blades accented by her silver-green eyes. She sighed as images from her dream continued to flash through her mind. It had been such a strange dream, but she had it before. Of this, she was sure. She decided to head downstairs to watch some TV and take something for the annoying headache. For the last few days, Neko had been getting killer headaches for no apparent reason. She was eating the same, getting plenty of sleep and she wasn't stressing, well, no more than any other typical seventeen-year-old. She let forth an annoyed sigh as she trudged down the stairs.

Neko called out to her family as she entered the kitchen, finding it deserted. Tan walls enhanced the entire room as the sun shone through the window above the sink making muted light patterns dance across the hardwood floor. Neko grabbed a glass and filled it with water, locating the ibuprofen on top of the fridge. She decided to take two extra-strength tablets, washing them down with the entire glass of water. She beamed when she realized her family had gone to the local farmers' market, leaving her the quiet house to herself. She was annoyed she would miss her Saturday morning boxing class, but her headaches made it impossible for her to even think straight, let alone focus on a punching bag. Neko sauntered into the living room. Her headache would soon start to subside so she sank into the cream-colored leather sofa and turned on the flat screen. She changed the channel to her favorite program and let the ibuprofen go to work.

After an hour, the headache had disappeared while Neko watched her show. Standing up, she promptly fell back down as her legs gave out from under her. Neko blinked rapidly while her head swarmed with vertigo.

"What the—?" Neko choked out, fighting the overwhelming sense of dread filling her mind.

"Get a grip," she snarled as she once again tried to regain her footing. On the second attempt, she managed to stand, and the dizziness diminished, only to be replaced by a loud buzzing in her ears.

'What's happening to me?'

Neko felt tears prickling her eyes as she made a mad dash upstairs towards her bedroom. Neko became increasingly confused once she got to the top of the stairwell and the buzzing faded, just as she stopped outside her parents' bedroom door.

'I should call Mom,' Neko decided as she walked towards her room but as she did so, the ringing returning louder and with it returned the headache from earlier that morning.

"What the hell?" Neko choked out returning to her parent's bedroom. Again, the pain decreased a fair bit, and Neko stared stupidly at the door.

"Okay." Annoyance laced her voice as she opened the door and stepped into her parents' orderly room. The white walls with dark green trim and immaculate oak bed set made the room look more like something out of a fancy hotel rather than from a normal house. Neko stepped farther into the room, and her pains faded into nothing as she focused on her parents' walk-in closet. Her eyes widened in shock as a radiant green light filtered out from under the sliding closet door.

The light was mesmerizing. Neko opened the door and stared down at the shelf before her. A glass jewelry box sat on the hip-high shelf and inside was the culprit. A small green emerald sat nestled amongst the cheaper jewelry, no bigger than her pinky and it was glowing!

'When did Mom get this?' Neko thought, she had never seen it before. She opened the jewelry box and snatched the glowing jewel that suddenly pulsed to life at her touch. Neko screamed in alarm and was unable to let go of the stone as something warm traveled up her entire arm followed by a pins and needles sensation as an unseen force hit her in the chest, knocking the air out of her lungs and sending her careening backwards. Neko's body felt heavy as a fierce wind tore at her. She found herself weightless, and seconds later, darkness consumed her mind.

Neko blinked, confusion creasing her brow as she found herself laying on her back staring up at a beautiful azure sky.

'How the hell did I get outside? The last thing I remember was that stupid stone.'

Neko gave a startled cry and bolted into a sitting position. Shaking her head, she took in her environs. She found herself in a field surrounded by stone pillars. Most of them crumbled and reminding her of ancient ruins. Feeling a cramp in her right hand, she glanced down and noticed the green stone still clutched in her palm, attached to it was a golden setting and a small golden chain. Neko chanced a better look at the stone that had seemingly lost its glow and now looked like an ordinary piece of cheap jewelry. Something told Neko this was not the case. As she held it up to inspect it, she noticed a small glow illuminating from inside the stone as if it were ignited with a tiny fire of green in the very center of the ovate stone. The setting reminded her of vines wrapping around the stone to keep it attached to the golden chain.

"It's just a stupid dream," she growled and got to her feet, stuffing the stone into her jeans pocket with more force than necessary. The sound of ripping material made Neko look skyward as she let out a sullen sigh, her pocket now ruined. She stared into the distance where she spotted a cloud of rising dust. After a few moments, she could hear a faint rumbling sound. Neko's eyes widened in shock as half a dozen men on horseback appeared over the rise, stopping some twenty feet from where she was standing, every muscle in her body tense. Once the dust had settled, Neko found she was facing some hostile-looking men. Glancing around nervously, she noticed all the men were wearing what looked to be medieval armor.

"Where…?" Neko started to speak, astonishment in her eyes. She fought the urge to scream and decided on balling her fists by her sides instead. Neko knew she had to find out what was going on and perhaps these men could help her if she asked them nicely.

"Hey girl, what is your name?" one barked out.

Neko stared at the man who had addressed her so harshly. He had removed his helmet, and she could see his features clearly. He looked to be her age, maybe a year or two older. His cerulean eyes were guarded as he observed her as one would a bug. He was obviously just as confused as she was about her sudden appearance. Suddenly, it felt less like a dream and Neko felt her stomach flip in apprehension. Deciding that maybe being nice would go over better than running her mouth, she complied.

"I'm Neko. Who are you?" She briefly paused and then added, "And where exactly am I?"

The male gave her a calculating stare, the slightest hint of a smirk on his lips as he watched her. Neko felt small under that gaze and averted her eyes, nervously starting to fidget under his scrutiny. Shifting from one foot to the other, she glanced up a moment later, and to her dismay, he was still watching her with mirth in his eyes.

"I am Prince Troy Vanuuse. May I enquire as to why you are on crown land? These ruins are sacred and peasants forbidden to trespass here. Only those of royal blood may enter theses hallowed grounds."

His tone was condescending, but there was amusement shining in his eyes. Neko felt herself blushing. She could sense that he was trying to get a reaction from her, and she of course, was playing right into it. Neko looked into the Prince's eyes making sure to watch his reactions. She knew she would have to be careful and watch what she said to him. Wherever she was, it was nothing like where she was from.

"I'm sorry. I didn't know. I didn't mean anything by it," she tried to placate the Prince, hoping he would not get too annoyed with her. The last thing she needed was an arrow stuck out of her rear end for back talking a Prince. He seemed to take her seriously and nodded with his arrogant smirk still in place. He gazed down at her from his black steed, giving her a stern look as all amusement vanished from his eyes.

"Do you know the punishment for your actions, girl?"

Neko inwardly cursed. Now, what was she supposed to do? The Prince had the upper hand, and he knew it, Neko was positive of that. She could feel tears prickling her eyes as she gave the Prince a pleading look. The image of her hanging flashed in the back of her mind.

"Please, I'm sorry. I didn't know. I'll leave, right now."

Troy gave her a curt nod.

"Very well, you are to follow me back to the castle. My father, the King, will determine the punishment for your actions. After all, these are *his* lands."

Neko caught the sneer directed towards her. Apparently, men in this time had no sense of chivalry like it often showed in the movies.

"But I haven't done anything wrong. You can see that!"

Neko cringed that her voice sounded so shrill, but she was starting to panic. What was going to happen to her? If she didn't think of something she would be beheaded or hung or something equally as horrible. A shiver ran down her spine as a god-awful screech pierced the air, effectively interrupting the conversation. Neko looked up, and her eyes found a dark shape in the horizon behind the group of knights. It grew larger as it approached them at a rapid speed.

"Your Highness, there she is—the dragon!" one of Troy's men yelled and pointed towards the huge flying reptile that was getting bigger by the second.

"She's a big beasty," another man yelled as Troy sneered and drew his sword.

"You."

Troy growled as he pointed his weapon at Neko. Her eyes went wide, and her face drained of all color at having the piece of sharp steel pointed in her general direction.

"Find a place in the ruins to hide while I slay this beast. I warn you now, try to run, and I will find you, girl."

Neko felt her jaw drop. She would have to be a complete idiot not to hear that threat. Troy was right. If she ran, he would find her, and this place was far too bizarre to be taking off on her own.

"Holy crap, dragons? I gotta be dreaming!" Neko exclaimed, continuing to stare at the approaching dragon and unable to look away. Troy gave a shout and spurred his horse into a run, the knights followed suit and raced off to fight the creature. Neko could only stare in bewilderment with her jaw to the ground, as she got her first really good look at the dragon. The creature was beautiful but deadly and here was Prince what's-his-face riding off to slay it because apparently, that's what princes did here.

"He's fricken' nuts!" Neko yelled, watching as Troy threw a spear of some sort at the huge flying creature. The massive beast was easily twice the size of an elephant.

"What did I just get myself into?" Neko pondered aloud as she stood watching the fight. Neko rubbed her temples and wondered who would win. Personally, she decided to cheer for the dragon.

Neko watched in a state of shock as Troy and his men attacked the dragon relentlessly for the better part of an hour. Little by little, she inched forward from her hiding place in the rocky outcrop. All she wanted was to get a better look, knowing somewhere in the back of her mind this was not the brightest of all things to be doing. Neko ignored her common sense and ventured into the open field. The dragon was now on the ground, hissing and biting at anything or anyone who got too close to her. The dragon was a beautiful emerald color, her scales glistening like tiny gems in the sunlight. Her neck was long and slender, just like the rest of her body. Somehow, to Neko, the dragon looked like it was young. Her wings were just as beautiful, and the membranes were a deep burgundy, the veins showing through the translucent flesh. Neko felt pity for the poor creature that now had a few spears jabbed into its vulnerable underside. Troy looked like he was enjoying the hunt as blood flowed freely from one of the wounds he had inflicted on the beast.

"Yep, he's off his rocker for sure," Neko stated as she realized the battle was quickly coming towards her.

"Oh crap," she hissed, watching as the dragon roared and reared onto its hind feet. Its tail lashed out violently and sent one of Troy's men and the steed he was riding sailing through the air. They landed with bone jarring impact and in a heap from which they did not arise. Frozen in fear, Neko stared up at the massive beast as the dragon roared in fury and turned towards the petrified girl. Neko's eyes met the dragons, its eyes a brilliant amber shade and slit, much like a snake's eyes.

"Get out of the way!"

Neko looked over as Troy yelled at her. He broke the trance and threw a spear into the dragon's chest. Rearing again, the dragon let forth a blood-chilling scream. Neko covered her ears but doubted she would ever forget that sound as long as she lived. It sounded too much like a human scream. The ground shook as the huge animal landed at her feet, its massive head no more than ten feet from where Neko stood with her ears covered. Neko slowly lowered her hands and let out the breath she had been holding, her entire body trembling.

Chapter Two

Troy dismounted his steed and fixed Neko with an icy stare.

"Did I not tell you to stay at the ruins, girl?"

Neko stupidly nodded her face flushing as she watched Troy's men approach their fallen comrades. She then stared at the dragon as it let out a tiny sigh. Neko felt ill. It was still alive!

"Move," Troy spat as he drew his sword from a leather scabbard on his belt. Without a second thought, he raised his blade and cleaved the dragon's head off with one blow. Neko could not handle it. She had to cover her mouth and turn. She made it a few steps before she retched. She could not believe how barbaric these people were.

"If you are finished, I have men who need a healer's attention."

She turned to face Troy, who glared at her. Neko remained still. She did not want to make him any angrier, and she had realized with dread that she was definitely not dreaming.

"Okay," she stated, anger lacing her voice as she followed him to his horse, noticing the four remaining men looked rather beaten up. Two lay on the ground, and they were not moving.

"Are they dead?" she whispered feeling a bit faint as Troy snorted and looked to his men.

"Clean up this mess. I will escort the girl to the castle. One of you give her your horse," he shouted out. Obviously, he had power. These men were at least twice his age and happily let him boss them around.

"You girl, get on that horse and accompany me to the castle. My father will want to speak with you."

Neko gave Troy a wilting look.

"My name is Neko," she ground out as she gave the brown horse a doubtful look, then put her toe in the stirrup and grabbed the leather saddle horn. Grunting, she awkwardly managed to swing her leg over the saddle and seat herself grabbing the reigns offered to her by one of the men. Neko grinned. She had never actually ridden a horse, so staying in the saddle on the first attempt was a small victory.

"Come along then," Troy stated as he kicked his horse, Neko copied him. She hollered in alarm as her horse bolted after the other one, thinking it was funny how horseback riding never looked that bumpy on TV.

It felt like hours later when in fact it was probably only a forty-five-minute ride to Prince Troy's castle. Neko gazed at the scene before her and once again found herself shocked. The building itself was more of a mansion, without the whole drawbridge and moat theme that she had assumed it would be. From where they were, the castle looked to be built on a ridge, giving a great view of the land for miles around. It had a stone outer wall and a large pair of wooden doors, to gain entrance to the estate, complete with armed sentries.

"Wow, you live here?" she asked as Troy answered her, a sneer in his tone.

"Of course I do."

Neko sighed, that had been the most he had said to her the entire ride. Apparently, awkward silences were common in this place. Neko focused back on the castle as the pair approached the gates. A guard spotted them and yelled over his shoulder. Immediately, the doors started to open inwards. The horses needed no guidance as they trotted into a stone courtyard and into the stables. A pair of stable hands approached the two riders, grabbing the horse's bridles so that Troy and Neko could dismount. Neko groaned. Her knees and hips felt as they were on fire.

"Come along," Troy growled, grabbing Neko by the upper left arm while dragging her alongside him as they passed through a door and into a poorly lit passageway. Neko was lost in a matter of seconds, all the halls looked the same, and how he knew where to go was beyond her. They came down a finer and wider hallway, complete with red carpet. At the end stood a set of wooden doors and outside them stood two guards in shiny armor.

"Prince Troy," one addressed him, both men bowing slightly as Troy pushed her forward.

"Keep an eye on her. I need to talk to my father for a moment."

The one guard grunted in acknowledgment as Neko spotted a nearby wooden bench and promptly sat down. Troy scoffed at her before he opened the doors and disappeared into a nice-looking room.

"Oh boy," Neko stated, something told her this was only the beginning of an interesting day.

Troy strode into the throne room muttering under his breath as he stopped before a dais. Sitting upon the throne was his father. Troy bowed before him.

"Father, we have an issue. While my men and I were hunting that bothersome dragon, we came upon a strange girl." Troy looked up at his father who didn't seem all that concerned.

"A girl you say, what is so special about this particular girl. There are so many in this kingdom."

"I understand that Father, but she is odd. She wears men's clothing and when I spoke to her, she seemed disoriented. Moments before that, I felt a surge of magical energy. Perhaps the two are connected."

The King chuckled.

"Is that so, my son? I assume you have brought her with you?"

Troy nodded as his father gave him a stern look.

"Well, then bring her in so that I may question her myself."

Troy looked to a nearby guard, "You heard my father. Bring in the girl from the hallway."

Moments later, the guard returned. Neko walked into the room behind him, her face pale.

"This is her?" the King questioned as he stared down at Neko. She looked the King in the eyes and noticed they were the same shade as Troy's. Neko blinked. The King looked vaguely familiar.

"Yes, Father. This is the one I caught trespassing in the ruins."

Neko looked from Troy to his father, "I'm sorry. I told your son I didn't know it was off limits. Please, I don't want to be hanged."

The King roared, mirth in his eyes as he looked down at the frightened girl who was near tears.

"My dear, I do not know what my son has told you, but if you were there by mistake, then there is no harm done and no punishment intended." Neko exhaled and fixed an aggravated look at Troy.

"Please child, tell me how you came to arrive here. Troy is correct in the fact that you are wearing most peculiar clothing."

Neko looked to the floor, not knowing why but she did not want to mention the emerald. Besides who would believe her? Even she thought it was impossible, and she had proof that it was real. She looked back up to the King. His eyes were kinder than his sons were. He had longer dark hair with some grey throughout. He also had a full beard and a small golden band around his head. Neko noticed he was the only one there and he was sitting in a single chair. The Queen was missing; then again, this wasn't exactly like the movies.

"I come from a land surrounded by water. I was walking on the beach, and there was this brilliant light. I followed it and found these ruins. I must have lost my footing. That's when I fell and when I opened my eyes I was at your ruins, which look a great deal like the ones I saw before I arrived here."

She watched the King's face as he nodded.

"I see. Those ruins are very old. It makes sense that there might be more around Arorus." Neko sighed in relief. At least he believed her.

"Troy, please find this girl..." The King paused and looked to Neko. "Child what is your name?"

"I'm Neko, Neko Norston." The King looked puzzled but nodded as she offered him a small smile.

"Yes, Troy, please find Neko accommodations, as it is nearly sunset. We will continue this conversation in the morning over breakfast. I look forward to it."

He gave Neko a polite smile as Troy looked rather annoyed but slightly bowed. "Yes Father, as you wish."

Troy motioned for Neko to follow him.

"This way," he ground out as she followed him down more hallways, still completely lost.

"What a day," she whispered under her breath as she watched the Prince stop at a doorway.

"You may stay in this guest room. I will fetch you in the morning so that we may dine with my father."

With that, he turned and stalked away leaving Neko to fend for herself. Neko blinked as the side of her leg started to feel warm.

"What?"

Neko hissed as she pulled the emerald from her pocket, the jewel pulsing with an inner green light.

"Great, this is all your fault," she growled at the stone and looked to where Troy had disappeared, her curiosity getting the better of her as she decided to follow him. Sleep was the last thing on her mind.

"Catch ya on the flip side, Kansas," Neko stated, stuffing the emerald back into her pocket as she grinned and raced after Troy.

Neko slowly followed the Prince down a series of similar looking stone corridors, small lanterns barely lighting the dim walkways. This place looked a tad creepier to her in the dark. Neko snickered, finding herself enjoying this game of spying on the grumpy Prince, wondering if it would kill him to be pleasant even for a few moments. She blinked as the stone against her leg continued to thrum with life, giving off a faint green glow as she followed Troy deeper into the bowels of the seemingly endless manor. Every hallway seemed to have the same red carpeting and bland granite walls, and the ever-present glass lanterns.

"I would hate to pay for the fire insurance in this tomb," Neko whispered remembering how her father was always talking about fire hazards his clients had when he insured them. Neko was pulled from her thoughts and froze at the sound of a door shutting. She slowly edged forward, careful not to make a sound as she peered around the corner. A set of massive wooden doors loomed before her reminding her of doors to a large library.

"Where are you going?" Neko wondered aloud, stopping before the doors that had vines carved into the ancient-looking wood.

"That's right because everything is ancient here," she muttered while slowly pushing on one of the doors. She opened it just wide enough to squeeze into the room, praying the door didn't squeak. Neko looked down as her stone started to vibrate, the green light pulsating as if it were a frantic moth attracted to the light.

"Crap," she hissed as she placed her hand over her pocket in an attempt to conceal the pulsating glow from the emerald. Her hand fell as she finally took notice of the room she entered. The entire floor was covered in forest green carpeting, and long bookshelves carved from the same wood as the doors covered the walls on both sides of her. On the shelves were hundreds of books and before her was what could only be the royal treasury.

"Wow," she whispered as she took in the far end of the room. In the center of a wide circle, there was a raised platform and on it sat a stone identical to Neko's. The stone was a deep amber color, and Neko watched in awe as the amber stone started to pulsate, its golden light filling the dimly lit room and reminding her of a disco. Neko heard Troy curse as he glared at the amber stone, blinking as Neko slowly approached.

"What are you doing in here? It is forbidden for anyone but the royal family to be in the treasury."

Neko pursed her lips. Why did Troy have to be so pushy? This guy had no sense of humor, and it was starting to piss her off.

"Chill out, okay? I'm not a thief. Look," she slowly held up her hand. In her palm, she held a golden chain, and her own stone began flashing wildly. "I think they're recognizing each other or something weird like that."

Troy stared wide-eyed at the stone she held, his jaw dropping as he had yet to utter a single word.

"Where did you get that?" he snapped, his eyes narrowing as he took a step towards Neko. She shook her head, startled by the anger that was radiating from the young Prince.

"Why are you so angry? I'll tell you, okay. Just calm down." Neko could feel her annoyance piquing as Troy took a deep breath and most of the anger faded, replaced with confusion as he furrowed his brows, obviously contemplating the situation.

"All right, tell me, how did you come to possess something like that?"

Neko looked to the stone that had dulled as she moved closer to the amber stone.

"Well, I found it in my mother's things. I didn't want to mention it before because it sounded stupid, even in my mind and truthfully I was scared of you, of this place, that I had gone off the deep end."

Neko sighed dejectedly as she looked to the Prince who seemed bemused.

"So, you did not come here by the ruins in your realm like you first claimed?"

Neko shook her head. "No. This stone was shining like the way it is right now. I went into my parents' bedroom, and as soon as I touched it, I woke up here, wherever here is and you know the rest."

Troy picked up the amber stone and raised his eyes to meet Neko's.

"I need to talk to my father, first thing in the morning. He must know about this. I believe that stone you have is a sacred element stone. The one I hold has the power of wind. I believe yours is the Earth Stone."

Neko raised an eyebrow, confusion evident on her face.

"So why would this Earth Stone be where I live? Shouldn't it be here with this one?"

"You would assume, but I am not sure. Only my father would know or know of someone who would understand it better that you or I do."

Neko slipped her stone back into her pocket. Troy mirrored her actions with the Wind Stone and gave her a serious look. "Perhaps it is best if you do not tell anyone else about that stone, at least not yet. If it got into the wrong hands, it could mean great misfortune for us all."

Neko felt a shiver run down her spine as the pair exited the treasury and stepped back into the hallway.

"I think it best if we retire for the evening, the ladies will see that you are fed. I will come fetch you in the morning. Wait for me in your chambers."

Neko nodded as the Prince gave her a no-nonsense look.

"All right, can you find your way back to your room?"

"I think so."

"Good. Then I shall see you first thing in the morning," he ordered as she headed back down the corridor towards her room, well aware of his stare that followed her until she turned the corner.

As soon as she was out of his line of sight, Troy grinned and held up the Wind Stone. It had been inactive for years, but now with Neko's sudden arrival the stone she carried had awakened the Wind Stone. It was a sure bet she would be able to help him find the remaining two stones.

"I would be unstoppable with all four," Troy mused, then looked towards the treasury door. "Too bad Father will not see it that way. He will want all the glory or, worse yet, give the task to brother," Troy grumbled as he pocketed the stone and headed towards his chambers. "Come morning, we shall be set out, and with any luck, Father will not notice for a day or so. Just enough time to catch the sailboats down the river and away from this dreary palace." Troy grinned and opened his door. He was tired, and he needed to have a good sleep to prepare for the following days ahead.

Chapter Three

Neko winced as sunlight assaulted her face. It was far too early, wasn't it? She groaned and threw back the large blanket that had practically smothered her the entire night. She cursed as she checked her watch.

"Six thirty, you have got to be kidding me," she grumbled and sat up when she heard a knock at her door. "W…who is it?" she asked as the door opened and Troy gave her an aggravated scowl.

"You are not even dressed?" he questioned as Neko flashed him an exasperated gaze.

"Hello, the sun has just risen. Sorry if I'm not up at the butt crack of dawn like you obviously were."

Troy took a deep breath. Getting angry with her would not speed things along, even though she was rude and had no business speaking to him the way she did.

"Hurry and get dressed. I will await you outside your room. Make haste," he shut the door with a thud as he left.

"Geez, he is so annoying," she growled as she got to her feet and pulled on her jeans, her black t-shirt already on. She had voted to use it as pajamas for the night. She groaned and grabbed her socks pulling them on. She then stuffed her feet into her black runners, wiggling each foot in them until they popped on, she didn't bother with the laces. They were pretty much one giant knot.

"Now off to have crumpets and tea with the good King."

Her sarcastic comment made her snicker as she did a quick check to make sure her stone was still in her pocket. She opened her door and almost collided with the fuming Prince who had been hovering just outside her room.

"Come along. We are running late," he grabbed her by the wrist, pulling her through the corridors as she staggered after him. She was lost in a matter of two turns, a few more turns and they entered a kitchen area.

"This is new," she observed.

"This is the kitchen and the servants' area. Hence, the dismal disarray."

Neko raised an eyebrow.

"What's with the vocab? They teach you that in 'How to be a Prince 101'?"

Neko did the quotations thing, which was lost on Troy. He gave her an even stare, expressing his disdain of the attempted joke.

"There is nothing wrong with being well educated."

He gave an annoyed sigh and sauntered through the kitchen, expecting Neko to follow his lead.

"Or a pompous ass, apparently," Neko muttered, but followed him through the kitchen and out a set of plain wooden doors.

"These are the royal gardens. We are going beyond here to the stables. My father has requested I take you to find the other two stones. He thinks once we have all four there will be a chance he can return you to your home as soon as humanly possible."

Neko blinked. A tiny bit annoyed that she had been left out of the morning conversation, not to mention his snippy comment.

"There's four of them?"

Troy released her hand. She continued to follow him as they jogged through the shrubbery and over the hand-laid stones that made up the pathways. Neko heard the shrill whinny of a horse as they arrived at the stables. The smell of hay and horse assaulted Neko's senses.

"We will be riding out alone. The guards have no time to escort us, and it would draw unwanted attention. I think I can manage a robber or two. They will get a thrashing if they are stupid enough to show disrespect to a crowned Prince."

Neko wondered why men were so egotistical in this place. Was it a crime to accept help when offered? Apparently, it was to this Prince.

"Uh…okay," she agreed, not wanting to get the Prince going on another tirade. "So, for me to go home, we need to find and bring back the other two stones to your father, right?"

They entered the stables.

"That is correct. My father thinks it is a good learning lesson for me as well. I agree, and it gets us out of this stifling castle."

"So why wasn't I included in your little discussion?"

Neko huffed as they walked down the stable corridor. He obviously wasn't going to answer her question. They approached three horses. One did not have a saddle. It was strictly intended as a gear horse.

"Is this going to be a long trip?" Neko asked as fear crept onto her face. Troy shot her a knowing grin.

"You are not getting cold feet now are you my lady? It is not a long trek to the sailboats." Neko hated that smug look on his face. He seemed to know this. His smirk only justifying her suspicions.

"You know you could try to be a little nicer. I don't understand what I did to make you so angry with me."

"It has nothing to do with you. My father does not give me the merit I deserve. He is always handing it to my eldest brother, and I am given the scraps."

"You have a brother? Does he live in the castle with you?"

"I have two brothers if you must know. Alexander is the eldest and Traven is the youngest."

They approached the two horses saddled and ready to go. Neko glanced at Troy.

"I suppose this is a bad time to tell you, but I've never ridden a horse in my life until yesterday."

Troy shot her a look as if she had sprouted a new head.

"Please tell me you jest."

Neko shook her head. "Sadly no, I like to look at horses, but not enough to go for a trail ride."

Troy cursed under his breath.

"This is no trail ride. Let us get you on the horse, and then I suppose I can teach you to ride while we travel."

Neko approached the docile looking horse to her left as Troy followed her.

"That is a mare. She will be your steed. She is a calm beast, so you should be relatively safe on her."

Neko looked to the other horse. He was a shiny ebony stallion and looked a bit flightily.

"I'm guessing my horse is a lot safer than he is."

Troy laughed. "He has been my steed since I was ten summers old. He is completely safe if I ride him."

Neko did not appreciate the condescending tone

"Well GFY"

Troy gave her a strange look and then hoisted himself into the saddle effortlessly, looking at her expectantly.

"You honestly think I'm going to be able to copy that. Yesterday was a fluke. So, I wouldn't hold my breath if I were you. Okay, so foot in there, grab horn thingy and into the saddle—simple. I did it yesterday."

Neko coached herself as she placed her foot into the leather stirrup. Hopping a few times, she grabbed the saddle horn and attempted to hoist herself into the saddle. She gave a startled squawk as she went up and over the back of the horse, falling onto the dusty floor. The grey mare looked down at Neko as if the girl had lost her marbles. Troy snickered at the display.

"That was truly pathetic. Try again."

Neko shot him a dirty look and got up, giving the horse a determined stare as she dusted herself off.

"Okay. I can do this."

The second attempt went better, this time she got onto the mare's back and gave a victorious arm pump.

"I did it. In your face."

Troy looked confused. The saying was lost on him.

"What is in my face?" she rolled her eyes, "Nothing. Forget it. It's just a thing I say."

Troy took the reins of his stallion.

"All right, we have wasted enough daylight. Let us be on our way. We should make the boat before nightfall."

Neko grinned as she and Troy made their way down the sandy cliff path. Wooden boats with bright red sails sat like little toys in the languid river.

"We get to go on one of those?" Neko asked as Troy looked skywards.

"Correct. We will launch at Tarik and from there, journey down the river Freirr for a few miles. Once we arrive at the village of Danusa, we will have a quick midday meal. We shall then decide our future path."

Neko was relieved they would be getting off the horses. They had been riding most of the day, and she was sure her hips and knees were bruised down to the bone.

"Good, 'cause I'm sick of riding. I hurt all over."

Troy snorted in disdain at her comment as he maneuvered his horse into the busy dockyards.

Neko could only stare in wonder as the vendors shouted their wares. All around her, people bustled. There were many shops lining the crowded streets, mostly for supplying those heading down the river. Neko turned towards Troy.

"So, what do we need to get for supplies?"

"We will need a map, some food, water and bedding. I doubt there will be lodging everywhere we go, so we shall need to camp out often."

He grinned looking to see what her reaction would be, hoping he had annoyed her even a little bit. Neko grinned right back. She was not about to let him intimidate her.

"Cool. I've camped before, so it's really not a big deal, for me anyways."

Neko could not help but feel smug at his indignant pout as he decided that the vendor to his right was more important than their conversation.

"And score one for the girl."

Neko smirked behind Troy's back. The Prince continued to ignore the strange girl.

Neko munched on a piece of bread and cheese as Troy bantered with the vendors for food. They had already found a map, and according to Troy, the price he paid for it was robbery. Neko had just shrugged. She had no idea what a gold piece was equivalent to in Canadian dollars. They had already gotten bedding and extra clothing, sending it ahead so that it was waiting for them on the riverboat. Troy glanced towards Neko. She was just finishing her small meal. Assured she was not going to wander away, he turned back to the food vendor.

"Have it sent to the first ship. We leave at first light. So, it had better be there."

The vendor bowed low.

"Yes, my lord. It will be as you ask. I will personally see to it."

Troy turned and approached the spot where Neko sat.

"All the arrangements are made. We shall head to the ship before sunset."

As they made their way towards the docks, Neko yawned as she looked across the wide river. The sun was just setting, and it cast a warm orange glow over the surrounding landscape. Stretching her arms high over her head, she yawned once more, feeling the fatigue of riding all day. Neko smiled as the horses ambled at a slow gait towards the awaiting docks. She could now make out people on the boats, preparing to set sail.

"Why do they sail at night? Isn't that a bit dangerous?" Neko looked to Troy who rode beside her, once again receiving an aggravated look from the Prince.

"We will not head out until dawn. We will sleep below deck for tonight, daft girl."

Neko felt her face heating up. Why was it that this guy could always make her feel so damn small?

"That makes more sense. Sorry I asked," she retorted, deciding to ignore Troy and take in the beautiful countryside. She soon grew bored of the scenery. It was all rolling hills and sandy cliffs, much like the rivers near her house.

"So how far away is this Danusa village you were talking about?"

Troy continued to stare ahead as he replied, "About two days sailing, we should arrive midday on the second day. The river is calm this time of year, and high waters will not be a problem for us."

Neko let out a deep breath and copied the Prince staring straight ahead.

"So, you said this stone I have, it's magical or something? What does it do exactly besides glow green and send people to other worlds?"

"It is a powerful magical instrument. There are four stones altogether. I've been told they are able to control the element for which each stone is named." Troy glanced over at Neko and then continued to stare towards the ships. "Your stone is that of Earth. It controls the very ground we walk on, provided whoever has the stone knows how to summon its powers."

"So just having the stone doesn't mean it will work for someone then?"

"True to an extent, the stone will not activate for just anyone. You must have some sort of magical potential for it to even acknowledge you."

"Then I have magic?" he gave Neko a withering look.

"Have we not just been discussing that?"

"Yes, but still… Look, this is going to take me some time to get my head wrapped around. Where I come from, magic and dragons don't exist."

"You forget, this is not your land and if you do not come to terms with this, you will be useless to me. The only way you are ever going home is by helping me find the last two stones so we can use the power of all four element stones to send you back."

Neko was silent for a moment.

"How does it work? Using all four stones to send me back I mean. Since only one brought me here, shouldn't it only take one to get me back home?"

"I do not know. Only someone who knows of theses rituals could answer that. Once we have all four stones, we will get to the fact of the matter and discover the stones' secrets."

"Do you know any more about the stones?"

Troy pursed his lips, his gaze straight ahead.

"Yes. Many years ago, there was a war over the stones. In the end, many died, and the stones were lost, hidden all across Arorus. As far as I know, the Lanarii have one, and that is where I would have us search first."

Neko stifled a yawn.

"Let me guess this place we're going. It's a long way from here, isn't it?"

"Of course, it is. Do you think you are hearty enough to make this journey?"

Again, there was that condescending tone. Neko swore he was doing it just to make her mad.

"Of course, I can. It'll be just like camping but with a smelly animal—and the horses."

Troy scoffed at her insult, then promptly dug his heels into his horse, making it break into a canter and leaving Neko behind. She rolled her eyes and continued at her pace. Her rear end was already asleep.

They arrived at the docks just as twilight settled in, the moon a sliver over the mountains. A few deck hands went about lighting lanterns that hung off wooden poles that lined the docks every ten feet or so. Neko groaned as her stiff legs protested her movement. They had left their horses in the care of the dockhands, who assured Troy the horses would be stabled near the rear deck of the massive riverboat. Neko stared up at the wooden vessel that was easily bigger than a yacht.

"It looked a lot smaller from the trail."

"That is because we were farther away this afternoon."

Neko resisted the urge to stick her tongue out at the irritating male.

"I swear you do that on purpose."

"What is it that I do?"

"Try to annoy me, duh."

Troy let a hint of a grin slip into place, causing Neko to go red in the face as she became even more flustered with him.

"Perhaps you are just looking into it too much," he snidely replied as they stopped before the riverboat, taking it in.

"Shall we?" he offered her his arm as Neko rolled her eyes and marched up the gangplank without him. Her ire was getting the best of her, and for once, she didn't care. Who was he to think he could say rude things and think she would bat her eyes and just let it go?

Chapter Four

The King sat on his throne, chin resting in his hand as he awaited his son's arrival. He sat up as he heard an enraged bellow and the large wooden doors to the throne room burst open as if they were made of matchsticks.

"Alexander."

He watched his eldest son approach the raised platform upon which the throne sat.

"Father, you have summoned me?"

Alexander stopped at the foot of the steps, bowing his head slightly before his gaze met his father's. The King looked into his son's ice blue eyes, wondering where his eldest son got his sadistic nature. Sometimes, he wondered about his son's mental state of mind.

"I have asked you here for one reason," the King started as he stood up and began pacing the dais, his hands clasped behind his back.

"Last night Troy brought to me a strange girl. Her attire was like nothing I have ever seen, most assuredly not from this realm."

Alexander shifted his weight from his right to his left foot as his father turned to gaze out the large window surveying his kingdom.

"What about this girl?"

The King turned.

"She seemed familiar, but from where I cannot tell. Regardless, this girl is a thief, and she has somehow conned your brother into stealing the Wind Stone."

Alexander cleared his throat. He did not particularly care for the good of the kingdom or the powers of the useless Wind Stone, but he knew the history about it well enough. Alexander blinked.

"Even if Troy has stolen the stone from the treasury, it has been inactive for years. What gain does it give him?"

The King sighed, and his eyes met his eldest son's.

"He must think she can help him find the remaining stones. Either to his gain or hers, it does not help us any. The fact of the matter is that he has betrayed me. I do not need to tell you just how powerful one would be if they got hold of all four element stones and activated their powers."

Alexander scoffed.

"But Father, the stones were hidden all over Arorus. The chances of them finding all four stones are slim."

The King's eyes went cold.

"It is not a chance I am willing to take, Alexander. I want you to find your brother and return him home to justice."

Alexander stood at attention as the King glared down at his son.

"Take four of your best men and track them. I want that stone returned to me."

Alexander nodded.

"What about the girl, Father?"

"Find out who she is and what she's doing. I want her here and completely unharmed. She could provide invaluable information regarding the stones."

Alexander blinked.

"But you said the stones—"

"I do not want Troy finding and controlling the stones. They would benefit me. Once you have returned your brother and the girl, then you will be given the task of finding the stones and bringing our kingdom to great prosperity."

Alexander bowed again.

"As you wish, Father. I will leave immediately."

"Very good my son. They were last seen heading towards the river. I do not doubt they will take the riverboats towards Danusa."

The King gave Alexander a smoldering look.

"Do not disappoint me, Alexander. There is no room for failure in this."

Alexander turned and vacated the grand room, his resentment piqued. Why did his brother have to be so stupid? Did Troy not realize that he would not get away with stealing one of the King's most valued trinkets?

"What are you up to little brother?"

Alexander growled as he stalked down the main hall. He had little time to get his men and supplies together before heading out to find and return his younger brother and the element stone he had stolen.

Neko sighed as she leaned over the railing of the large riverboat. They had just landed in the village of Danusa, mere hours before sunset. Neko stretched and watched as men started unloading what cargo they could before nightfall. It had been a two days' journey on ship and Neko had hardly seen Troy. Apparently, he had been off "making arrangements and tending the horses" the entire time.

"Probably off playing croquet with all the other stuck up royals," Neko muttered as she took a deep breath and looked around, hoping to spot Troy returning from the village he had disappeared into just over an hour before.

Neko pulled her emerald from her pocket and examined it.

"It looks normal enough, I guess."

She turned it over in her hand as the fading sunlight glittered on its smooth surface.

She unclasped the chain, placing it around her throat as she decided to wear the necklace for safe keeping.

"I can only imagine the fit he'd have if I lost it," she muttered as she tucked the stone under her t-shirt, thankful the chain was a little longer so she could conceal the jewel. For some reason, she felt the strongest urge to protect the small gem.

The sun had long set, and dark was encroaching with a bluish glow over the land when Troy finally returned nearly three hours later.

"Where were you?" Neko asked, slightly annoyed she had been waiting for him for so long. Troy shot her a disgruntled look.

"I had to find lodging for the night. Unfortunately, the inn is full, and we would have better luck sailing down to the next village. Chino is also closer to the forest that we must travel through to gain access to the Lanarii domain."

Neko rolled her eyes.

"And it took you like three hours to do that?"

Troy took a deep breath. Running her through would not help him locate the remaining two stones.

"Let us dine. I grow weary of your constant babbling."

Neko felt her temper rear its head as she planted her feet and gave the Prince a fiery look.

"No."

Shock was evident as his eyes met hers.

"Pardon me?" she frowned at him, her eyes full of outrage.

"I've been nice to you ever since I got here and all you can do is call me down. I am not one of your servants who you can order around."

Troy blinked as she continued her barrage.

"Why can't you at least try to be nice to me?"

Troy felt his resolve fading. He was tired and hungry and decided maybe appeasing her would be better than fighting with her for the rest of the night. The girl had a temper on her and was not afraid to voice her opinions, to his greater annoyance.

"You are right," he stated in resignation.

"I have been taking my frustrations out on you, and it was wrong of me, I apologize."

He smirked at her flabbergasted look.

"Uh…y…yeah sure," she stuttered as Troy offered her his arm.

"Shall we go have an enjoyable dinner and drink? Let us start anew."

Neko took his offered arm and linked hers in his, a deep blush dusting her cheeks.

"Okay," she stated as the pair strolled off the wooden docks and into the still bustling village.

As they made their way towards the inn, Troy glared ahead. It would be easier for him to get along with the girl if she were not so damn temperamental. He was not used to having women resist his princely charms, and it irritated him to no end. He returned from his thoughts to hear the girl chattering about some idiotic thing called a car.

"Are you even listening to me?" she asked as Troy turned to her and flashed her his most sincere smile.

"Forgive me Neko. My mind was elsewhere. I am famished."

Neko let out a sigh, her breath feathering her bangs as they stepped into the inn.

"That smells yummy," she stated as the smell of warm stew assaulted both their senses. Troy had to agree. He was ravenous.

"Let us dine. Then you may tell me about this thing you call a car."

Neko beamed as the pair took a table and settled down for a nice meal.

Neko grinned at Troy as they made their way down the Freirr River.

"So, this village, Chino, is it like Danusa?"

Troy shook his head, staring out over the large river behind them.

"It is a great deal smaller. They are a fishing village located where the Freirr divides and the Aleeraz branches off to the east."

"So, what will we do once we get there?"

"We need to obtain more information on the Lanarii. We must find out how to get to their stronghold in the forest. Only they know where that stone is."

"So, we're sailing down another river?"

"You do not like the boat?"

"It's kinda boring."

"I would agree," Troy chuckled, "but it is the quickest way. It will only be a few more days' travel I suspect."

"Where does this river come out?"

Troy pulled forth his map.

"You see here? This is Chino."

He showed Neko as the pair leaned in closer, examining the map.

"Okay, and we're going to this lake, or rather, this place here."

Neko pointed to the small lake town on the map.

"Yes, this is Larrow. It is a small mining village, slightly smaller than Danusa."

"And then we're going on horseback to where?" she let the question hang as Troy pointed towards a black dot smack in the center of a large forest.

"Here. This is the approximate location of the Lanarii Palace, here, in the village of Rinnyus."

Neko whistled.

"Wow. That's a lot of forest."

Troy rolled the map up, returning it the inside of his cloak.

"It is, but there is no other way to get that stone, and we need all four."

Neko yawned and simultaneously stretched.

"I know. Well, at least it means we get off this stinking ship."

Troy chuckled, finding himself enjoying the company of the strange girl. He growled as he caught himself. He was not going to befriend her. He did not need a distraction. His task was simple, get the stones and use them to gain control of his father's kingdom. It was his turn to make the rules, and he would not bow to anyone again.

"Troy, are you okay?"

Neko asked as she placed her hand on his arm giving him a small shake.

"I am fine," he snapped, wrenching his arm free of her grasp.

"We will soon arrive in Chino. We should prepare."

Neko watched as Troy turned and stomped away. She had not missed the anger that flashed in his eyes.

"What's your deal?" she growled as she rolled her eyes and followed the temperamental Prince below deck.

Two days later, Neko and Troy arrived on the banks of the village of Chino. Their boat had arrived just past noon. So, they had some time to take in the village.

"We will need to replenish our food supplies before we set sail again."

Neko glanced around as the pair strolled into the small village.

"We shall get the needed supplies and then you will get proper attire for the journey through the forest."

Troy eyed Neko's outfit with disdain.

"Excuse me but this is all I have, and I don't have any money whatsoever."

"I am a crowned Prince. It is nothing for me to get you the gear you need. Think of it as payment for helping me find the stones."

"Don't you mean if? What makes you so sure we'll find them? It's not like they have a huge neon sign above them saying 'magical teleporting stones here.'"

Troy gave an exasperated sigh, glaring at Neko.

"Keep your voice down. The stones we have will react if the others are near, just like how your stone did in the castle."

Neko crossed her arms over her chest.

"Hey genius, I had to be practically on top of the other stone for mine to react, so it's not going to be a walk in the park."

Troy gave Neko a flat look.

"Let us just try to find out some information regarding the Lanarii palace first."

"All right. Lead on then."

She gestured with her arm, annoyance flashing in her eyes as Troy sauntered past her and together the pair made their way deeper into the village. As the pair chatted, they were unaware of the two people shadowing them.

"Are you sure that is the Prince?" one of the men watching Troy asked. He was in his twenties, with an average build and chestnut hair that hung in his chocolate eyes. The other man was a few years older, with sandy hair and dark green eyes. He was skinnier than the first male and nearly two inches taller.

"Yes, Skylar, I am sure that is Troy. I just heard him confirm it to that tart."

Logan sighed glaring at his younger companion.

"Give me some merit. I heard the two of them mentioning stones. It might be the same ones Arran is interested in."

Skylar ran his hand through his hair.

"All right Logan, I need you to go get Arran. Tell him what I told you. Get him to meet me here as soon as he is able to, and I will keep track of these two."

Logan nodded as he gathered his things.

"I will make haste. Be careful."

They clasped hands in a loose handshake as they parted ways.

Arran sat at a table near the back of the small tavern. He and a few of his men had stopped for a pint after a long day's travel. The group had arrived from Bingstur, on their way to Port Ednus. A ship carried much-needed supplies for him and his rebels.

"Sir!"

Arran turned as one of his trusted men approached him. His cheeks flushed from his hasty search for his leader.

"Logan, what is it?" Arran asked, alarmed as he started to unsheathe his dagger.

"Skylar and I were at the docks. We happened upon Prince Troy."

Arran sheathed his blade.

"And?"

Logan took in much-needed air as he continued his message.

"Well, he was talking about looking for some stones. Skylar thought they might be the stones like your stone."

Arran glanced at the three men in his company.

"Where is he?"

Logan gestured behind himself.

"They looked like they were heading into town for supplies."

"They?"

"Yes, the Prince and a girl. I think they arrived on the last riverboat from Danusa."

"I have heard enough. Do you know how much money a Prince's ransom is worth? It would keep us going for a long while and save us a perilous journey to Port Ednus."

The others chuckled as Arran looked to Logan.

"Take me to Skylar. I assume he is keeping an eye on our friends?"

"Follow me. I will lead you there, sir," Logan stated proudly as his leader offered him a rare smile.

"Good work," Arran complimented as he followed the younger man into the still bustling streets.

Neko smiled as she took in the beautiful black cloak she wore.

"Is it to your liking?" Troy asked as Neko ran her hand through the warm fur.

"It's beautiful."

Troy glanced over at the tailor.

"I will take this along with another for myself."

Troy pulled forth a small leather pouch.

"Yes, as you wish, milord," the elderly tailor stated as he accepted the coins without question.

"Neko, it is time we head to the inn. We have an early start in the morning, and we need our rest."

Neko followed the Prince back out into the street.

"I'm starving."

"As am I."

As the pair headed towards the inn, Neko stopped, feeling eyes on her as goose bumps ran down her arms.

"What is it?" Troy asked noticing she had frozen where she stood.

"I…I'm not sure, I just got the willies for a moment, like we were being watched. Stupid, right?" she laughed, her cheeks dusted red from her flushed face.

Troy rolled his eyes at her odd behavior.

"Why would anyone be watching us? No one knows that we are here."

"I thought you said your father sent us here?"

Troy mentally berated himself for his slip up and her sound memory.

"Well, of course he knows. I meant no one else, you daft girl."

Neko felt her anger rear its ugly head again.

"I am not dumb. What's with you? It's like your nice one minute and then biting off my head the next. Are you bipolar or something?"

"Bipolar?"

Neko threw her arms up in the air.

"You're just so."

She clenched her fists for emphasis.

"Completely arrogant and rude, it's like you have no consideration for anyone but yourself!"

Neko stopped her rant, realizing she was making a scene and causing a few people to give her judgemental stares. Neko felt her face heat up as Troy raised an eyebrow at her display.

"If you are quite done with the dramatic monologue about my behavior, can we go back to the inn for our dinner?"

Neko sighed. Her shoulders slumping.

"Yes. Sorry I was acting like a jerk."

Troy fought the urge to sneer at her as they once again started walking towards the inn.

As they sat and enjoyed their meal, Neko decided to bring up the Lanarii.

"So, who exactly are these Lanarii and how hard will they be to find?"

Troy paused mid-chew to give her a flat look. He finished his bite and sighed.

"They are a very secretive bunch who do not like to divulge anything to anyone but themselves. They are a selfish people and finding them will not be as you say, a walk in the park."

"So, they're like Arorians?"

"You are gravely mistaken. They are a completely different race, one of barbaric woodsmen. They refuse to follow the decree of the kingdom and think they are above the ruling family because they have been here before we came into power."

"The ruling family being yours?"

Troy grunted and took another bite of his food as Neko leaned back in her wooden chair and took in the poorly lit inn. It was a large area with a bar, about ten tables and a large fireplace near the rear of the room. Everything looked to be made of sturdy wooden slabs and had the whole rustic cabin feeling to it. Neko cringed. There was even a huge stuffed black bear standing nearly seven feet tall and looked like a three-year-old had stuffed it. Neko stared as a pair of men entered the inn. One was tall and blonde-haired, and the other one was shorter and had shaggy brunette hair. Neko blinked as the blonde's frosty gaze met hers, he looked at her with scorn.

Neko jumped and looked to Troy as he rapped his fork on her plate, drawing her attention.

"Best you finish your meal while it is warm," he chided as Neko returned her gaze back to the blonde, only to find he and his friend had disappeared.

"Uh…yeah, sure thing."

She took a small bite of stew, shaking her head. Something felt strange to her, but she could not put her finger on it. Neko pushed her half-eaten bowl away. She had suddenly lost her appetite.

"I gotta go make a pitstop."

She stood up, and Troy flashed her an annoyed frown.

"Pardon me?"

Neko rolled her eyes and let out an exasperated groan.

"Gotta go pee," she whispered as she headed towards the back of the inn, leaving Troy to finish his meal.

Skylar took a seat in the shadows near the back of the inn. He had spotted Arran entering the inn, and Logan pointed to where the oblivious Prince sat at the bar, finishing his meal and pint. Arran and his men sat with Skylar, making sure to keep to the shadows.

"There is the Prince," Arran stated as he turned towards Skylar.

"Where is the girl?" he asked as Logan gestured to the lavatory.

"Go and get her, perhaps we can use her as leverage against the Princeling."

Logan got up and discreetly made his way towards the back of the inn.

Arran looked to Skylar.

"Did you find anything more out about why he is here?"

"Yes. Apart from the stones, the barmaid informed me they were talking about finding the Lanarii just now as they ate dinner."

Arran rubbed the stubble on his chin, ire flashing in his eyes.

"If he was talking about stones then I have a good idea about what he wants with the Lanarii. I doubt Lord Riken wants anything to do with the corrupt son of the King."

Skylar gestured towards the Prince.

"Shall we go introduce ourselves sir?"

"Yes. Let us go and do that."

Arran jeered as he rose and approached the unaware Prince.

Neko yawned as she exited the bathroom, or rather, what passed for a bathroom around those parts.

'That was nasty,' she thought as she rounded the corner and ran into someone. Neko stumbled backwards and looked up, her eyes meeting the dark orbs of the brunette she had seen with the blonde earlier.

"Sorry," she blurted out as the male gave her a knowing grin.

"No harm done, my dear, but I could use your assistance with something."

"With what exactly?"

Neko's eyes went wide as he pulled forth a wicked looking dagger from a sheath on his side.

"I just need for you to come along with me, quietly."

Neko took a step backwards.

"No," she stated, looking for an exit as the male smirked and lunged at her. Neko screamed and fell backwards, tripping over her own feet as she landed in a heap on the cobblestone floor, her back against the wall as the guy gave her an amused look.

"I will not harm you, if you do as I say. Now, on your feet girl."

Neko bit her bottom lip as she got to her feet, her eyes on his blade as the fellow growled in annoyance and grabbed her by the forearm, pulling her back against his chest, then resting the blade on the small of her back.

"If you scream or try to escape, I will gut you. Do you understand?"

Neko nodded, tears welling in her eyes as her heart hammered in her throat.

"Okay, okay I'll be good," she whispered as the guy grabbed her by the back of her cloak, pushing her out into the inn and towards Troy. Neko watched as a man approached Troy. There were six of them all together. The obvious leader started talking to Troy. He was slightly taller than Troy with dirty blonde hair and piercing turquoise eyes. His hair was a little on the shaggy side, and he had a five-o-clock shadow. Neko gulped. He looked mean, and when his eyes met hers, a jolt ran down her spine.

"And why would I do a damn thing for you?" Troy spat as the man gestured towards Neko.

"Because if you do not, I will have her killed."

Troy turned, his gaze catching Neko's frightened stare.

"Fine. Just do not hurt her."

Troy turned, the group heading towards the doors.

As Arran took another step towards Neko, Troy's stone lit the room with a blinding yellow light, startling the patrons. Neko screamed as she felt a burst of heat and her stone lit with a green flash of light, just as blinding as Troy's stone. Neko felt the fellow behind her jump back from the light, and it was then she saw a flash of red coming from under the leader's tunic. Neko struggled with the man holding her captive, his hand still twisted in the back of her cloak. Neko watched as Troy drew his blade and went after the leader, her jaw dropped as all the men attacking them were sent sprawling backwards by some unseen force. The leader lunged at Troy, sending the grappling men towards Neko.

"Neko, run!" Troy shouted as he pushed the leader into the bar, sending the man over the bar and careening to the floor. Neko growled and pulled against the man holding her. She let her arms go lax, and the male hung onto her cloak while she finally managed to free herself. Troy was ahead of her and slashed at the male who had been holding her. Troy grabbed her hand as she felt something latch onto her leg.

"I do not think so!" the leader growled as he held onto her foot in a crushing grip. Neko felt a rush of adrenaline course through her as she struggled to break free.

"Neko, now!" Troy snarled, jerking on her arm. Neko gave a yell, and with her free foot, she planted it right between the leader's eyes. He instantly released her. Troy pulled her to her feet, and the pair raced out the back door of the inn and into the street.

"Head for the river!" Troy ordered as the pair took off into the night.

Chapter Five

"Arran...Arran!"

Arran groaned and opened his eyes, pain splitting through his head as he blinked, someone gently shaking him.

"What happened?" he asked, sitting up as Skylar sighed.

"They have escaped sir."

"How did this happen?"

Skylar looked to his feet.

"Troy had the Wind Stone. He used it to push us back so he and the girl could escape."

Arran winced and brought his hand to his forehead. Blood came away in his hand.

"That little bitch," he snarled, remembering that Troy's companion had kicked him hard enough to knock him out.

"She had the Earth Stone!" Arran hissed as a sly smirk lit Skylar's face.

"Perhaps, but sir…"

Skylar pulled forth an amber gem.

"They did not get away completely unscathed."

Arran smirked, mirth in his eyes.

"How in the hells did you get your hands on that?"

"It was not I," Skylar paused a moment, chuckling.

"During the fight, Troy must have dropped it. I found it on the floor."

Arran took the offered stone, noticing the chain attached to it had been broken.

"Sir!"

Arran looked up as Logan raced into the room.

"We need to leave. The royal guards will be here any moment."

Arran placed the Wind Stone into his cloak and got to his feet, taking one last glance around.

"Where are the others?"

Logan spoke up, "Two were killed. The others have headed back to base, and we should be going as well."

The three men exited the rear of the inn and slipped into the shadows just as the King's guards arrived at the front doors of the inn.

Neko leaned over, her hands resting on her knees as she sucked in much-needed air, her stomach turning and threatening to eject her dinner. She had never been so frightened in all her life.

"Oh my God, they were going to…to kill us!"

Troy shot her a deadpan as he reeled in rope from the boat they had commandeered.

"I highly doubt that he wanted to ransom me to my father."

Neko stood up straight.

"Why?"

Troy looked heavenward.

"Because I am a crowned Prince and he is the leader of the rebels. His name is Arran, and he is opposed to anything to do with the royal family."

"Oh...so do you think they're going to follow us?"

Troy glared at her.

"I do not think they would give up so easily, but we have a head start. So, perhaps if we are lucky, we will lose them in the Sytonii Forest."

Neko leaned against the railing of the small boat.

"I'm sorry I lost my cloak."

"After that pathetic display, you are only sorry for losing a damn cloak?"

"What do you mean pathetic display?"

Troy glared at her, his temper now rather short.

"How did you let yourself get caught so easily?"

Neko felt her cheeks heat up. He was being mean, again.

"I'm sorry if I'm not just like you. I can't fight with a sword! Okay? But that guy scared the hell outta me. I thought he was going to stab me!"

Neko felt the tinge of tears as her eyes blurred, the adrenaline finally wearing off.

"I didn't ask for this, to come here. I just want to go home where there's wi-fi and pizza and frickin' hot running water!"

Neko let a frustrated sob escape her as she sat on the wooden deck of the boat. Bringing her knees into her body, she started sobbing in earnest.

"Why did this stupid crap happen to me?" she asked between sobs as Troy stood where he was, staring down at the distraught girl.

"Neko we must make arrangements for our journey. We do not have all the supplies needed to travel. We cannot remain where Arran and his rebels would find us. You need to get a hold of yourself. You are not a child. Stop acting like one."

Neko wiped her eyes on the sleeve of her thin hoodie as she sniffled and slowly got to her feet. Her eyes met Troy's, and she nodded.

"You're right. Crying about it isn't helping, and I don't want to go through that again."

Troy watched Neko as she sighed and kicked her toe at the ship decking.

"What are we going to do, Troy? Can't we go back? Maybe your father can help—"

"It would still take us weeks to return on foot, and it still leaves us with the problem of having no food or supplies."

Neko wrapped her arms around herself as Troy turned and started pacing the deck.

"Maybe you can teach me how to fight like you. You were really brave back there. You saved my life."

Troy blinked and then spoke, "We do not have time for fighting lessons, right now. What we must do is hit for Larrow as quickly as possible. Once there, we will have to acquire supplies and head into the forest."

Neko shivered as a small breeze picked up and tussled her hair.

"Troy?" she asked as the Prince turned, his blue eyes guarded.

"What?"

"What was that back there? Why did the stones go berserk?"

Troy busied himself with tying some of the ships rigging ropes down to the railing of the small, three-man boat.

"They lit up and reacted to one another, just like in the palace."

Neko shook her head.

"But it was more than that. Couldn't you feel the static in the room? I saw five full grown men go sailing through the air just after I felt the stones pulse!"

Troy turned, his eyes alight.

"What do you mean, the pulse? How could you possibly feel that?"

Neko's eyes met his, a firm look in them.

"I don't know. I just felt it, okay? There was a red light too. Did you see that?"

"Damn that Arran, he must have had a stone as well. We are lucky he did not have a chance to use it on us."

Neko brushed her fingers over her stone. It was cold to the touch.

"At least we have our stones."

As she spoke, Troy felt for the stone at his neck, fear filling his eyes as he searched frantically for the now missing gem.

"No!" he screamed. "This cannot be happening. I had it at the inn. Then Arran attacked me, and then I lost track of my damn stone!"

Troy gave an enraged holler and kicked at the side of the ship. Neko could only stare as Troy gave another yell and continued to rampage on the tiny boat.

"Troy, please calm down."

Neko tried to placate the Prince without setting him off anymore.

"Do not tell me to calm down, not when that bastard has my stone!"

Neko bit her bottom lip and waited until Troy calmed down on his own.

"I'm sorry you lost your stone, but we need to get away from this Arran guy. What if he wants my stone too?"

"You are correct, Neko. Forgive my outburst. We must keep moving and keep our stone away from that thieving jackal."

Neko groaned and stared over the river.

"Now what?" she asked as Troy came to stand beside her, his gaze also fixing on the inky river before them.

"We cannot do anything but get to Larrow and make haste for Rinnyus and the Lanarii."

Arran kept a watchful eye as he and his two companions made their way through the grassy plateau. The only sound was the occasional snort from their steeds. They had left the night before last and were making good time on their journey towards the Lanarii forest of Sytonii.

"Are you sure they went down the river?" Logan asked as Arran turned towards him.

“As sure as I breathe. They stole a ship and took off like the cowards they are.”

Logan shifted in his saddle as he shot Skylar a questioning glance.

“Forgive my insolence sir, but you seem to be in a rather foul mood, even for you.”

Arran gave a humorless chuckle.

“Am I now? I suppose my mood has been sour since our encounter with the Prince. I am ill at ease with what he is plotting.”

Logan raised an eyebrow.

“Plotting sir?”

Arran paused as he kept staring straight ahead. Spotting the deep green trees of the Lanarii forest in the distance, he knew they were getting closer to their domain now.

“He is after the stones. He obviously did not know I was in possession of the Fire Stone, but he must know that the Lanarii have the Stone of Water. I will not let him gain any more stones.”

Skylar looked to his leader.

“How do we know if the Lanarii will even accept our help?”

Arran smirked.

“Because before the war, the Lanarii and my people were allies. It benefits no one if the King gets his greedy hands on the element stones. That is what started the entire war, to begin with!”

Logan looked towards the treeline.

“Basically, we are to tell the Lanarii about Troy’s plot, and band together with their King to capture Troy taking the remaining stone of his?”

“It is my sworn duty as the last heir of my family to protect the stones from anyone wanting to use them for ill deeds. They were not created for world domination, and they are tools meant to help the people, not oppress them.”

Skylar let out a deep sigh.

“But to involve the Lanarii, surely we can handle this matter ourselves. It is only a Prince and a little girl.”

Arran glared at Skylar.

"Yet, when it was six against two they still managed to escape us all. Underestimating your enemy is the quickest way to get yourself killed. You would do well to remember that"

Skylar accepted the verbal assault.

"You are right sir. Forgive my impertinence."

Arran waved it off.

"And forgive my criticism towards you. I am not frustrated with you. I am angry that I let my guard down. They should have been captured easily."

Logan cleared his throat.

"Begging your pardon sir, but they did use the stone's powers."

Arran thought for a moment.

"You are right. I wonder though, how could Troy know how to summon the Wind Stone's powers? Only his father, the King, is gifted in the dark arts as far as I know and the stones have been quiet all this time. I can summon their powers because of my bloodline, but how is Troy drawing the stone's powers?"

"Perhaps it was a fluke. A lot was happening in that moment."

Arran rubbed at his chin.

"Perhaps. I do not doubt that the little Prince is following in his father's steps. We must focus on getting to Lord Riken's palace and informing him before they arrive and catch him unprepared."

Skylar looked to Logan, who, in turn, looked to their leader who continued watching the forest line.

"Let us make haste. We can reach the treeline before sunset and with any luck, reach Rinnyus before sunset tomorrow."

Arran gave a holler and kicked his horse into a run, his men right behind him as the trio thundered across the grasslands leading towards the looming Sytonii Forest.

Alexander sauntered into the inn as if he owned it, his four elite guards behind him as he cleared his throat. The entire room went silent as the King's eldest son spoke. Noble and peasant alike recognizing him.

"Innkeeper, me and my men are hungry. Fetch us some food and make ready rooms for the night."

The small man trembled before the imposing Prince.

"Of course I would, my lord, but the rooms are full you see."

Alexander pulled forth a wicked looking dagger, the blade around five inches long and the colour of coal, a slight curve to the blade and the pommel was set with a beautiful garnet stone.

"Then best you make some rooms available before my men do."

The innkeeper gulped and nodded.

"Yes, your majesty, right away."

The man took off as if the hounds of hell were on his tail. Alexander smirked and turned to the rest of the patrons.

"I am looking for some people."

He walked up to the bar and stabbed his dagger into the wooden countertop. Spotting a shot glass, he downed its contents.

"They are traveling lightly, two people, a young man, and his lady friend."

He looked around. No one made a sound as all eyes focused on the warrior.

"They would have passed through here a few nights ago."

Alexander looked up at the russet-haired barmaid who averted her eyes.

"You."

He freed his blade from the wood and pointed it at her. All colour drained from her freckled face.

"What do you know about this?"

The barmaid's voice trembled as it seemed his icy eyes bore into her soul.

"Two nights past a couple came here. They were approached by some rebels, and then they started a brawl."

Alexander continued watching her.

"Then what?"

The barmaid shrugged.

"They all took off before the guards arrived."

Alexander stood up, towering over the frightened woman.

"This couple, where did they go?"

The barmaid took a step back, bumping into one of the ale barrels, her heart hammering in her chest.

"They stole a fishing boat and went down the river, towards Larrow or Bingstur I suppose, but that is all I know. I swear milord."

Alexander returned his dagger to its sheath attached to his leather belt.

"I believe you. Now fetch us our meal and a round of ale, wench."

Alexander turned and headed for the nearest empty table, his men following suit.

"Eat up boys. We leave for Bingstur at dawn."

Lord Riken gazed out over Lake Tariin. It was nearing early evening, and the forest was alive with the chorus of thousands of crickets. Riken focused as movement near the northern border caught his eye. He smirked approvingly as his archers also spotted the movement and closed in silently, their bows aimed and arrows ready to let fly. The Lanarii disappeared into the foliage, the forest silent as Riken waited, his hand resting lightly on the handle of his katana. He did not have to wait long as three men entered the Lanarii village, Riken's men behind them, their bows aimed should any of them get the idea to attack his village.

"What business do you have in my forest, boy?" Riken spoke, his baritone deep as his tawny eyes met Arran's displeased gaze.

"Lord Riken, forgive my abrupt entrance, but I have no time for pleasantries. A prince by the name of Troy is on his way here as we speak. He seeks the Water Stone you possess."

Riken narrowed his eyes.

"Who are you?" he asked as Arran shook off the hand of the Lanarii warrior who had a decent grip on his shoulder.

"I am Arran, of the clan Destayy."

Riken perked up at the information.

"The Dolphinian Prince, yes I have heard of you, although you have left that title behind."

Arran sighed and ran his hand through his messy locks.

"My parents would not have left you to care for the Water Stone if they did not trust you."

"You are correct, but what can I do?"

Arran took a deep breath.

"I would ask your assistance to capture and relieve Troy of the Earth Stone he has in his possession. I have the other two with me."

Arran pulled forth the leather cord that had both the Wind Stone and Fire Stone attached.

"And what do you plan to do once you get the stone from Troy?"

Riken pondered as Arran looked to the Lanarii King.

"I would take them somewhere safe, where they would not be found, at least not by tainted hands."

"I agree with you, son of Trydus. These are no mere trinkets, as you well know."

Arran smirked.

"So, you will help me?"

Riken gave a slight incline of his head. His golden hair pulled back into a loose ponytail at the base of his neck ruffled slightly in the light evening breeze.

"Yes Arran, I will assist you. However, it is late, and it would be wise to start for the temple at first light."

Arran gave the Lanarii a puzzled look.

"The temple?" he questioned as the King tilted his head.

"That is where we have hidden the Water Stone, away from prying eyes, awaiting the guardian to come and claim it."

Arran ran a hand through his hair.

"As you wish. We will leave first thing tomorrow morning then."

Lord Riken gestured towards the large wooden lodge behind him.

"Come, you and your men look weary. I shall have dinner and mead prepared for you and beds for you to sleep in."

Arran gave the King a thankful look.

"Thank you for your hospitality, Lord Riken."

The Lanarii King offered a kind smile.

"Come, let us dine and further discuss this, Troy."

Neko stared across the vast expanse of the pristine Lake Ladorius.

"Wow! It's so calm. It looks like a mirror!"

Neko looked to Troy. The pair had just arrived in Larrow and were heading into the small city to gather supplies and continue into the Sytonii Forest.

"Yes, yes, yes, it is wonderful. Come along. We have no time for dillydallying."

Neko snickered and then started laughing.

"Are you serious? Did you just say dillydallying?"

Troy shot her a look of aggravation as the pair stepped off the small boat on which they had arrived.

"Are you hard of hearing suddenly?" he barked as Neko rolled her eyes.

"Who the hell pissed in your cornflakes this morning?" she grumbled as he trotted on ahead. If he heard her comment, he did not acknowledge it.

The duo arrived in the town center in record time. Troy wanted to get in, buy their supplies and get out before they drew any unwanted attention.

"Why are we being so sneaky? You said we have a head start on them."

Troy glared at Neko.

"Those damn rebels are everywhere. There is no telling if they are here in this very town. We need to keep moving. I do not need to explain to you our dire situation. If Arran gets the stone, then you will never get home. Do you want that?"

"Of course not, I want to go home!"

Troy stopped at a food vendor, haggling prices on dried venison with the shopkeeper as Neko turned to gaze at the rather large town now that she had a moment to get her bearings. The place reminded her of stone ruins as if the town had been built on top of a much larger metropolis.

"Hey, Troy." Neko waited until he turned to her, "Why does this place look like ruins?"

Troy held a large package of dried meat in his hands as he handed the shopkeeper a few gold coins.

"Because it is built on top of the ruins of a large capital, it was once called Ciinta."

"Ciinta?"

Troy started walking, so Neko fell into stride with him as they headed deeper into the bustling town.

"It was a place where all the races came to meet, and then the war happened. It was destroyed along with the peace treaty of the races."

"Like a world war?"

"I was very young when it happened. All I know is the entire land was fighting, and many of my people were killed."

Neko blew her breath up into her bangs.

"Wow. We had a war like that in my world, two actually, but that was way before I was born."

Troy zeroed in on a clothing vendor. He handed Neko the venison and smiled politely at the elderly woman.

"Perhaps you can assist me. I need a warm cloak for my friend here and some bedding and packs to carry everything in."

The woman looked the pair over, her brown eyes full of life.

"Ye two would not be looking to head into that cursed forest would ye?"

Troy gave the woman a guarded look.

"What business is it of yours, woman?"

The woman held her hands up in a placating manner.

"No need to get huffy, young sir. I was just curious. Many venture into that place. Many do not return. The Lanarii do not care for outsiders."

She looked at Neko as she spoke.

"Are ye sure ye want to trespass in their domain?"

Troy glared at the woman.

"We do as we please. Now, how much for the supplies I want?"

Troy pulled forth his coin purse, signaling the conversation was over.

"Unless I should take my business elsewhere."

The woman shook her head.

"No, no. We are finished here. That will be twenty-five gold pieces."

Troy looked a bit green.

"Pardon me?"

The old woman grinned, holding out her hand.

"Ye will not be finding a better clothing stall than mine, seeing as tis the only one in this area and ye look to be in a hurry, lad."

Neko covered her mouth with her hand, hiding the smile. This old lady was sly and reminded Neko a great deal of her ninety-four-year-old grandma back home.

"Just give me my things," he snapped, dropping the entire gold purse into the woman's hand.

"Damn thieving old hag," Troy snarled as he found what he wanted and stuffed them into the leather satchel. He tore the venison bag from Neko's grasp, stuffed that into another leather pack, and shoved it into Neko's arms along with another beautiful cloak, this one a deep grey. Neko tried to stifle her giggle, but it bubbled out, causing Troy to shoot her an aggravated glare.

"Can you handle packing the food? If you lose it, we will not get to eat."

Neko felt her jaw drop as Troy shot the old woman another dirty look before stomping towards the far end of the town, near the treeline.

"Ye best be careful, child. That one has not your best interests in mind."

The woman shot Neko a sad look.

"Heed me, child—"

Troy turned and yelled at Neko, "Time to go!"

He glared at Neko as she gave the woman an apologetic smile and trotted over to Troy.

"Sorry, holy bossy much?" she snapped as Troy turned his nose up at the old woman and exited the area, the two walking side by side.

"What did that old crow say to you just now?"

Neko sighed and adjusted the pack she held over her shoulder.

"Something about you being mean to me."

"Let us be on our way. We have been here too long. We need to get into the treeline before dusk."

Troy stopped before a chestnut mare with cream-colored mane and tail tethered to a vacant stall.

"Troy, what are you doing?" Neko asked as he glanced around and untied the horse from the post.

"I am just borrowing it," he growled as he clicked and the horse willingly followed.

"Troy!" Neko harshly whispered as she gave a panicked looked around, expecting someone to come running after them.

"Quickly now," he stated as Neko stomped her foot.

"Great. Now I'm going to get charged with grand theft pony," she spat as she raced to catch up with Troy.

Chapter Six

"Eh, you two."

Neko paused as a man in his mid-forties beckoned her and Troy over towards him as he ambled towards them. He wore rags and looked to be rather skinny.

"I saw you two, buying all that gear. You must be heading into the woods, to find the Lanarii?"

Troy approached the man.

"What do you know? Perhaps some information to my liking will merit you a few decent meals."

Troy gestured to the pack Neko carried. The man smirked, showing off the two teeth he still had in his head.

"I know lots. I hear lots. No one sees me. I am just a lowly beggar."

Troy turned up his nose.

"I can see that. Do you know where the Lanarii would keep something valuable, worth hiding in their wretched forest?"

The man smirked wider. Neko cringed at the smell of this man. He was nearly bringing tears to her eyes, and she was a good ten feet away from him.

"Well, I heard talk about a temple they have there, to worship their own gods I suppose. Perhaps they have hidden this valuable thing there."

The beggar thought a moment.

"That is what most people heading into the forest are looking for, some vast treasure the Lanarii horded in the chaos after the war."

Troy gave the man a hard stare.

"What else?"

The man glanced at the pack Neko held.

"I would be willing to tell you more if I got rewarded first."

Troy growled but walked over to Neko and pulled forth a rather large ration of dried meat from the bag she carried.

"Troy," Neko protested as he shot her a deadly look.

"We need this information."

He handed the large chunk of meat to the dirty man who grabbed it and horded all but one piece away in his raggedy clothing. He took a few bites of meat before he started to talk again.

"Yes?"

Troy prompted as the man swallowed the huge chunk he had taken whole, Neko scrunched her nose. This man reminded her of a starving dog devouring its last meal.

"The few who have returned say this temple is near Rinnyus, alongside the small lake. The entrance is a cave hidden by a waterfall. The entire temple is inside this cave, but it is guarded day and night, and no one has ever set foot in there except the Lanarii."

Troy looked skyward.

"That is all?" he sneered as the man shook his head.

"It is all I have heard. Not many have returned from that forest. You two most likely will not. You will be fodder for the Glodiirii."

Troy turned on his heel.

"Come along Neko. We have wasted enough time with this peasant. We need to find that cave."

Neko followed him, eager to get away from the beggar. That man gave her the creeps.

"At least stinky was helpful," Neko blurted out as Troy found himself smirking at her candid remark.

"Yes. He was quite ripe, but now we know exactly where to look for that stone. I know the stone is in that temple, especially if it is constantly guarded."

"What if that guy was wrong? He was hurting for a meal. What if he made it all up?"

Troy smiled, nothing nice about it.

"I never forget a face. If his information is incorrect, he will be dealt with."

Neko made a mock frightened face.

"You know you're not as scary as you think you are."

Troy glanced at her from the corner of his eyes.

"Oh really? I seem to recall you in tears the first time we met."

"Yeah, 'cause I just got dumped here, and there was a freaking dragon roaring at me!"

"I recall it almost fell on top of you when I killed it."

"That was pretty bad ass I have to admit."

Troy grinned as the pair walked through the stone archway and towards the treeline. Neko absently stroked the mare's neck.

"So, what should we name him?" Neko asked as Troy gave her a confused look.

"She is not a pet, and you should not name her. We might have to use her to keep us alive."

Neko glared at Troy.

"That's not even funny."

"I only jest. There are plenty of things to eat in the forest and fish to catch from the abundant streams."

Neko laughed as she realized he had finally loosened up and found his sense of humor.

"You know that's the first joke you've told me since I met you."

Troy paused a moment and his smile faded.

"Troy?" Neko asked looking around for any signs of trouble. "What's wrong?"

Troy shook his head.

"It is nothing. I thought I saw something. Come along. We need to quicken our pace. The trees are still a few hours walk, and sunset is fast approaching."

Neko smiled and together the pair headed towards the imposing treeline of the Sytonii Forest.

Alexander reigned in his mount as he spotted some specks in the distance, heading straight for the Sytonii Forest.

"That's them, the young feller and that girl. They asked about the Lanarii temple. Tis all I know."

Alexander sneered down at the beggar one of his men held.

"Then you are of no further use to me, peasant."

He chuckled, and with a heavy boot, he kicked the slight man full force in the chest. The man fell into a graceless heap on the ground where he fought to get his breath back.

"Move out. The sooner we get them, the sooner we go home."

Alexander spurred his horse into a brisk pace, not looking back to see if the peasant man was alive or dead. Frankly, he did not care.

Neko took a long drink out of the small spring that flowed near their makeshift camp for the night. They had arrived at the forest with some daylight left and so they had trekked into the forest a little way and set up their camp on the outskirts of a small meadow.

Troy tended the small fire they had built to keep themselves warm during the chilly late spring night. Neko sat in front of the fire, staring into its mesmerizing flames.

"Do you know how to get to the Lanarii village from here?" she asked, her gaze still on the fire as Troy sighed and threw another small branch onto it.

"It is right in the very center of this forsaken forest," he growled as Neko wrapped herself in her cloak, tired but not ready to stop watching the flames dance, their shadows bouncing off the nearby foliage almost in a frantic way.

"I think this forest is very peaceful. It feels so calm here. I've never felt this with any of the forests back home."

Neko took a deep breath, inhaling the fresh scent that only a forest could provide.

"The trees are so big, and Troy, this place is magical, don't you think?"

Troy snorted, kicking at the dirt beside the fire.

"Yes, magical, full of magic, magic Lanarii who would just as soon cut off your head than to help you."

Neko finally looked at Troy. His eyes guarded in the fading light.

"You really hate them, don't you?"

Troy threw another stick into the fire.

"They think because they can hide in this forest that they should not follow their King or his rules. They are barbarians and have no respect for the ruling family. They think they are above us."

Neko's shoulders sagged as her tired body finally decided it was time to rest.

"When I am King, I swear, I will burn this forest to the ground, and then they will have no place to hide."

"Well, good thing you're not the King then," she retorted, annoyance evident in her tone as she leaned against the tree she was sitting near and closed her eyes. She was ready for a nice long sleep. Troy watched her a moment, then shook his head as he too found a comfortable position to sleep. He doubted he would get much sleep this night. That was fine with him because once he got the Water Stone, he could afford to rest properly.

Neko opened her eyes to the sound of the brush rustling and sunlight shining on her face, almost blinding her. She glanced around in alarm as she noticed Troy still sound asleep beside her.

"Troy," she whispered. "Troy!" Neko growled and gave him a solid shot in the shoulder.

"What?" Troy hissed, opening his eyes as Neko shook his cloak.

"There's something nearby. I just heard it in the bushes!" she harshly whispered as Troy stood up, looking around as he drew his blade. A soft chuckle made the pair look to their left.

"There is no need for that, Troy. I am offended you drew your blade on your big brother."

Neko also stood up, taking in the appearance of the newcomer. His eyes were ice blue, framed by short sandy locks. He was tall and built, nearly six-foot five if Neko had to guess. Neko's jaw dropped. This guy was a brute.

"That's your brother?" Neko asked in shock, as he finally noticed her, a smirk played on his face as Neko realized he had also drawn his blade.

"You must be the little thief Father was talking about."

Neko blinked as she took a step closer towards Troy.

"Father is very angry with you Troy, stealing from him of all things."

Neko looked to Troy.

"Troy, what did you do?" Neko asked as Troy glared daggers at his older brother.

"I do not have it."

Alexander's smirk dropped, a nasty sneer replacing it.

"Is that so?" He whistled, and his four men slowly emerged from the nearby forest.

"Crap."

Neko blurted out as Alexander focused on Troy.

"Why would you steal that stone, Troy? It is not as if you can summon the powers it possesses. What did you think you two could do? Get all four stones and rule by yourselves?"

Troy growled and made a fist as Neko's jaw dropped.

"What's he saying, Troy?"

Neko looked to Alexander and back to the Prince.

"I thought you said your father wanted us to get the stones to take me back home. You said he knew what we were doing!"

Troy glared at Neko.

"Shut it, Neko."

Alexander held up his hand.

"No Troy, please explain what you are trying to do here. Obviously, you have your own agenda. Father thought the tart might be why you took the stone, but I can see she is also a pawn of your scheming."

Alexander looked towards Neko.

"Where is the stone, girl?" he asked her as Troy nudged Neko with his elbow.

"Tell him nothing."

Neko feebly laughed.

"You say that like I have a choice. I really don't want to get my head hacked off today, okay?" she spoke fast as Alexander chuckled and pointed his blade at her.

"Smart girl. Now tell me where the Wind Stone is."

"Troy was right. We don't have it. Arran has it. We lost it a few days ago."

"As in that scum sucking rebel leader!"

Alexander thundered, causing Neko to flinch. Troy took a step forward, his blade raised.

"Neko, get behind me, now."

His tone was so serious that Neko instantly obeyed and ducked behind the Prince.

"So, it comes down to this, you raising arms against me Troy, not a good idea little brother. Father wants you back in one piece.

So, you can make it easy and come along willingly, or I will beat you into a pulp and drag your sorry carcass back—your choice."

Neko trembled. This man scared the crap out of her. Troy, on the other hand, looked ready to fight as he planted his feet and took a fighting stance.

"Neko, get back," Troy ordered as Neko backed up towards the tree she had been sleeping against, keeping it to her back as Alexander and Troy started to circle one another, the men with Alexander cutting off their escape into the meadow and the forest beyond that.

"I have been spoiling for a good fight," Alexander sneered as he lunged. Troy blocked the forceful blow making the two blades ring and sending sparks to the forest floor. Neko felt her stomach turn as the pair continued to exchange blows, ones that if they were not blocking would surely sever a limb or worse.

"Stop it!" Neko shrieked. The pair ignored her and continued fighting.

"Know it all little bastard," Alexander hissed as he slid his blade against Troy's and used a cheap shot to kick his younger brother square in the knee. Troy staggered back as his injured knee buckled but he managed to deflect the blow meant to cleave his head from his shoulders.

"Give up, Troy. You cannot best me. You never could."

Alexander gloated using his blade to send Troy's clattering to the ground some five feet away. Neko felt panic welling in the pit of her stomach as Alexander went in for the killing blow.

"Stop!" Neko screamed as her stone burnt against her chest, and that blinding green light filled the entire meadow. There was a loud crashing noise as the very earth itself reared up, and a rather large vine caught Troy's brother across the back, propelling him some ten feet before he fell into a tree trunk and knocked himself out.

"Troy!" Neko shouted as she raced to help the dazed Prince, grabbing his blade as she raced by it, passing it to him to sheath as she helped him to his feet.

"Come on!" Neko screamed as Alexander's men regained their senses and came at the pair.

Neko blinked as an arrow with black feathers struck one of the guards straight in the chest.

"Lanarii. Neko, we need to go," Troy hissed in pain as Neko put his arm around her shoulders and helped him to hobble back into the cover of the brush. Neko could hear the yell of Alexander's men as they attacked whoever had shot that arrow.

"Get on the horse, quickly," Troy ordered, untying the mare as he climbed on the horse and Neko followed suit. Troy urged the horse into a run, and together the pair disappeared into the forest as the last of Alexander's elite guards fell to the fighting prowess of the Lanarii warriors.

Chapter Seven

Troy cursed as he pulled on the reigns, stop-ping the mare in the center of a small glade.

"We should be far enough away. Besides, those guards will keep the Lanarii busy for a while," Troy hissed as Neko got off the horse and tried to help him to the ground.

"I do not need your assistance," he snarled as he landed on his feet, his knee sending a jolt of pain throughout his entire body.

"That was a pretty hard kick, Troy. I can help you I do know a bit of first aid."

Troy gave her a screwy look.

"First aid?" he asked as Neko furrowed her eyebrows.

"It's like a lesson you go to, to learn how to treat minor injuries like sprains and getting cheap shots in the knee by psychotic big brothers."

Troy gave her a tight smirk as Neko gestured to a nearby rock.

"You should sit down and rest it for starters. You're lucky he didn't break your leg."

Troy ground his teeth as he awkwardly took a seat on the nearest flat boulder. Neko knelt before him and started to help him take off his boot. She was relieved that his pant legs were rather wide, she didn't much feel like telling him to take his pants off. In fact, as she rolled his pant leg up, she could feel the telltale heat of a blush creeping up her neck, and she was sure her face was making a very good impression of a tomato.

"Neko, you look flushed."

There was something of amusement in his tone that made her look up. As her eyes met his, she could see mirth in their cerulean depths.

"It's nothing, just a side effect of life-threatening situations," she quickly snapped as she took in his knee.

"This looks painful."

Neko quickly changed the subject as she gently held his calf muscle, examining his kneecap.

"Okay, so when he kicked you, do you remember feeling or hearing any snapping noises?"

Troy shook his head.

"It is not broken."

"I know that, but sometimes if there is a snapping or popping noise, it could mean a torn ligament."

Troy looked down at her as if she had grown another head.

"It's a fancy word for the muscles around your knee," she answered his unasked question as he sighed and shook his head.

"No. I heard nothing."

Neko gently massaged his knee. She could see where a bruise was forming.

"Well, it's not swollen, so that's a good sign."

Neko released his leg.

"Can you try bending it for me? If it hurts, then stop, okay?"

Troy obliged her request and slowly extended his knee, wincing slightly as he returned it to the previous position.

"It is tender but does not hurt as much as earlier."

"I think you're okay, just bruised it is all, which is a good thing. You're very lucky. That jerk kicked you hard."

Troy had to agree with her there.

"Yes, he can be a meat-headed imbecile at times, but do not let that fool you. He is as cunning as a fox, which is why he is dangerous. Thank you, by the way. I saw what you did to save me."

Neko placed her hand behind her head and chuckled lightly.

"Yeah about that, I have no idea how I did it. I guess that's what you meant by being able to summon its powers, eh?"

Troy groaned and stretched his leg out, testing his injured knee.

"There's a test they do to check your injuries. I think it's called the McMurray test. You just gotta move your knee around and listen for clicking. I think you're okay though. Maybe we can just wrap it and put a cold compress on it."

Troy snorted and stood up.

"It is fine, Neko. I can already put weight on it."

Troy demonstrated as he stood on both his legs, no pain on his face.

"Well, that's good news. All the same, maybe you should take it easy for a few days."

Troy scoffed as he sat back down and started unrolling his pant leg.

"I thank you for your concern, but it is unneeded. We do not have the luxury of resting, not when we still have to find that temple."

Neko rolled her eyes.

"Whatever. So, what's your master plan oh great one? We did find the Lanee or whatever they're called, and then we ran away from them since they decided they wanted to bust an arrow in our asses."

Troy finished putting his boot back on and continued to sit on the rock, giving the girl a hard stare. He could tell she was mocking him and he did not understand her odd words.

"It is the Lanarii, and since we have yet again lost all of our supplies, I suppose the best thing we can do is retrace our steps and perhaps tail the Lanarii back to their village. With any luck, they will lead us straight to the temple."

Neko glared at the Prince, throwing her arms up in the air.

"Are you completely insane? Did you not see what they just did to those men with your brother? And you want to follow them. What if they see us? What if they try to kill us, again?"

Neko crossed her arms glaring at the ground as she muttered.

"'Cause apparently, everyone we meet wants to kill us."

"Are you frightened of a few woodland sprites?"

"It's not the ones I can see that worry me."

Troy snorted and got to his feet fixing her with a haughty stare.

"We can make some camouflage, and if we stay behind them, they will not think we are reckless enough to follow them."

Neko seemed to ponder this a moment before nodding.

"Yes, you have a good point, but won't they be long gone by now?"

"No. They will have to do a body count of Alexander's men. If Alexander is alive, which he probably is, they will capture him and take him to their village to have judgment passed upon him by their King."

"What about the horse?"

"She is too loud in the forest."

Troy removed the saddle and bridle and then smirked at Neko.

"It will give any nearby Lanarii something to chase."

He gave the mare a solid slap on the rear end causing her to whinny in protest and take off into the forest, breaking and snapping the foliage as she plowed through the area.

"Now, let us salvage what we can from the supplies we do have."

Neko glanced down at the satchel hanging across her left shoulder and nestled against her right hip.

"Well, at least I managed to hold onto this."

She gestured to the pack she had by her side. Troy glanced up and grinned.

"That is a good thing. Now we do not have to waste valuable time gathering food."

Neko stopped and watched Troy as he turned to face her, wondering why she had stopped walking.

"Hey, Troy, I think I'm gonna need some sort of a weapon before we keep going, given the trouble we seem to attract."

Troy gave Neko a once over.

"Perhaps you are correct. Here. Do not lose it."

He unbuckled a small, sheathed dagger from his belt handing it to Neko who took it, giving him an unimpressed look.

"What the hell am I supposed to do with this, butter bread?"

Troy took a long deep breath.

"No, if you would just trust what I say, the size is not important."

Neko raised an eyebrow, her mouth taking over.

"Sure, that's what all the guys with short swords say."

Troy decided to ignore her crass statement and snatched the blade back, removing it from the sheath to show it to Neko. The blade was only three inches long but had waves down the entire blade with a deadly sharp point. The silver blade had a slight red tint to it. The handle bound in leather had a small pommel on the end with an obsidian stone embedded.

"You see this blade, although small, is deadly. It has been coated in a poison that will momentarily stun an enemy, giving you a chance to escape. Case in point. Back at the inn, I should have seen you were fitted with some sort of protection."

Troy offered Neko the dagger again. This time she carefully took the blade, examining it.

"I did not think we would have attracted this much attention in so little time." He admitted grudgingly.

Neko carefully sheathed the blade and secured it to the waistband of her jeans, offering Troy a pensive smile.

"Thanks. I'll take good care of it."

Troy gave a stiff nod.

"See that you do, it was a gift from my mother, and you may borrow it only until we find you a suitable replacement."

Troy straightened his shoulders and started walking. Neko just smiled and shook her head as the pair started their trek back towards their old camp. Hopefully, with any luck, they would quickly find the Lanarii and be able to follow them back to the temple.

They arrived at their old camp in good time.

"Wait," Troy hissed as he grabbed her by the arm and the pair crouched in the underbrush.

"Look," Troy whispered, pointing to a group of four Lanarii surrounding something some twenty feet away.

"Disgusting, forest dwelling dung heaps."

Neko cringed as Alexander's voice thundered, masking any sound of their approach.

"We should take him to Lord Riken," one of the Lanarii spoke, ignoring Alexander who sat with his hands bound behind his back and a nasty cut above his right eyebrow.

"Do you filthy heathens know whom you are dealing with?"

"At least his big mouth will hide any noise that we might make," Neko retorted as the pair continued watching from their hiding spot.

"We do not care who you are. You are trespassing into our domain. Therefore, whoever you are beyond this place has little meaning to us."

Troy snickered as Alexander's face went red. He started screaming all sorts of profanities and insults at the Lanarii who ignored him with a will power Neko had never before seen.

"Wow, your brother has some impressive vocabulary going on there."

Troy scoffed as the pair slowly followed the group of Lanarii and their vulgar prisoner.

"He is a tactless brute. He cares not for anyone but himself. Do not trust him or his false words."

"Oh yeah, about that, he was right when he said your father didn't know what we were doing."

Troy knew that accusing tone all too well and he cursed that girl for having such an impervious awareness of what his brother had said before their duel.

"I am sorry I lied to you, Neko, but please let me explain."

Neko folded her arms across her chest, her annoyance at its peak.

"Well, then, enlighten me," she sneered as Troy ran a hand through his locks, his eyes meeting hers, which were ablaze with ire.

"My father had the Wind Stone in the treasury for years, and I was afraid if he found out you had the Earth Stone he would want that too, and then you would have no way of getting home again."

Neko's annoyance faded into bemusement.

"My father is not as nice as he seems. Look at how he set my brother upon me. He is a power-hungry tyrant."

"So that's why at the castle you were so angry towards him."

Troy pointed towards the Lanarii.

"Come along. We need to keep pace, if you wish to further discuss this, we can later."

Neko shook her head as the pair slinked after the retreating Lanarii.

"It's fine Troy, but next time, just tell me the truth, okay?"

"We have an accord."

"All right, an accord it is. Now, let's go find that temple."

Arran impatiently kicked at the ground as he, his two men, and Riken along with two of his Lanarii guards stood nearby the pool and small waterfall that concealed the entranceway to the temple.

"What if they come another way? We have been here half this day and seen nothing," Arran grumbled as Riken chuckled.

"A patient hunter must sometimes wait for the prey to find them. We know where they want to go. They will come here and this way, it is the only way in from Larrow."

Arran offered the Lanarii King an apologetic look.

"I do not understand why we do not acquire the Water stone first."

Riken rubbed his chin, fixing the Prince with a calculating stare.

"You want the stone Troy has in his possession, correct?"

"Of course, I do."

Riken gestured to the temple.

"Then we await him here. Once he is relieved of his stone, we may venture into the caves at our leisure for the last stone. It will do us no good if we go to get the Water Stone and miss the chance to capture Troy."

Arran felt like a fool, a small child reprimanded for his insolent behavior.

"You are anxious to return the stones to safety. I understand your fear, young Prince, but you must keep your wits about you and focus on the task at hand."

Arran exhaled, giving the Lanarii King a humble expression.

"Forgive my tirade. You are correct. I am worried about the stones."

"Perhaps we should send the men out with their bows. We will have the element of surprise when Troy does arrive."

"That is a good idea."

Arran made a gesture towards his men.

"You heard Lord Riken. Go find a place to keep watch."

Skylar and Logan nodded and trekked into the surrounding forest, Riken's men doing the same, leaving the King and Prince to wait by the entranceway. They had not waited long when Arran spoke up.

"What will you do with Troy once he is—"

Riken cut Arran off by raising his hand, signalling silence.

"Do you hear that?" he asked as Arran focused on the noises of the forest.

"...me...were watching them too!"

Arran blinked, that feminine voice familiar.

"...were not for your breaks every ten minutes."

Riken gestured they should find cover. The pair ducked behind a large rock outcrop as the voices got closer.

"It wasn't every ten minutes! Why do you have to be so...so..."

Troy cut Neko off.

"So, what?" he sneered, his knee was still tender, and it had put him in a foul mood despite the girl's attempts to keep the peace between them. Now they had lost sight of the Lanarii that had captured Alexander, and they were wandering around lost in the forest. Neko gave an enraged shout.

"So damn mean. You know, I've done nothing to you, and you still treat me like I don't know anything!"

Troy blinked as they stopped in the clearing, a clear pool of water and waterfall looking rather inviting.

"Uh... wow," Neko stated, cutting her rant short as she took in the serene area. "This place is something else."

Her voice was full of wonder as she stood before the falls, admiring its alluring view.

"Yes, it is awe-inspiring. Perhaps you should focus less on staring with your maw wide open collecting flies and focus more on locating that cave."

Neko shot Troy a disgruntled scowl.

"And maybe you should focus less on being an ass."

Troy turned, anger in his eyes, but paused, Neko gasped and pointed, grinning ear to ear.

"Troy look!" she waved to the darkness beyond the curtain of water falling from the ledge above.

"It's a—"

Troy cut her off approaching the cave.

"It is a cave behind a waterfall," he stated with glee in his voice as Neko followed him towards a large boulder.

"That is far enough," Arran growled as he and another man stepped into view. Both had their blades drawn.

Neko stared at the other man, realizing that he was a Lanarii. There was something daunting about the way he held himself. He was a few inches taller than the rebel leader but lankier. He had long wheat-coloured hair pulled back in a ponytail with honey-coloured eyes that were guarded.

"Not good," Neko hissed as Troy drew his blade, glaring at the pair.

"Surrender Troy. You are surrounded, and it is two against many."

Riken's gaze caught Neko's and she could not look away. Something about his stare made her freeze in her tracks as if he could see into her very soul.

"Neko!"

Troy's voice and a well-placed elbow to her ribs snapped Neko from her trance.

"We need to get to the trees," he whispered as Neko turned and groaned spotting four men approaching. They were surrounded.

"Slight problem with that," she murmured as Troy glanced over his shoulder cursing as they backed up, the six men closing in on them.

"Surrender Troy. You have nowhere to run."

Neko felt her heart in her throat as they tried to find any means of escape.

Troy stood before her, his blade raised as they backed against the bank. The only way out was to jump into the water and try to swim across and get into the forest beyond that.

"Go now!" Troy yelled as he pushed Neko forward and jumped in after her.

"Swim!" he yelled as they made a mad dash for the far bank some thirty feet away. Neko fought to keep her breathing normal as the frigid water made her entire body tingle. Thankfully, the adrenalin masked most of the coldness, and she focused on one thing and only one thing, escape.

Neko and Troy made it to the other bank quickly, the six men racing to catch them.

"Run!"

Troy yelled as the pair dashed towards the cover of the dense trees. Neko did not look back as she tore into the forest. She could hear angry shouts behind her, and a blazing heat on her chest informed her that once again her stone was doing something to protect her. She ran for what seemed like forever, not even stopping when a low branch caught her in the left cheek, making the entire side of her face sting. When she finally stopped to catch her breath, she paused looking back only to see that Troy was not beside her. Neko looked around frantically. She couldn't even call for him without risking capture. Neko shivered as the adrenalin finally faded, and her legs felt like jelly. She let herself fall to the forest floor. She had left him behind with those men. Troy was gone. She was completely alone, soaking head to toe, freezing and lost in a forest filled with hostile rebels, and who knew what else.

"Just perfect," she whimpered, tears cascading down her cheeks as she let forth a sob. What was she supposed to do now?

Arran cursed as he lost track of the tart. She did not look it, but the girl could move. Arran profaned and slashed at a tree with his blade. It did not help that vines and rocks seemingly kept popping up and further hindered his success at capturing the girl who ran like a possessed thing. He arrived back at the falls in a disgruntled state, even thought they had easily captured Troy. Riken glanced up as Arran returned alone.

"She gave me the slip."

Arran answered the Lanarii King's unspoken question.

"Well, that is most unfortunate because he does not have the element stone, meaning she does."

Troy sat on the ground, his hands bound behind his back, much like his brother's had been hours before.

"Tell me, does that putrid little tart have the Earth Stone?" Arran growled at Troy as he stood towering over the Prince.

Troy replied by spitting on Arran's boots. It was the last thing Troy saw before his world went dark.

Arran looked towards Riken who shook his head.

"I suppose we should get him back to the village. He will be questioned and dealt with, as for the girl."

Riken glanced into the forest. The sun would soon be disappearing and covering the area in the dark.

"She could not have gone far. I will track her. The rest of you head back to the village."

Arran looked towards the Lanarii King, a protest dying on his lips as the King spoke, "I travel quicker alone."

Riken gave a curt nod and turned, heading into the forest Arran had appeared from minutes before. Arran sighed and turned as two Lanarii gathered the unconscious Troy between them and started their short trek back to the Lanarii village of Rinnyus.

Neko shivered as she wrapped her arms around her torso. She was soaked through. She groaned and removed the sodden cloak around her shoulders, letting it fall to the forest floor with a squelching noise. She rubbed her hands together as her teeth chattered.

"I need a fire," she said to herself as she gathered a few dry sticks. Neko cursed as she realized that her lighter was probably ruined and sitting at the bottom of the waterfall pool along with the pack of venison, she had dropped while trying to escape the Lanarii and rebels. Everything she possessed now consisted of the clothing she wore, her dagger and the emerald.

"Just great," she spat, tears of frustration filling her eyes as she kicked at the pathetic attempt for a fire pit, her temper getting the better of her as she gave an enrages holler. She froze as a movement to her right caught her eye. She felt her heart quicken as she ducked, trying to conceal herself in the forest as she drew the dagger at her side, making sure not to accidently cut herself on the blade. Scarcely breathing, she watched the spot. Slowly, she sat up and crept backwards, her chest warming where her stone sat. Neko turned, ready to run, only to come face-to-face with the Lanarii with the amber eyes.

"Oh, crap," she whispered as she scrambled to get away, screaming as her foot caught a rock and she fell backwards. The Lanarii approaching her, his blade drawn as she pointed her dagger in his direction.

"Surrender. You have nowhere to run."

His voice was calm, and she almost wanted to believe him.

"Stay away from me."

She meant to sound fearless, but it came out a whisper as she backed up, the hard ground biting into her elbows.

The warrior did not listen as he closed in on her, intent on grabbing her before she got the urge to run or attack him. He could tell from her posture and the way her hand that held the dagger shook that she was trying to put on a brave front.

"Don't touch me!"

This time she did scream, and Riken jumped back alarmed as a blinding green light emanated from her chest, dazing him. It was only his finely tuned senses that helped him avoid a vine that shot out of the ground straight for his face. He landed in a crouch as the green light faded and the girl scrambled to her feet, her dagger raised and fire burning in her grey eyes. She was panting for air as she looked around wildly for the Lanarii. Riken slowly stood, taking in her state of disarray. Her hair plastered to her head and a rather large gash on her cheek had crusted blood on it. She was shivering, and her lips had a slightly bluish tinge to them. She seemed to be just as alarmed by the vines as he was.

"I will not harm you if you surrender."

Riken's tone calmed as he slowly sheathed his blade. The girl seemed to calm down slightly, distrust in her eyes as he slowly approached her. Her attire was rather odd. She wore light blue pants and a funny shirt with a hood on the back.

"You are cold and wet. If you stay out here like this, you have a great chance of getting sick."

The girl continued to stare at him with wide eyes as he stopped five feet from her.

"I am Riken, King of the Lanarii, and you have my word no one will harm you if you surrender your blade and come with me."

The girl's expression remained the same as he awaited her answer.

"That stone you have, you managed to activate it. Quite a feat."

"You mean the vine?" she asked. He nodded.

"You summoned it. You willed it, and it obeyed your will to be protected."

He slowly unclasped his cloak, holding it out to her.

"Here. You are shivering."

She narrowed her eyes, obviously not trusting him, as the stone pulsed to life, seeming to resonate with her heartbeat. Riken offered her a calm look.

"If I meant you harm, I would not be trying to help you."

The girl seemed to agree with that as she reached out and snatched the cloak, wrapping it around herself. Her eyes were still on Riken as he held his hand out, gesturing to her dagger. Neko sighed. She had nowhere else to run and staying the night in the dark forest was not on the top of her to-do list. She returned her dagger to its sheath and then handed the covered blade over to the Lanarii. He took it and tucked it away into his belt giving Neko a curious stare.

"What is your name?" he asked as she shivered.

"My name is Neko," she replied, his cloak instantly warming her as she inadvertently inhaled the scent of pine needles that clung to it. Riken smiled at her.

"Well, then Neko, I need for you to come with me. Your friend is alive, I can assure you."

"Why are you being so nice to me?" she blurted out, causing Riken to chuckle.

"I am a very good judge of character. I am at ease with you. Therefore, I will treat you respectfully unless you give me cause not to."

"Troy told me you would just as soon kill us than to help us."

"You should not believe all you are told. What do you feel? What does your gut tell you?"

Neko thought a moment as she got to her feet.

"That you mean me no harm," she stated as Riken nodded approvingly.

"Come now. You will need clean clothing and a good hot meal. It is a short journey to Rinnyus."

Neko followed the Lanarii King into the forest, the encroaching darkness no longer drawing fear from her.

Chapter Eight

Troy groaned as he slowly opened his eyes. His head ached something fierce, and his shoulders felt like they were on fire. As he looked around, he noticed another person sitting across from him with arms bound behind him, a wooden pole holding him prisoner. As Troy's vision cleared, he recognized the other prisoner.

"So, he lives."

His older brother sneered as Troy found himself also tethered to a wooden post in what looked to be a storage building of some sort.

"Alexander."

Troy bit out as he tried his restraints finding that they were not budging.

"Do not bother. Those imps know how to tie ropes."

Troy cursed, leaning his head back against the post.

"Where is your little friend?"

Alexander leered as Troy shot him an annoyed scowl.

"How the hell should I know, she took off into the forest when we were attacked."

"I imagine you could not run so well with an injured leg and all."

Troy glared at his brother.

"Perhaps we could put aside our differences and band together to get out of this place."

Troy cut to the chase as Alexander thought a moment.

"What do I get out of it?"

"For starters, revenge."

"Then you mean to go through with it, overthrowing Father?"

Troy gave him a guarded look.

"And if I am?"

"Perhaps it is time that fossil was dethroned. If you can get us out of here, then I will offer my allegiance to you, but in return, I want one of the stones."

Troy glared at his brother.

"After you tried to kill me?"

"Do not be so dramatic. What other option do you have at the moment, Troy? We are surrounded by the enemy."

"Fine. Let us just worry about escaping first. Shall we?"

"Fair enough. What did you have in mind little brother?"

Neko glanced up, watching the back of Riken's head. For some reason, she had taken an instant liking to him. She felt a pang of guilt. He was supposed to be the bad guy. He stopped, looking back at her over his shoulder.

"Do you need to rest a moment?" he inquired as Neko shook her head.

"No. I'm good."

"We can stop if you like. I can see just as well in the dark. I have walked this forest for many years."

Neko sighed and nodded. Finding a log, she sat down. She felt exhausted.

"I'm sorry. I just feel so tired."

Riken turned to face her.

"You summoned the power of the Earth Stone. The fact that you still remain standing is impressive. You do not give yourself enough recognition."

Neko felt her cheeks warming at the complement.

"I guess so."

Riken gave her a calculating stare.

"You do not understand the magnitude of that stone. Yet, you summon the stone's powers like a reflex."

Neko's eyes met the Lanarii's.

"Are you really a King?" he offered her a kind smile.

"Yes. Do I not look the part?" he teased as Neko softly smiled.

"You just seem so young is all."

"In human years, I am quite old, but as a Lanarii, I am considered a young adult."

"So, your age would be…?" she couldn't help being so nosy, but she was curious, and this Lanarii didn't seem so bad. Plus, she had never met one or known them to exist a few weeks earlier. Looking at him, he reminded her of an elf, and she wondered if the Lanarii were a certain type of elven people.

"I am nearing my second hundredth year."

Neko felt her jaw drop and then words flew from her mouth without her filtering them.

"Holy shit!" she froze and covered her mouth with both her hands.

"Sorry," she whispered as Riken blinked then chuckled.

"It is refreshing to speak with someone in such a frank way. I take no offence, Neko."

Neko giggled nervously.

"It's just, wow, two hundred! That's like really old. I mean not that you look old like you look good for two centuries and I'm just gonna shut right up now," her voice tapering off as she felt like her face was on fire and noticed Riken smirking down at her.

"You are a most peculiar girl, Neko."

Neko looked to the ground and then back up at Riken.

"So, are you like an elf?"

The look Riken shot her could have curdled cream.

"The Lanarii are nothing like the elves."

Neko blinked.

"Oh?" she questioned as Riken sighed and his glare disappeared.

"Forgive my outburst. You see, many think that the Lanarii are a specific breed of elves, which we are not."

Neko nodded, not sure what else to do.

"We are not even a distant relation. Our people go back hundreds of years, elves are darker beings and have an immense hatred for any race other than their own. We keep to ourselves but will not attack senselessly like the elves."

Neko glanced down, she gasped, and her head shot up as a loud howl pierced the night's silence.

Neko stood straight up, her eyes wide as she looked to Riken who rested his hand on the hilt of his sword.

"What was that?" she asked as a shiver ran down her spine. Another howl filled the silence, this time sounding closer.

"They are the Glodiirii, wolves of the ancient woods."

Neko thought a moment, the name familiar.

"The old guy mentioned them in the village, but they're just wolves," she stated as Riken shot her an irritated stare.

"They are not just wolves. They protect this forest from outsiders. They must have caught wind of the earlier battle. Quickly, we must make haste. Even the Lanarii do not cross their path if they can avoid it."

Neko stumbled as Riken seized her by the right wrist, pulling her into the forest.

"Why are they so scary?" Neko asked feeling like something was watching her.

"They are the size of a bear, and they do not like men in their forest. You have heard that the Lanarii are responsible for people going missing in the Sytonii, which is not the case. Most likely they have run into the Glodiirii."

Neko winced as his grip tightened and she stumbled.

"Slow down would ya?"

Riken only seemed to quicken their pace.

"We play a dangerous game. We must leave this area."

Neko felt sick as they raced through the dark woods. She could not see anything and trusted that Riken knew where he was going. Riken came to a screeching halt as they stopped in a small glade.

"Riken?" Neko asked as he cursed in his native tongue.

"We cannot go further. They have us surrounded," he growled as he drew his blade. Neko felt her heart in her throat as she caught a flash of holographic green, eyes in the forest all around them.

"Now what?" she asked as Riken released her wrist and took a fighter's stance.

"I will try to fend them off, but I am one against many."

Neko screamed as she heard a savage growl rip through the air. Again, she felt her stone warming against her skin as more snarls joined the first, there must have been ten or so wolves, circling them just outside her field of view.

"What about the trees, can't we hide in the branches?"

Panic laced her voice as the growls and snarls seemed to increase in volume.

"They are closing in now. We would never make it in time."

As he spoke in resignation, a huge body came charging towards them, Neko screamed in terror and the entire area filled with a flashing green light.

"What in the hells was that?"

Alexander growled as he and Troy both saw the quick flash of green light emit from somewhere off in the distance.

"Lightning?"

Troy offered as Alexander shook his head.

"That was no lightning, and there is not a cloud in the sky."

The oldest brother snarled as he looked around. He and Troy had been moved out into the open to be better watched by the guards. When checked hours before, Riken's men had discovered Alexander nearly free of his ropes. Arran had been livid and ordered his men to watch the brothers every move.

"Did you see that!"

One of Arran's men stated, looking to a Lanarii who nodded.

"The Glodiirii are restless, they call to each other."

Arran growled in annoyance and looked to the Lanarii that spoke.

"What about Riken?"

The Lanarii looked anxious.

"Usually the Glodiirii do not bother the Lanarii, but they are ill at ease, and I fear they stand between our King and his path home."

"But he is the King of the Lanarii, why would the wolves attack him?"

The warrior gave Arran a flat look.

"Perhaps the Glodiirii are not perusing him but the one he set out to find, the girl."

"This is not good, should we go after him?"

"You and your men are safe here, venture outside theses walls and not even we can protect you from the Glodiirii. We must wait and hope that Lord Riken has found refuge in the forest away from their wrath."

Arran glared over at Alexander who chuckled at the irate Prince.

"Is there something that amuses you?" Arran asked as Alexander gave him a calculating stare.

"For the leader of the rebels, I thought you would be taller."

Troy smirked at the indignant look Arran shot the eldest brother.

"Leaving us so soon?"

Alexander taunted as Arran turned and left the area, he was in no mood to deal with the idiot sons of the King. Alexander grinned at his brother.

"With any luck, those mongrels got the Lanarii King."

"We better pray they have not because if Neko is with him then so is the Earth Stone and we both need that stone to arrive here safely if we stand any chance of escape."

"Do you actually think the little brat is capable of rescuing us?"

Troy elbowed his brother.

"We do not need her to save us per se. We only need the stone she has, once she arrives we will have to escape our bindings, grab the stones from Arran and make for home, Father cannot know of our plan to dethrone him."

"And how pray tell do we escape? They are watching us like hawks not to mention those beasts running around the forest."

Troy glared at a nearby rebel.

"You asked me to trust you. Now it is your turn to trust me, brother."

"As you wish, I am curious to see what scheme you have up your sleeve little brother."

Neko slowly opened her eyes, blinking she found strong arms wound around her and as she looked around she noticed two things, one she was practically being smothered by someone she had only just met and two they were not being ripped apart by huge wolves. Neko pushed at the King's chest. He realized they were both unharmed and released her, allowing her to regain some of her personal space. He gazed around, his eyes resting on what had saved them, large pillars made from the earth itself had seemingly sprung up, surrounding them in a small enclosure, keeping the Glodiirii out but also keeping them trapped with the ancient wolves standing just outside, looking rather perplexed.

"What is this?"

Riken wondered aloud as he looked down at Neko who looked just as confused. It was then he noticed the fading green glow coming through her shirt just above her breasts.

"You have summoned the Earth Stone once again."

It was a statement Neko realized as his eyes gave her a piercing stare.

"And if I did?" she asked her voice hitching as the King gave her a serious look.

"Calling upon the powers of that stone is dangerous for a human. The ancient powers are not meant for your kind to be foolishly summoning."

Neko gave him an irritated look, her eyes meeting his in a searing gaze.

"Is it foolish to not want to get my head gnawed off?"

Her voice was quiet and calm, but Riken could see the anger pooling behind her silvery eyes as a Glodiirii snarled in the background.

He paused, realizing she was fighting the urge to let her emotions go, the wolves could sense panic and it would only further their efforts to rend the pair limb from limb.

"I understand your point of view. Perhaps we shall further debate this once we are able to move about freely."

Neko sighed and turned, taking in the feral beasts, which were far from feral once she happened to catch the eyes of a white one.

"He is the alpha."

Riken offered, catching her stare as Neko gazed into deep amber. There was an intelligence in those eyes that she had never seen in any animal from her world. It was breathtaking, reminding her of the dragon she had seen earlier.

"You're right. They are not mindless animals, they are beautiful."

Riken blinked, most humans only saw voracious beasts with the intent to kill.

"That may be, but there is still the matter of being surrounded by them, they will not let us go."

Neko continued to stare at the alpha, her hand slightly dropping as slowly the earth spikes lowered and she drew a shaky breath.

"What are you doing?" he hissed grabbing her by the upper arm causing her to wince as his grip left bruises. A nearby wolf snarled causing Riken to release her immediately.

"Please, we mean no harm."

Neko spoke, her tone taking a regal quality as she slowly held a steady hand out towards the alpha. The alpha gave her a knowing stare and then to Riken's astonishment he walked forward to scent Neko's outstretched hand. She gave a shaky breath.

"We got lost, we didn't mean to disrespect your forest, and we'll leave, just please let us pass through safely."

Riken watched as Neko paused, as if listening, but that was impossible, humans were deaf to the language of the ancient animals. Most likely, she was just talking to keep herself calm.

Neko stood still as the alpha approached her, his face inches from hers, he could kill her in a heartbeat, and yet she let him look her in the eyes, Riken had to admit, he was captivated by her courage. His eyebrows nearly disappeared into his hairline when she reached forward and stroked the white wolf's cheek, smiling when the wolf allowed her to touch him.

"Thank you," she whispered as the wolf took a step back and signalled to his pack. Within moments, they had faded into the fog that surrounded the area as if they too were only part of the mist. As they departed so did the unnerving fog.

Chapter Nine

Neko and Riken stayed as they were for a few moments, making sure the wolves were gone before they both let out the breath they had been holding.

"How did you do that?" Riken asked as Neko grinned.

"My silver tongue?" she offered as Riken shook his head.

"You used the element stone to calm them?"

"No. It was so weird, like a dream. I swear I could hear him talking to me, like inside my head."

Riken was clearly confused with what she was telling him.

"It wasn't so much in words as it was pictures and feelings. I could just sense he realized we were lost and not trying to hurt anything, so he told us to go, but then he showed excitement to meet me, which I didn't really understand. We should probably get moving before he changes his mind."

Riken stared at her as she started speaking rather quickly, the excitement evident in her voice.

"I can't believe he let me pet him. It was so cool and...Riken?"

"That stone, I must ask that you give it to me for the time being. You understand I cannot let you into my village where there is the potential you could attack me or my men."

Neko blinked. His tone was kind, but he was deadly serious.

"And if I say no?"

"You would not be allowed to enter Rinnyus I am afraid."

Neko bit her bottom lip.

"Will I get it back?"

Riken gave her a hard stare.

"I am not sure yet. I have a hunch about where it is that you come from, but I must reserve my judgment until I can prove what it is I wish to say."

As he spoke, Neko happened to glance down at a small plant just below eye level. It was like nothing she had ever see at home. It had small green leaves that almost had a silver hue to them and from the leaves sprouted a single flower. It reminded her a great deal of a tiger lily but with a smaller blossom and a deep silver colour, making her think of moonlight. She reached out to pick the flower deciding it would make a nice souvenir once dried and pressed. Riken glanced up just to see Neko reach for the flower. He recognized the plant immediately and lunged forward, knocking Neko's hand away from it, cursing as the plant brushed against the back of his hand, burning his skin where it made contact.

"What was that for?" Neko snarled, annoyed with the Lanarii's peculiar behavior. Her sneer fell as she watched his face contort in pain.

"Riken?" she asked as he leaned against a tree and slid to a sitting position, cradling his injured hand.

"That is moonsbayne. It is very poisonous."

Neko felt her stomach turn.

"Oh my gosh, what do we do?"

Riken gave her a serious look as he lifted his uninjured hand towards the forest trying to keep his breathing slow and even. Panic would only quicken the poison.

"Listen very carefully to me. You need to go into the forest and find a plant. I do not have much time."

Neko awed at how calm he was. Even as he spoke, she could see his complexion was turning a deathly parlor.

"There is a plant that grows on the forest floor, a moss, but it is almost black in colour. You cannot mistake it. Grab it and get it back to me as quickly as you can."

"Wait, you want me to go out in that forest alone? I can't... I don't know—"

"If you do not help me, I will die. The poison acts quickly. It will render me unable to move and eventually stop my heart."

Neko scrambled to her feet.

"Okay, black moss. Just hold on!"

Realizing how grim the situation was, Neko raced into the woods, scanning the forest floor for the black moss. She felt a sense of desperation when she could not locate the moss immediately. She knew it had only been a few minutes, but it felt like an entire hour had passed. She paused as she glanced to her left and there sitting on a rock near her feet was what looked to be moss, and it was black! Neko squealed in delight and ripped a large chunk from the rock as she raced towards Riken who sat some eighty feet away. She fell to her knees as she held the moss towards Riken who gave her a tired look.

"Neko, I cannot do this without your help. I cannot move," he wheezed as he looked down to his feet.

"On my belt is a dagger. I need you to take it now."

Neko gulped but did as he asked. Once she held the dagger, his eyes met hers.

"Now you need to cut my arm, making a deep enough incision to draw blood."

Neko's jaw dropped in aghast.

"I can't cut you!" she shrieked as Riken gave her an exhausted stare.

"Then I will die. The healing extracts in that moss need to go directly into my blood to neutralize the moonsbayne."

Neko bit her bottom lip, her heart racing as she looked down to the small silver dagger in her hand.

"All right. I'm so sorry for this."

She winced as she held the tip of the dagger to his forearm.

"Can I cut you here?" she asked as Riken wheezed again, his eyes dulling as he spoke barely above a whisper.

"Yes. Hurry Neko."

Neko groaned and pressed the blade into his arm, drawing a bead of blood as she squeezed her eyes shut.

"Open your eyes!" Riken hissed as Neko's eyes shot open.

"Now!" he urged as Neko scrunched up her face and quickly pulled the blade across his skin, opening a wound about five centimetres long. She gagged as blood ran from the wound. She dropped the dagger and took the moss, ripping it up into smaller pieces. She looked to Riken for further instructions, but his eyes were slipping shut.

"Riken!" Neko yelled as the Lanarii's eyes slowly opened.

"Get the fluids into the cut."

He gasped for air as Neko reacted, squeezing the moss until black liquid dripped onto the seeping cut. Neko placed the moss on top of the cut and looked to Riken who gave her a relieved stare.

Neko watched in fascination as Riken's skin returned to a healthy glow, only ten or so minutes had elapsed since she had given him the moss extract.

"Wow, that was intense."

Riken opened his eyes a crack, offering her a weak chuckle as the feeling returned to his limbs and he found it easier to breath.

"Thank you. Your quick actions saved my life."

Neko looked over towards Riken from her sitting position beside him.

"You're welcome, but why did you do that. Why not just let me touch the plant and heal me instead?"

Riken held up his injured arm.

"And do this to you? Only a coward would do something like that."

Neko offered the Lanarii a thankful smile.

"You know you could have just let me touch the plant and took my stone. Why didn't you?"

Riken shot her a piercing gaze.

"I am not a deceiving individual. I have no reason to cause you harm."

Neko thought a moment and then beamed at the Lanarii.

"Okay, I got it. If I agree to give you my stone, I have one condition. You give me something you value, then we can trade back once you do your thing."

Riken smiled. This girl had a funny sense of humor. He took a moment then answered her.

"That is a fair trade. I will give you the armor of Annalise. It is back in Rinnyus."

"Like actual armor that you wear?"

Riken shot her an amused look.

"What else would you use it for. It is made to fit only one, so you would not be able to wear it I'm afraid."

"No offense but how can I lug heavy armor around with me and I can't even wear it?"

Riken sighed, a nostalgic look filling his tawny eyes as he slowly got to his feet, testing his strength.

"It is Lanarii armor, very light and very well crafted."

Neko shrugged as she followed Riken who had taken back his dagger and was now on his feet. He started walking once again, this time at a slower pace.

"Hey, don't you want to rest a bit more?"

"We have already tarried too long. I am well enough to make it back to Rinnyus. We are close as I recognize this area. Perhaps another half hour or so of walking."

"All right, lead away. I don't know about you, but I am ready to sleep where I fall."

Riken tapped his chin thoughtfully.

"Perhaps in summoning the Earth Stone, it drained some of your manna."

"Manna? What's that?"

Riken continued walking as the pair conversed.

"Manna is the energy that exists in this world. It is in everything, from trees to the grass to all things living."

Neko thought a moment before she asked her next question.

"So, it's like life energy, and by using this stone I have, it took some of my energy and transferred it into the power I summoned to make those bar things?"

Riken shook his head.

"No. That would have completely drained your manna reserves. The element stones all have their own self-sustaining powers. Your manna is simply used to trigger the stone's powers into being."

Neko's eyebrows furrowed.

"That's so strange but really cool."

She grinned as Riken stopped, recognizing one of the paths that led to his village.

"We are not far now. I recognize this pathway."

"Here, might as well take it now. I have nothing to hide from you, just so you know."

Neko took off her necklace and held it out to the Lanarii. Riken offered her a kind smile and took the stone from her.

"Forgive my bothersome request, but I am responsible for the safety of my village and the people in it."

"No biggy. I understand. I'd probably do the same thing in your shoes."

The pair continued walking in silence for a little way. Neko took in the sights and sounds of the forest as darkness encroached.

"Soon, you will be able to spot the village. It is not too far now."

Neko strained to see past Riken's shoulders, even attempting to walk on her tippy toes a few steps. Riken chuckled at her antics before she made an "Oh" face and took in the glowing village.

"That's your village?" Neko asked in wonder as she stopped to admire the beautiful view.

"It's…is it supposed to be glowing like that?" she asked, confusion creasing her brow as Riken nodded.

"It is, we have lanterns that light the entire village with that silver light. It is especially impressive in the darkest of the night."

Neko whistled. "It reminds me of the ice castles from the fairy tale books I used to read as a kid."

Riken gazed towards the village.

"Shall we move on? I believe we are owed a hot meal, a nice bath, and a long sleep to refresh us. It has been a rather long and trying night."

Neko yawned as they approached the main gates. Two Lanarii guards patrolling the granite stone wall almost fully concealed by the vines that grew up the sides.

"Halt. Who goes there?" one of the Lanarii boomed as Riken raised his hand in greeting.

"It is Riken."

The warrior did a double take and motioned to the other guard.

"Open the gate. Our King has returned," he yelled as the wooden gate set in the stonework slowly swung inwards, revealing more of the Lanarii village. Neko's jaw dropped from the sheer beauty of the area. The silver lanterns glowed with an ethereal light, making the entire area look as if bathed in the light of a full moon.

"Is the village to your liking?"

Neko vigorously nodded.

"Like I said. It's a freaking fairy tale book."

Riken nodded to a few Lanarii that bowed as he walked past.

"I assure you, Neko. This is no fairy tale book."

Riken stopped as a blonde Lanarii ran up to Riken, relief in his eyes.

"Thank the stars. You are alive. We heard the Glodiirii and thought the worst."

"We are quite fine. Could you please see that our guest here gets fed and a place to sleep. We will address this once Neko, and I have rested."

The blonde looked to Neko then back to Riken.

"Sir, are you sure that is a wise idea?"

Riken held his hand up.

"She is here as our guest, Landis. Please show her the same courtesy you would me."

The other male bowed stiffly. There was no masking his displeasure. Riken looked to Neko.

"I will send for you once you have rested. Then I will fulfil my end of the bargain we made."

Neko blinked and nodded, well aware of the stare she was getting from the other Lanarii. Riken gave her one last smile before he turned and disappeared into the village. Neko remained where she was standing, not too sure what to do with herself.

"If you would follow me, miss."

Landis sneered as Neko slightly bowed her shoulders and followed the clearly annoyed Lanarii, much like a scolded child would follow an angry parent.

Arran stood up as Riken appeared where the rebels were currently spending the night.

"You made it back. I was beginning to wonder if the Glodiirii got you."

Riken sighed as Arran gave him an expectant stare.

"Did you find her?"

Riken nodded and held up the necklace.

"Yes, she is with Landis, and now we have the Earth Stone."

Arran grinned.

"Great. Now we can discuss what to do with the princelings. I would wager their father would pay a mighty steep ransom for their safe return."

Riken raised an eyebrow.

"And why would we do that?"

Arran looked dumbfounded.

"So, I can pay for food and supplies for my men. You will be getting a cut for your assistance as well."

Riken shook his head, his temper starting to slip.

"I will not be taking a cut; we are not ransoming them. We are not brutes like they are and I will not belittle myself by acting like the foolish humans. You should know better Arran."

Arran spluttered, but regained his composure. "We cannot just release them. They would retaliate. They know where your village is. Do you think they would hesitate to come back and take their revenge, we must silence them then."

Riken shot Arran a wilting glare.

"The forest is large, and with the Glodiirii, they would be hard pressed to return here. We are by no means defenseless."

Riken glanced at the moon that was now rising quickly.

"I have been in the forest most of the night. I am weary. So, let us finish this discussion when I am well rested. I have a few things I wish to ask you, in private."

"Fair enough. I will await your summons."

Riken tilted his head in thanks and turned, heading towards his quarters, he was in terrible need of a well-deserved rest.

Neko was stunned into silence. She had heard of the star treatment before, but this was getting a bit ridiculous. Riken had called it a village but where she stood now reminded her of a five-star hotel room. Landis had been more than happy to drop her there with a female Lanarii and place the burden of "Neko's nanny" on her shoulders.

"This is to your liking?" she asked, her voice soft as Neko turned to face her.

"Yes, it's great. Thank you."

Neko grinned holding her hand out to shake.

"I'm Neko. Who are you?"

The woman gave Neko's hand a strange look, causing Neko to laugh nervously and take her hand back.

"My name is Sornna."

"Right. Cool."

"What is cool? The sleeping area?"

"No. Cool is like a word people from where I come from use to describe something good."

"I do not understand. Why not just say good?"

Neko shrugged, feeling a bit foolish.

"Everything is great. I think I can handle it from here. Thanks for all your help," Neko stated, wanting to be rid of the stoic Lanarii woman.

Sornna bowed slightly.

"As you wish. I will fetch you when Lord Riken summons you."

With that, she was gone, leaving Neko standing in the room, her eyebrows raised.

"Okay, creepy lady," Neko growled as she took in the room once again.

"Talk about poker faces, would it kill them to smile once in a while?" she grumbled as she found what looked to be the bathroom, complete with a washbasin and homemade soap.

"Score."

Neko happily washed down and then paused spotting what looked to be a rather nice dress sitting out on a wooden chair near her bed.

"No way," she whispered excitedly as she picked the dress up staring at how well made it was.

"This is really nice and clean. I don't care. I'm using it," she concluded as she stripped off her muddy clothing and pulled the dress on over her head. Neko blinked, looking down. The material felt cool against her skin like silk but not slinky. It was the strangest material she had even seen or felt. It felt heavy and looked to be durable. Its color was a light greenish grey. It had a v-cut front and a V-shaped accent that went under the breasts and tied into the back of the dress. The sleeves were a generic tank top style with half cut t-shirt sleeves, the material slightly see through and three-quarter arm length. The skirt was a medium flare and ended mid-calf. Neko glanced down towards the foot of the chair noticing a pair of silver slippers.

"Hey, these look just like flats," she stated picking up the sleek footwear.

"And they look to be my size. How the hell did they know my size?" Neko wondered as she slipped the shoes on. Not surprisingly, they fit like a glove.

Neko yawned and looked over to the bed, her body screaming for rest. Neko trudged over to the bed and fell face first into the soft surface, groaning in sheer pleasure as she snuggled into the mattress that smelled like fresh air. Moments later, she was fast asleep.

Riken stood in his bedchambers, now washed, wearing a clean outfit and having eaten a well-needed meal. His eyes came to rest on a wooden chest, accented in gold and silver metals. Waves of nostalgia made him wish for simpler days. He took from his dresser a small metal key and placed it into the lock on the chest. Slowly, he turned the key, the telltale click of the lock disengaging. Slowly, he opened the lid revealing the contents of the strongbox, the armor he had promised Neko, or rather, chainmail vest. He ran a hand over the woven fiber. One of the best blacksmiths in Rinnyus had constructed it.

"Annalise," Riken whispered picturing the face of the Lanarii woman in his mind as he forced himself not to get lost in his emotions.

"It has been so many years; yet, your face never fades from my mind," Riken mused as he took the armor from its resting place, setting it out on the dresser top.

"All that time put into a piece of armor none can wear. Why did you make such a thing?" he wondered as he took a deep drink of his honey mead. His eyes drifted upwards, his mirror catching the reflection of his features. He stared at his image a few moments, tawny eyes full of unshed tears. He walked across the room and took from his worn tunic the necklace Neko had given to him. The stone had a lackluster appearance now that it no longer hung around the girl's throat. He stifled a yawn as he took the stone and placed it into the now empty chest. He also took the dagger she had given him and placed it alongside the stone. Once he had secured the stone, he glanced one last time at the Lanarii armor and resigned himself to get some well-needed rest. No doubt tomorrow would be a demanding day.

"Miss…miss, please wake up."

Neko was brought from her deep sleep by a childish voice. Slowly, Neko opened her eyes and glanced towards the figure standing three feet from her head.

"Yeah?" Neko asked, her voice deep with sleep. The girl looked to be no older than twelve if Neko had to guess.

"Sorry to have awakened you, but Lord Riken has summoned you to an audience with him in the Palace."

Neko yawned and sat up, her hair defying gravity as she rubbed the sleep from her eyes.

"Okay, give me ten minutes."

"I will await you in the hallway."

With that, she was gone, leaving Neko to stretch and yawn once again as she got to her feet. Neko washed her face and hands. Looking in the small mirror, she sighed and attempted to comb her hair down with wet fingers, managing to look somewhat presentable.

"What I wouldn't give for a proper brush."

She whined as she turned and headed back into the main room, smirking slightly at the thought of seeing the Lanarii King. She liked his company. He was a lot more cheerful than Troy. Neko blinked, in all the excitement she had forgotten about her friend.

"I'm such a jerk. I hope he's okay."

Worry creased her forehead as she stepped out into the lavish hallway. Just like everything in this village, it was well crafted.

"Follow me, miss."

The girl spoke as Neko obligingly followed the Lanarii girl down the hallway and into the small and crowded street outside. In the daylight, it looked a lot less mystical to Neko, but because the forest was so dense, it still gave off the illusion that it was dusk in the village.

"How long did I sleep?" Neko asked, not expecting the girl to answer her.

"You were asleep for most of the day. It is just past afternoon meal."

Neko blinked.

"A whole day?" she asked as the girl nodded, leading them down the pathway towards a large building rising on what looked to be a large boulder.

"Is that where we're going?"

"Yes. That is the King's palace."

Neko gazed in awe. It was massive, almost like a fortress.

"There you are."

Neko jumped as Riken seemingly appeared from thin air. She did not miss the smirk he flashed her at her jumpiness.

"I trust you slept well?" he asked as Neko nodded, her cheeks heating up.

"Yeah. I must have been more tired than I thought."

He gave her a once over.

"Good. I was afraid the dress would not be to your liking."

"Are you kidding? It's the coolest dress I've ever seen, and the material, well uh…thank you."

She stumbled over her words, annoyed that she couldn't even talk properly.

"That is good. I will escort you to the palace. We have a few things I would like to discuss with you and Arran."

Neko froze.

"Arran!"

Anxiety filled her head as Riken gave her a steady look.

"Yes. I need to speak with the both of you."

Neko tensed, her eyes hardening as Riken took in her stance. She was not impressed.

"Neko, what is it?"

"You damn well know what, that…that jerk tried to kill me! I'm not going anywhere near that tool."

She crossed her arms in front of her chest, refusing to take another step. The Lanarii girl, sensing an ensuing argument, wisely turned and left the pair to themselves.

Riken exhaled. He had overlooked that Neko would be a bit cross with Prince Arran.

"I understand your concern, but this is my domain, and you are under my protection. He will not harm you, Neko. I give you my word."

Neko shot the King a dejected scowl.

"I don't understand what he has to do with any of this."

"Everything. Neko, I have a theory about who you really are, and he is a big part of it, so come with me, and the three of us will discuss this matter."

Neko uncrossed her arms and rolled her eyes.

"All right, fine. I'll go, but I'll tell you right now. I won't like it," she snapped as Riken fought the urge to smile at her indignant pout.

Arran stood in the central meeting chamber of Riken's domicile. Various chairs and couches dotted the large meeting hall. Arran decided to sit down while he awaited the Lanarii King's arrival and his private conversation. Arran stood up as Riken entered the room, a frown appearing on Arran's face as he noticed Troy's tart following the Lanarii King into the room.

"What is she doing here? I thought she was locked up with the brothers."

Neko bit her bottom lip, keeping her retort to herself.

"She is here by my request. I need to speak with both of you. I believe I know just where it is that Neko comes from."

Neko sighed eyeing the rebel leader. He didn't look as scary as he did the last time she had seen him. Now he looked slightly affronted, and his expression made her want to laugh. Instead, she opted for covering her smile and coughing.

His stern gaze caught hers.

"Is there something amusing to you, tart?"

Neko felt her jaw drop at the obvious insult.

With Riken standing two feet away, she felt bolder and threw an insult of her own back at the irate Prince.

"The only thing I find funny here is your face."

She knew it was childish, but she couldn't help herself.

Arran actually looked stunned, and Riken felt a slight headache coming on. These two both had a stubborn streak a mile long.

Getting them to cooperate would be a rather trying ordeal on Riken's part.

"That is enough!" Riken's voice boomed as the other two froze. Neko's face paled, and she took a step away from the Lanarii. Arran set his jaw and nodded, sensing the King's aggravation.

"You are correct King Riken. Forgive my lapse. It will not happen again."

Neko swallowed the lump in her throat and looked to her feet. They seemed very interesting at that moment. Riken took a deep breath and gestured to the small table in the far corner of the room.

"All right, let us all take a seat and converse in a civilized manner."

Neko nodded and together the trio took their seats. Neko sat in a large plush chair. Riken sat in another chair, and Arran grabbed a couch, reclining in a relaxed position.

"Let us begin then."

Riken was sitting across from Neko. He looked to her then to Arran.

"Last night, I witnessed Neko summoning the Earth Stone."

Arran blinked, then looked to Neko, shock in his eyes.

"That is impossible. She is just a child."

"I know that, but the truth still remains. We were attacked by the Glodiirii, and if she had not intervened, we both would be dead, and this conversation would not be taking place. I witnessed the entire thing. She summoned the stone with very little manna."

Arran shook his head.

"That cannot be true. She is a tyro. It would have taken all her manna, only—"

Arran stopped staring at Neko for a moment, then to Riken.

"Surely you are jesting. She cannot be of Dolphinian blood. Look at her."

Neko felt her temper rear its head.

"Sitting right here buddy."

Neko gave a rude wave as she looked to Riken.

"What's a Dolphinian?"

Arran snorted, clearly annoyed by her.

"I am a Dolphinian. My ancestors are the ones who became the guardians of the element stones. You may be able to summon the stone's powers, but that does not make you a descendant."

Arran looked to Riken.

"How can you entertain this notion. There is no proof."

Riken sighed, giving Arran a tolerant stare.

"There is no denying her abilities, but perhaps a test of sorts."

Neko and Arran both looked to the Lanarii King.

"A test? What sort of test?" Neko asked as Riken and Arran shared a look.

"You want to send her into that cave to get the Water Stone?" Arran concluded as Riken nodded causing Arran to laugh.

"That is absurd."

Riken looked to Neko.

"If you can find the Water Stone and face the trial in the temple, it will prove beyond a doubt that you are a descendant."

"And if I can't?"

Arran sneered at her.

"Then you die. Only a descendant could do it, which means that the King here is pretty sure you are of rightful blood."

Neko shot Riken a fearful look.

"And if I refuse to go into that cave?"

Riken offered Neko a kind smile.

"Still doubting your worth, Neko? You summoned the Earth Stone. You can summon the Water Stone as well. Use its powers to aid you in the temple, I have faith you will succeed and prove Arran wrong."

Arran rolled his eyes and stood up, towering over the girl as he shot her an arrogant stare.

"She is nothing more than Troy's little lackey, a common little tart."

Neko felt her anger spike.

"Screw you," she spat standing up and glaring up at the Prince, her fists clenched. Arran laughed.

"You want to hit me, then go on."

He leaned down towards her, tapping his cheek, giving her a condescending look. Neko gave an enraged holler and complied, hitting him solidly. Riken's eyebrows raised as Arran staggered backwards and fell into his seat, a stunned expression crossing his face as a small cut appeared on his cheek.

"Damn," he hissed cupping his face as Neko flexed her fist, glaring at him. Neko turned and stormed out of the room, leaving two shocked men in her wake.

Riken looked to Arran who shook the cobwebs from his head.

"That girl can throw a punch."

Riken chuckled at Arran's flabbergasted expression.

"You did ask for it."

Arran snickered. He was still shocked she had actually punched him.

"When I told her to hit me, I thought she would just slap me."

"That is your mistake. We will continue this later. I should go find Neko."

Arran got to his feet.

"Perhaps tonight after evening meal?"

"That is acceptable. We will reconvene then, in my personal study."

With that, Riken made his exit. Once his back was turned to Arran, Riken smiled, he had not seen such an amusing thing for a long while.

Chapter Ten

Neko stormed down the walkway and into the street. No one paid her any attention, and she was glad. She didn't want to talk to anyone at the moment. She winced. Her right hand hurt, and she had actually broken the skin on her knuckles striking that jerk.

"Stupid idiot," she snarled as she stopped, groaning aloud. She didn't know how to get back to the lodge she was staying in.

"Just freaking perfect," she ground out as a familiar voice caught her ears.

"You hairless pigs."

Neko followed the ranting voice. She found the owner of the voice in an open area not far from where she had been standing.

"I demand to speak with your leader."

Neko stepped into the area. Four armed Lanarii and the two men of Arran's from the pub in Chino stood guarding Troy and Alexander.

"Troy," Neko stated, walking towards the irate Prince.

"Neko?" he asked, his eyes lighting up as Neko approached her friend.

"You're okay. I was so worried when you got caught," Neko stated as the guards allowed her to stand before Troy.

"I'll talk to Riken. See if I can get him to let you go."

"You are on a first name basis with that barbarian?"

Neko blinked, shocked by his snide tone.

"He is not a barbarian. He helped me get out of the forest."

"They are not our friends, Neko. Look what they did to me. It is all a ploy to get us to lower our guard."

Neko gave him a baffled look.

"But—"

"—Did he make you give him your stone?"

Neko averted her gaze.

"He did take it from you. They do not trust outsiders."

Troy berated Neko.

"And now they have all four stones, and you're never going to get home."

Neko felt her resolve crumble.

"But he said he wouldn't hurt us. Maybe if I just ask him he could—"

Troy cut her off, unsure why he was getting so worked up with her for trusting that damn Lanarii.

"What, send you home? They will not lift a finger to help us. Now that they have the stones, they have no use for us. What do you think they will do? They certainly will not release us."

Neko felt ill.

"Riken wouldn't do that, Troy. Not all Lanarii are like you say they are."

"Get him to prove it then, ask Riken to release me. He will not, and he will give you any excuse. Ask him; you will see."

"You are wasting your breath brother. She has joined them and sentenced you to death," Alexander cut in, glaring at Neko, her eyes refusing to meet his.

"I haven't," Neko weakly protested as Alexander snorted.

"Liar."

Neko looked up to Troy. He actually looked hurt.

"All I wanted was to help you, Neko. You betrayed my friendship, and now I will pay the price."

Neko shook her head. Determination flashing in her eyes.

"No, I didn't betray you. I'll talk to Riken. He'll release you, Troy. You'll see. I promise I will get you out of here. Okay?"

Troy sighed in dejection.

"You can try. The King will not let me go. They have played upon your kind nature."

Neko gave Troy a stern look. Her annoyance showing in her stance.

"I will free you, Troy. I made you a promise, and I will keep it. Please just wait a little longer."

Alexander snorted.

"Do not listen to her brother. She is in league with them."

Troy looked to Neko.

"I want to believe you, Neko. Please hurry and get me out of here."

Neko nodded and stood up.

"I will," she said. "I'll go right now and find Riken. Okay? I'll be back as soon as I fix this."

She turned and left, intent on finding Riken and giving him a piece of her mind.

Troy smirked across to his brother who chuckled.

"I have to admit, that was a good idea to get yourself freed. Well played," Alexander stated, making sure to speak low enough, so the guards didn't hear him.

"Like I said, leave our escape to me."

Neko was so intent on what she was going to say to Riken that she didn't see the other person before she had run smack into him. She would have fallen had two strong hands not firmly gripped her upper arms, steadying her.

"Neko?"

Her eyes traveled up, meeting the tawny eyes of the very person she was seeking.

"Riken."

Her tone hardened as she pulled out of his grip.

"Neko what is wrong? You look upset."

"Of course I am. I just discovered that you have my friend tied up like a common criminal."

Riken sighed, his eyes reflecting slight annoyance.

"It is for the safety of my people."

"He has no weapons. How can he possibly be a threat to your people?"

Riken gave her a placid stare.

"He will be detained until I figure out what is to be done with him."

Neko felt her jaw drop.

"I didn't want to believe him, but he said you would refuse to let him go. Troy was right. You have all the stones now. Why would you want to help us if you don't have to?"

Riken felt a twinge of remorse.

"That is not correct, Neko. I have no reason for an ulterior motive with you."

Neko glared up at Riken, her eyes fierce.

"Then let my friend go, or untie him at the very least. He can't hurt anyone especially with all the guards I saw running around here."

Riken looked skyward.

"Neko, I will not release him, at least not yet."

Neko felt tears welling in her eyes.

"Why not?"

Her tone was piercing as Riken fixed her with an icy stare.

"Because I have made my decision and I am done arguing with you. I will not release him, and that is final."

Neko's face fell at his refusal.

"You're nothing but a barbarian."

Neko quoted Troy's earlier accusation taking slight pleasure in the shocked look that crossed Riken's face. Her heart quickened at the rage that pooled in his eyes, making them burn like molten metal. She couldn't look away as they both remained motionless, staring at one another. The stalemate was broken when Neko's stomach decided to make its demands very clear in a very loud way. Neko bit her bottom lip, a blush dusting her cheeks as all Riken's previous anger faded. He gave her a kind smile.

"When is the last time you had a decent meal?"

Neko blinked, clearly confused by his sudden change of emotions.

"Uh…a few days ago I think," she stated as he sighed and nodded in confirmation.

"I think we both need to take a moment. Come. I will get you a proper meal, and we can continue this whilst breaking bread."

Neko nodded and followed the Lanarii, feeling rather foolish for getting so angry with him. As they entered the palace, Neko sighed and decided to apologise.

"I'm sorry, for what I said earlier. You're not a… a barbarian."

Riken gestured to a hallway. As they followed it down, they came to a set of what looked to be stained glass doors. Beautiful leaves in green glass accented the door. Neko stared as they entered a personal study decorated in light green wooden panels and a small hearth had a little fire going, making the room seem very homey.

Riken waved over a nearby Lanarii. Neko recognized Sornna as Riken asked her to bring them something to eat and drink. She bowed and left, her stoic mask in place. Riken gestured to a pair of armchairs sitting across from one another, a small marble coffee table between them.

"Please, have a seat, Neko."

Neko slowly took a seat, looking anywhere but at the King.

"Nice study, lots of books," she stated the obvious as Riken chuckled, also taking a seat as he watched Neko nervously fidget in hers.

"Thank you. This room is one of my favorites in the palace."

Neko took a deep breath and forced herself to look at Riken, not surprised as his eyes were already on hers.

"I do understand your concern for your friend, but I have a duty to my people that I must fulfil."

"I know. I was just angry. Troy has helped me get this far, and I owe it to him to at least try to free him."

Riken rubbed his chin thoughtfully.

"I will make you a deal, Neko."

Neko perked up as he continued.

"When you retrieve the element Stone of Water and prove your lineage, I will release your friend on the condition that he is shadowed by one of my men."

"That would be great! Thank you."

Riken smiled at the exuberance of the girl before him.

"As for the other, he is a vile man, and I will not free him in my village."

Neko's expression dropped.

"I second that. He's a creep."

Riken looked up as Sornna returned, a platter laden with food in her hands. Neko felt her mouth water as she barely contained herself while Sornna set the platter on the table. Riken gestured to the food.

"By all means, you must be famished."

That was all the prompting she needed before she tore into the food, realizing just how ravenous she was. Riken couldn't help but chuckle at her immense appetite. It explained her earlier short temper. He too would be in a foul mood had he not eaten for two days.

"This is so good," Neko stated between bites.

"I am glad you like it," he stated as he poured them both a glass of mead Sornna had just brought out.

"I suggest sipping this. It is rather potent," he cautioned as he slid the silver goblet towards Neko who gingerly raised it to her mouth and took a small sip, grinning as the flavors burst on her tongue.

"This is really good too."

She took another sip, this one larger than her first. Neko set the goblet down and continued to dine with gusto. Riken watched in awe as Neko finished her meal, she had not been lying when she had said she was starving. She seemed a great deal more content now that she had a full belly.

"Thanks for that; it was awesome."

"You are most welcome, Neko."

Riken glanced out of a nearby window. The sun was almost gone behind the mountains, meaning it was late afternoon. Neko glanced down at her watch, thankful it was a waterproof one and hadn't been ruined in the water during her and Troy's attempt to escape. The watch read 16:12 as she stretched, her belly feeling rather full.

"What is that?" Riken enquired as Neko held her wrist up.

"What? Oh, this? It's a watch. It tells time."

Riken gently took her wrist, looking at the digital watch.

"A sundial? Where is the fin?"

Neko giggled and took her hand back.

"Don't need it. The symbols are what tell you the time. It's kinda hard to explain just how it works, but there's lots of this kinda stuff back home."

Riken leaned back in his chair.

"Such a strange place you hail from. What is it called?"

"I come from a place, well a village really, called Lumis."

"I have never heard of this Lumis you speak of."

Neko sighed, sadness creeping into her silver eyes.

"Well, it's not really from here. I come from a very faraway place."

Riken gave her an expectant look.

"How far away?" he queried as Neko gave him a flat look.

"Try worlds."

Riken, caught off guard by her remark, gave her a questioning stare.

"Worlds?"

Neko pursed her lips.

"I know it sounds stupid, but it's the truth. That damn stone brought me here, to Arorus."

Riken believed her. The truth was evident in her eyes. It was just such an odd thing to hear.

"The stones are very powerful. If you were brought here, then you are here for a reason."

"Yeah. I'm starting to get that, but I'm just an ordinary teenager or, at least, I thought I was."

Riken offered a kind smile. She was modest to a fault.

"You have summoned the Earth Stone's powers. You are more than just ordinary."

Neko felt her cheeks heating up as Riken watched her flush, a smile on his face.

"We have a few moments before Arran arrives. Would you care to join me for a walk? I have something I would like to show you."

Neko compliantly followed Riken back into the luxurious hallway. He led her to a wide set of stairs, both ascending them as the pair chatted. Neko followed Riken through a large wooden door inlaid with gold and silver.

"Come in," he offered as he stepped aside to allow Neko in through the doorway first. Neko was shocked at the size of the new room.

"What is this place?"

Riken chuckled and walked over to the large bed complete with a canopy.

"These are my chambers."

"As in your bedroom?"

Her face paled as Riken nodded and picked up the armor he had set out on the end of his bed.

"That is correct. Come here. This is the armor that I was telling you about."

Neko gulped but did as he asked, standing awkwardly at the foot of the bed, staring down at the copper-colored armor.

"It looks like a tank top," she observed as she gently ran her fingers across the cold material.

"It is finely crafted metal. It wears like clothing, but it is very strong, like chainmail."

Neko looked up at Riken, her eyes meeting his.

"Seriously, this can stop a sword or an arrow?"

"Yes, I have armor similar to it, and it has been an advantage to me for many years."

"Wow, sure looks like a tank top to me."

Riken gently folded it and picked it up, handing it to Neko.

"We made a deal. This is yours to hold onto."

Neko took it from him.

"You really mean it when you say it's light. Holy crap."

Riken grinned and walked over to his dresser, placing his hand on top of the chest that contained Neko's stone.

"The Earth Stone is in here, for safe keeping and I have the only key."

"Good to know."

Neko glanced around the room.

"So…I suppose we should go now?"

Riken caught onto her nervousness.

"Why, are you nervous?" he asked as Neko dropped her head.

"Oh, not really. Just, we're kinda in your bedroom alone and yeah it's just kinda awkward for me."

"Do I frighten you?"

Neko felt her blush returning with a vengeance.

"No. It's not that I'm scared of you. It's just, I don't know, it's a thing."

Riken raised an eyebrow.

"A thing?" he chuckled, enjoying taunting the flustered girl. Neko's eyes narrowed as she caught onto his little game.

"Ha ha ha, you're a real card. Can we go now?"

Riken opened the door and let her exit first following her into the hallway.

Neko and Riken arrived back only to find Arran seated in the study and patiently awaiting their return.

"Finally. I thought you had forgotten," Arran stated as he glanced from Riken to Neko. Neko smirked as she looked at the damage she had done to Arran's face. Arran caught her smirk and glared at her.

"You think yourself clever, girl?"

"I know I'm clever and I'm one hundred percent sure you deserved it."

Arran narrowed his eyes.

"A slap not a bloody punch."

"Well, then maybe you shouldn't tell someone who's into boxing to hit you."

She received two blank stares. Arran asking the question first.

"What is boxing?"

Neko rolled her eyes, wishing for people who knew what modern things were.

"Boxing is a sport where I come from. Two people put on big padded gloves and basically beat the hell outta each other until one person gives up."

Both men looked slightly confused.

"You willingly fight? But you are a girl."

Arran seemed genuinely confused as Neko shot him a deadly look.

"Yeah. It's called equality. You know, where women have all the same rights as men do. Besides I'm not advanced enough in my training to fight other people yet. I'm a beginner. So, all I do is fight a punching bag."

Neko glanced over to Riken who chuckled.

"Shall we continue. Can I trust you two not to get into another fist fight?"

"I'm cool," Neko retorted raising her hands up as Arran blinked at her odd vocabulary.

"I will contain myself, King Riken."

Riken took a seat. Neko and Arran followed suit as the trio continued their earlier discussion.

Chapter Eleven

Riken focused his attention on Arran.

"If you would be so gracious, Prince Arran, I would like for you to explain to Neko the events leading up to the war and how the stones ended up where they did."

Arran gave Riken a screwy look.

"Why would I tell her that?"

Riken sighed and decided to let them in on his suspicions.

"I believe Neko here is not just a descendant of your race, Arran, but the next chosen guardian of the element stones."

Arran's jaw dropped.

"Are you out of your mind? That is the most outlandish thing I have ever heard!"

Riken gave the irate Prince an even stare.

"Think about it for a moment, Arran. Neko summoned the Earth Stone with very little manna. You yourself said all three stones reacted in the pub, while they were all close to Neko. And just moments ago, Neko informed me that the emerald she entrusted to me transported her here. Do you not see? It makes perfect sense."

Arran stared at Neko who shrunk in her chair.

"Is this true? You were transported here, from where?"

"Like I told Riken, where I come from is definitely not from this world. The stone I had lit up, and I went from standing in my parents' bedroom to an open field, and that's where I met Troy."

Arran was in disbelief.

"This cannot be possible. Look at you. You are not even trained. Why would the stones choose you?"

Arran looked towards Riken.

"Do you have any more notions about her?"

Riken sighed and gave a curt nod.

"In fact, I do."

Riken stood up, hands clasped behind his back. He walked over to the hearth, staring into the fire, his back turned towards the others.

"Before your mother died, Arran, she took the stones to hide, yes?"

Arran looked to Neko then back to Riken.

"Of course she did. She brought one to you."

Riken turned looking at Neko.

"When I first met you Neko, you seemed familiar, and now I know why. When the Queen arrived here, she was in a panic and with her was a little girl, the Princess."

Neko blinked, her stomach twisting in apprehension.

"What are you saying?" Arran growled as he looked over at Neko.
"You are a smart man, Arran. Look at her. Surely you can see the similarities between her and your mother's appearances."

Arran gave Neko a scrutinizing stare as the Lanarii King turned to face the Prince.

"It cannot be so. My sister was killed with my mother when King Arwin took the Wind Stone."

Riken turned to face the Prince.

"Your mother's body was found. Your sister's body, however, was never found. Almost as if she had disappeared from existence."

Riken let the words hang as Arran's eyes widened.

"As in sent somewhere else?"

Riken nodded and glanced at Neko.

"Almost the same way Neko was brought here."

Neko covered her mouth with her hand as Riken continued his deduction.

"If that is true, then Neko must have had the Earth Stone with her when she was sent to her world, and now the stone has brought her back to fulfil her destiny as guardian, which means…"

Arran stared at Neko in astonishment.

"She is my sister."

Neko felt like she wanted to puke.

"What?" she asked, her voice wavering as Riken gave her a look of concern. Her face had gone deathly pale as Arran growled in frustration, "This makes no sense. Why does she not remember this?"

Neko sighed giving her explanation.

"When I was young, I hit my head. I have no memories of anything before the age of ten."

Arran glared at her.

"How convenient. I must say that Troy thought of everything when he trained you. I do not believe for a moment that you are who you claim to be."

Neko blinked, the anger in Arran's eyes making her flinch.

"I never claimed anything; you and Riken did," Neko defended. Her tone hardened as she stared at the Lanarii who looked a bit taken back.

"Perhaps, then, let us make sure. Let her do the trial in the temple. If she retrieves the stone then there can be no doubt of her true identity," Arran scoffed, giving Neko a disgusted look.

"Let the filth try. I refuse to acknowledge her as Dolphinian blood."

With that, Arran abruptly stood and made his exit, leaving Neko and Riken alone in the study.

Neko was in a state of shock. She could hardly believe any of it. It sounded so bizarre. Yet, it made everything fit into place. Riken gave her a soft look.

"Perhaps a good sleep will help Neko. In the morning, we will travel to Katrii falls. There, you will go into the temple and retrieve the element Stone of Water."

Neko sighed and got to her feet, the armor she held clutched to her chest protectively.

"Okay. That sounds really good. Uh…can I get someone to show me the way back to my room…uh…lodging place?"

"There are plenty of guest rooms here in the palace. You are welcome to spend the night here. I will have someone fetch your things for you if you wish."

"That would be great. Thanks."

Neko paused a moment, her eyes serious.

"Why are you being so nice to me, even after what Arran said about me being a fake?"

"Prince Arran holds a lot of anger from the events of the war. He does not trust easily, but I trust my judgement, and I am very sure of your lineage. Tomorrow will be all the proof Arran needs to see the truth."

Neko gently set the folded armor at the foot of her bed. This room was just as lavish as the previous one she had been staying in. She took a deep calming breath as she sat on the bed, running her fingers over the metal material of the armor.

"I wonder why no one can wear this? I guess its all part of being in a realm full of magic. It looks like my size though."

Neko smirked as she stood up, stripping from her dress.

"I bet it wasn't made for a man."

Neko held the shirt-shaped garment up, trying to figure out how to put it on. In the end, she settled for pulling it over her head and putting it on just as she would a tank top. As the material fell to her waist, she realized two things, one, the material felt warm and two, it was constricting around her.

"Oh no."

She started panicking, trying to get the garment off before it got too tight on her.

"This was such a bad idea," she panted as she realized she couldn't remove the armor no matter how she pulled on it.

"You have got to be kidding me!" she exclaimed as she let go of the material and glanced up into a nearby mirror, staring at her reflection.

"It looks just like a shirt," she observed, and she turned, looking at the armor from all angles.

"It's really not that bad," she mused as she ran a hand down the armor. It felt cool to the touch.

"I don't know what Riken was going on about. This thing fits me like a glove."

Neko yawned and looked down at her watch noticing it was nearing 10:00 pm.

"Okay, time for sleep. I'll deal with this thing in the am."

Neko walked to the bed and leapt onto it, sprawling out on her back as she stared up at the celling through the canopy and waited for sleep to claim her.

Morning arrived all too fast as the constant bleeping in her ear alerted Neko that, yes, it was a weekday and her watch was going off, meaning it was 7:45 am.

"Shut up," she hissed as she rolled over and blinked, staring up at the canopy above her bed, jumping as a knock at her door echoed through the room. How had they known she was awake?

"Hello?" she asked as the same Lanarii girl from the day before entered the room. In her arms, she held Neko's clothing, washed and folded as Riken had promised.

"Lord Riken requests your presence for morning meal, miss. Once you are dressed, I will escort you."

Neko blinked and yawned, covering her mouth to be polite.

"Okay, I'll be out in like five," she stated watching the girl leave as she forced herself to crawl out of the warm bed.

"What I wouldn't give for a coffee right about now."

Neko glanced over to her blue jeans, t-shirt, and zip up hoodie. She grinned when she found her socks and runners under the folded laundry. Neko quickly threw her blankets to the side, remembering she still had that damn armor on. Neko grabbed the bottom of the material and once again tried to remove the garment over her head, but it was still sticking to her like a second skin.

"Well, so much for that idea."

Neko grumbled as she decided to put her t-shirt over the top and ask Riken about the strange armor during breakfast. Once she had her shoelaces properly tied, Neko opened the door and found the girl waiting beside the doorway.

"This way, miss," she politely stated as Neko followed the girl down into a breakfast area. There was a circular dining nook with huge windows going some twelve feet up, making the entire room dazzling bright.

"Did you sleep well?"

Neko nodded and took a seat. Riken looked like he had been up for hours, and Neko wondered if the Lanarii needed to sleep as much as humans did.

"I slept like a rock," Neko stated as she spotted what looked suspiciously like eggs, bacon and toast.

"Please eat. You will need your strength for today."

Neko gave an audible groan and slouched in the bench seat.

"Please don't remind me. This is so going to suck."

Riken raised an eyebrow.

"Suck what precisely?"

Neko felt her cheeks heating up.

"Oh, just forget it," she growled burying her face in her crossed arms as Riken looked on with mild concern.

"Neko, are you feeling all right?"

Neko looked up, her chin still resting in her arms on the table.

"Yeah, just a lot to take in, you know?"

Her silver eyes met his tawny ones.

"Hey, so I have a question, completely theoretical."

Neko tried to sound nonchalant, Riken focused on her, awaiting her question.

"That armor you gave me, has it fit anyone, like ever?"

"No. It would not fit any who tried it. Why do you ask?"

Neko gave him a sheepish look.

"Well, I was just curious. Why would someone make it if it didn't fit someone beforehand?"

"Annalise was somewhat clairvoyant. All she would tell me is that she was making it for a time when someone would need to use it."

"Annalise was a person? I thought that was the name of the armor."

Neko laughed as Riken smiled fondly at the mix-up.

"Yes, she made the armor. We call it the armor of Annalise as a tribute to the memory of Annalise. She passed on not long after completing the armor, during the Great War."

Neko felt a bit foolish. The armor she was wearing was for someone else, and here she was playing dress up in it. She really needed to learn to grow up sometimes.

"I'm sorry about that."

"Thank you. It was a long time ago, but I still miss her fiercely."

Neko let out a puff of air, feathering her bangs, something she constantly kept doing, and now she felt like a real jerk. She decided to tell Riken about her wardrobe malfunction with the armor later on. Right now, she really didn't want to lose what respect he had for her. Riken stood up, looking expectantly at Neko.

"Shall we depart? I thought we could walk there. I am afraid there are a few Lanarii who wish to see you finish the trial. So, it will be a bit bigger group than I had previously thought."

Neko felt her stomach turn.

"What? Like how many?" she whispered as Riken shook his head.

"I cannot say. After Arran left, he began telling anyone who would listen that you were challenging the temple today."

Neko felt her annoyance peak.

"He's trying to get me to fail. He hates me, and he thinks I'm some kinda con artist."

Riken gave her a sympathetic pat on the shoulder.

"Do not let it hinder your judgement. He does not matter in this moment. Focus only on your task at hand. Do this, and you will be successful."

Neko sighed and together the duo withdrew from the palace and entered the village streets.

"We will exit through the east gates. There is a path alongside the stream that will lead us to the entrance of the temple."

Neko compliantly followed Riken through the streets. They did not meet many as they approached the Eastern gates. They were open and no guards in sight.

"Where is everyone? Isn't it dangerous to leave the gates open and unguarded?"

Riken gestured to the pathway.

"There is no other way to the temple save for going through one of the other two gates in this village. It is a canyon of sorts, boxed in by treacherous mountain ranges. Our temple is a sacred place for my people. We guard it very well."

Neko remained silent as they walked for a while. Riken seemed to enjoy the silence and took in the sights and sounds of the forest as they continued on their path.

Chapter Twelve

After a half hour of walking, Neko and Riken finally arrived at their destination. Neko glanced around not recognizing the area.

"This isn't the cave from the other day," she stated as Riken chuckled and walked ahead of her. Riken could see Arran and his two men standing near the temple entrance along with a rather large gathering of Lanarii warriors.

"The cave you are speaking of is a decoy. We made it that way so anyone crafty enough to get that far would be deceived into thinking he had found the temple, therefore, leaving the real temple undiscovered and safe. As I mentioned before, the only way into this temple is through Rinnyus."

Neko groaned as she spotted the crowd. Arran saw her and shot her a rather sardonic stare. Neko felt her resolve crumbling.

"See. He really does hate me. Look at that smug bastard."

Riken hummed as they stopped before the entrance to the cave. This one did not have a waterfall hiding it, just a bubbling brook beside it with a small pool that looked to be about twenty feet across and ten feet deep with pristine water. Neko focused on trying to spot fish rather than to look at Arran's haughty expression.

"I hope you're ready to be found out for the fraud that you are, girl," he growled as Neko finally looked up, her eyes meeting his. Arran was shocked that instead of unshed tears he was looking into angry silver orbs, ire filling her eyes as she actually curled her lip at him.

"I hope you're ready to eat those words when I get that stone. Your mouth is certainly big enough to swallow all your pride."

Riken fought the urge to laugh aloud, but he could see her entire body was trembling. She was putting on a brave front, and perhaps it was her way of getting herself prepared for the task at hand. Arran laughed in her face.

"We shall see. Go on then. Prove me, wrong little girl."

Riken placed his hand on her arm.

"Ignore him. It is now time that you prove your mettle."

Neko took a deep breath and turned towards the large mouth of the cave, pillars carved from the mountainside loomed over her, casting their shadows at her feet.

"I can do this."

She surprised herself at how steady her voice was. As she approached the tunnel, she realized it was a rather long corridor carved into the mountainside, torches lighting the dank area with a tiny bit of light.

"So, I just go right in?" she asked looking back towards Riken who shook his head.

"I cannot aid you Neko. You must do this task alone."

Neko groaned and slowly stepped towards the shadows. She felt her foot slide, as she gave a piercing yelp; she fell to the unrelenting ground, her knees sending a sharp jolt of pain through her body. She looked over her shoulder, seeing Arran and his two men snickering at her clumsiness.

"Are you still sure she is the guardian?" Arran asked Riken who shot him an unimpressed gaze.

"Damn it," Neko ground out, trying to keep her cool. It was too late as she felt her anger rearing its ugly head. She got to her feet and gave a savage snarl as she stormed into the cave. She could hear Arran's laughter fading as she trekked further into the cavern.

"Stupid jerks," she grouched as she slowed her pace and glanced around. Her knees still hurt, and she didn't doubt she had skinned them. On the bright side, her foot wasn't hurt. She was just a big klutz. She felt like she was being watched and it was giving her the creeps. Being all alone in a dark cave wasn't helping either.

"Okay, it's a temple. So, they come here all the time. Therefore, it's not like there's going to be dragons or whatever in here. I just have to find the stone and keep calm."

Neko spoke to herself in hopes of breaking the haunting silence that filled the cave. Neko froze as she came to the last torch.

"What?" she asked as she realized that she was in a large circular chamber. In the center was an altar with offerings set out on a small table before it. This area was well lit because of a rather large opening in the ceiling of the room some forty feet above Neko's head. The chamber had three tunnels that branched off from it, all of them going deeper into the cave. She could not see any more burning torches save for the ones in the large chamber.

"Are you frigging kidding me?" She felt her frustrations return as she growled and wrestled a nearby torch from the sconce on the wall.

"There is no way I'm going any further without a light," she mumbled as she randomly chose the left tunnel. This was going to take a lot longer than she had expected.

Neko was starting to panic. She didn't know how long she had been wandering around the caves. It could have been an hour or five, she inwardly cursed herself for not taking note of the time when she has started this ridiculous endeavor. She was certain of one thing, and that was her torch had nearly burnt out. She couldn't have doubled back to get another one even if she tried. She was completely lost in the labyrinth of tunnels that filled the cave. Neko let out a pitiful groan as her torch finally fizzled out and she was shrouded in complete darkness. She stepped backwards, feeling the cold rock against her back. She slowly slid down the smooth surface and brought her knees to her chest, wrapping her arms around her knees as she buried her face in her arms. She squeezed her eyes shut wishing herself away from this horrible, dark cave. She gave an aggravated sigh, wishing for something wasn't going to help. If she wanted to get out, she would need to make a plan. She focused on listening to the sounds of the cave. There really wasn't anything else to do at the moment. She could hear the constant drip of water echoing somewhere, and the caves amplified even the slightest noise, making it sound like people talking.

Neko lifted her head, staring around frantically.

"Hello?" she yelled, trying in vain to see anything other than darkness but all she got was the return of her echo. Neko froze as gradually the cave around her faded from black to a silvery glow. Neko slowly gazed up and her breath caught, above her, hundreds of tiny crystals dotted the roof like stars in a night sky.

"Wow," Neko stated in awe, as she looked around, able to see quite well in this grotto.

"This is just like the lanterns in Rinnyus."

She grinned and scrambled to her feet, dusting the seat of her jeans as she followed the illuminated tunnel. When she came to a junction, she paused, taking in the area, she noticed only one of the passageways had the crystals on its ceiling.

"That's really smart," she mused, realizing the Lanarii used the crystals to find their way in the caves, anyone venturing in would refuse to go in without a torch and so they would never be able to see the glowing trail markers. Neko continued to follow the marked tunnels, feeling rather confident that she was making headway. She also noticed there were some bigger crystals, about the size of footballs randomly placed in the tunnels. She stopped at one. Tapping it with her toe, she wondered if they too were meant as some kind of markers.

Neko went rigid as she felt a tremor run from the bottom of her feet to the top of her scalp. She had felt the same pulse from her Earth Stone when she had first activated it. Only this felt like goosebumps when one gets cold. Neko stood a moment trying to figure out what was happening to her. Then she felt it, a pulling of sorts, something in her mind telling her to keep walking. Neko felt a calmness envelop her as she listened to her instincts. Soon, she found herself standing at a dead end. Neko blinked wondering where she had made a wrong turn. She paused, barely making out the bottom of a set of stone steps carved into the very sides of the cave wall. Neko stepped closer, realizing that a thin line of the glowing silver rocks trailed upwards, following the narrow steps that seemed to wind up into the shadows above.

“Seriously?” Neko grumbled as she placed her one foot on the first step, testing it to see if it would hold her weight. Neko took another step and waited a moment. It seemed sturdy, so she climbed a few more steps. Twenty steps up and like an idiot, she decided to look around. She shifted, and a piece of the step under her foot gave way, making her fall forward painfully landing on her hands as she let forth a startled scream that echoed off the stone walls. It took Neko a good three minutes to gather her courage before she decided to continue upwards, the strange pulling feeling getting stronger as she decided to continue crawling up the remainder of the steps on all fours. If she fell from there, no one would ever find her. After about ten minutes of slowly climbing she made it to the top of the stairs. She didn’t even want to think about how she was going to get back down the crumbling staircase. Once at the top, she found herself staring at a narrow stone bridge maybe only two feet wide that spanned about fifteen feet across a bottomless chasm. Neko took a deep breath, wanting to turn back but at the end of the bridge was an open archway and beyond that, she could see light illuminating a large chamber. Neko felt her energy renew as she stepped out onto the bridge. Slowly, she stepped out. Inch by inch, she made her way across, focusing on the bridge before her, refusing to look down and knowing she could not afford to lose her concentration. Once she had traversed the ledge, she took a few steps and then Neko was through the archway. She found herself in a large grotto, easily double the size of the altar chamber. She stood staring at the beauty before her. There were thousands of glowing crystals on the grotto roof some fifty feet above her. Not only were there silver crystals but a rainbow of them, red, blue, purple green, all illuminating the area with a ghostly light making it look like a full moon was shining down on this completely different world in the dark. Neko could see a large body of water that filled at least half of the grotto. In the center was a small island covered with the silver crystals. In the center sat a raised stone dais, and on that Neko could see the faint blue light of the Water Stone. As she neared, the stone reacted, just as the others had, throwing a bright blue pulsating light beam through the entire chamber.

"I found it."

Neko felt half relief and half dread. She still had to cross the water, and she did not like the idea of swimming in a dark cave pool, not knowing what was swimming in there with her. Neko stopped at the edge of the pool, staring longingly over at the Water Stone that had ceased the light show and was sitting there almost patiently, awaiting her to come and claim it.

Neko decided she was going to keep her clothing on in case there were snakes, bugs, or whatever else in the water. She decided to keep her shoes on too. She did not want to cut her feet on any sharp rocks that might have been in the pool. With a resigned sigh, she walked into the water. She cursed finding that the water was on the chilly side. Thankfully, she was a good swimmer and eager to retrieve the stone and leave the creepy cave.

⁂

Arran lounged back on the boulder he had been sitting on for the last two hours. He glanced over at Riken who had been standing motionless beside the water pool for the last hour.

"How long are you giving her?"

Riken continued to stare into the deep pool.

"She has until dusk. If she does not return on her own, then I will go in and find her."

Arran stood and stretched, his muscles stiff from sitting so long.

"Well, I am not about to hold my breath. Once she fails, then what? Will you still dote on her or will you tie her up with her devious partner?"

Riken turned, giving Arran a heated stare, annoyance in his golden eyes.

"Why do you distrust her so much? What is it that she has done that makes you desire her to fail in her quest?"

"She is a pretender, one of Troy's little pawns. That clumsy little tart is not my sister. That is not Seaonna."

Riken rubbed his chin, deep in thought.

"And if she does return with the stone, then what? Will you renounce your accusations or will you find some other fault of hers to dissect?"

Arran felt himself flush. He did not want the Lanarii King to think him an insolent individual.

"No. It is as you say. If she retrieves that stone then there can be no doubt of her status in my family. If she returns successful, I will award her the other two element stones I wear with me. After all, it means she is the true guardian, and the stones are hers by birthright."

"You show good character, son of Trydus. I would expect no less of you."

Riken turned back to the cave entrance.

"You will see; she will return victorious."

Arran also looked towards the cave entrance.

"How is it that you can be so unwavering in your faith in her?"

"Because Arran, I saw what she did in the forest, how she was treated by the Glodiirii leader. Not even the bravest Lanarii are permitted to lay a finger on him and yet he allowed her, which is all the proof I needed."

Arran felt ashamed after hearing the King's revelation. He knew about the Glodiirii and their reputation. No one could fool the forest guardians.

"Well...no one informed me of that detail," Arran amended as Riken chuckled and awaited Neko's return.

Neko shivered as she waded further into the underground pool. The water was already reaching her hips, and she would kill to be able to jump into a nice warm Jacuzzi. Clenching her jaw, Neko kept moving, trying her best not to disturb the stagnant water. Once she was up to her chest, she slid into the water, deciding on doggy paddling instead of flapping her arms around and causing a commotion that might attract unwanted attention. As she got close to the island, she realized she would have to heave herself up out of the water, as there appeared to be no incline to use to get onto the island. It took her only a moment to find an area to scale safely. Neko grabbed a solid looking crystal and succeeded to get her torso onto the island. With a bit of kicking, she managed to get her legs out of the water and then she was on land. She decided to take a short break before she continued any further. She was cold, wet and tired. After she had caught her breath, she got to her feet, making a disgusted face as she realized she was covered in dirt as well as being drenched. She stood before the dais, staring at the small gemstone no bigger than her pinky finger. She spoke as she reached for the stone, "For such a small stone, you sure are a pain in my ass."

She paused just before she took the stone, her mind reeling. She had watched one too many adventure movies about raiding lost treasure troves and what not. She sure as heck didn't need a huge boulder coming out of nowhere and turning her into a pancake.

She nervously glanced around, not sure how to proceed. She tightly smiled and fidgeted. She finally snatched the stone and held it to her chest, waiting to see if she had sprung any booby-traps. After about a minute, she let out the breath she had been holding. She curiously looked down at the stone. It was a clear sapphire color, and she noticed that it had the same mount on it that the Earth Stone had, almost as if it had been fashioned to be on a chain. Neko shook herself from her stupor and decided it was time to leave. She tucked the gem into her bra. There was a pocket for the padding; so, she stuffed it in there, thinking that would be the safest place for the stone until she could get a proper chain for it. As she got her courage up to go back into the frigid water, she froze at what she saw on the far bank blocking her way back outside. Some sort of four-legged creature paced the bank, growling but refusing to set foot in the water. Neko crouched down, fighting to get her breathing back to normal.

"Oh crap. Oh crap. OH CRAP!" she whispered frantically as she looked up, the creature still pacing the far shore.

She looked behind her, noticing another tunnel but once she got out of the water, that thing would be on her.

"I did it. I got the stone. Why did that thing come out now, and what the hell is that?"

Neko grimaced, wishing this was just one really bad dream brought on by too many sweets before bed. Neko rubbed her face in frustration. She was so close, and now she had this thing to deal with. She had nothing but the Water Stone that apparently was like the other stones and only worked when she was about to get herself killed, and she thought to herself, that there was no way she was letting that animal anywhere near her.

Neko shivered as a draft blew against her back. Blinking, she slowly turned around and analysed the pedestal where the Water Stone had been sitting. She held her hand out, confirming that, yes, there was a breeze coming from under the stand. Neko checked to make sure the creature was still on the bank. Then, with a solid kick, she sent the pedestal toppling over where it landed with a soft thud in the damp soil, revealing a bottomless hole the rough size of a manhole cover. Neko winced as the dais rolled down the one side of the twenty-foot round island, making a loud splash as it fell into the murky depths. Neko frightfully looked up, watching the snarling feline-bear looking creature take a few steps into the water towards her. The creature lifted its head, its nose twitching like crazy as it tried to find her exact location. Neko needed no more prompting as she scrambled to get down the opening. Feet first, she slipped down until she was hanging weightless with only her hands to support her weight. She tried to feel for a foothold but was not so lucky. She felt panic welling in her gut and then she heard a soft growl and looked up. She screamed as a huge muzzle full of razor sharp teeth came at her, and she let go, scared the creature was going to tear off her arms. She screamed in fear as she plummeted into darkness. A few moments of blind terror and then she hit water. As soon as she realized what had happened, she fought to get back to the surface, taking in a huge gasp of air as she broke the frigid water. She saw light and swam towards it, realizing with glee it looked like there was an exit, sunshine lighting the smaller cave as she finally made her way to shore. She staggered towards the exit, relief flooding her as she stepped out into the light, fresh air filling her lungs as she took in the forest, she was never so happy to see trees in all her life. She quickly looked down, patting her chest to make sure the Water Stone was still safe.

Neko flopped down back first in the nearby patch of grass. She had noticed the hole she had fallen through was surrounded by solid rock. There was no way that thing could follow her. It was far too big to get through that opening. Neko lay there for ten minutes, regaining herself before she heard voices coming from somewhere nearby. Curious, she got to her feet and followed the voices. In seconds, she came to a ledge and stared down. Below her, some twenty feet, was the temple entrance and the pool of water.

"It is nearing dusk. She has failed," Arran protested when Riken shook his head in disagreement.

"We should go in after her." Arran prodded.

Neko grinned. They hadn't seen her come out or did not expect her to come out the way that she had. She felt very self-assured in this moment. She had done it all by herself, despite Arran telling her she would never get the stone.

"Hey Arran," Neko taunted in a sing-song voice," I hope your mouth is able to fit your foot in it."

Neko watched as twenty sets of shocked eyes set upon her. In her hand, she held up a tiny blue stone. Riken smiled up at her. She was soaking wet, hair plastered to her head, dirt, and forest all over her clothing, on her face and in her hair, but she wore a triumphant grin.

Riken looked over to see Arran staring up at Neko in an awe-struck silence, his jaw catching flies.

"Now, can someone please get me down from up here?"

Chapter Thirteen

It was well into dusk when the group from the temple returned to Rinnyus. Neko's breath caught as she once again took in the splendor of the beautiful village, the silver lights making it glow.

"You have done well, Neko," Riken offered as Neko flashed him a grin.

"Thanks. Did you know about that secret passageway under the dais?"

"The trials in the temple were to make one use their surroundings to their advantage. They were designed to make the guardian trust in themselves, rather than prove themselves in battle."

Neko gave him an inquisitive look.

"So, I was never supposed to fight that cat thing after I got the stone?"

Riken stared straight ahead and continued their conversation.

"You could have if that was what you thought was best. You already had the stone, so it was pointless to fight the Katherr, but you could have defeated it with the Water Stone. Any life, even that of an animal is precious. The fact that you took the passive path shows me a great deal of your character."

Neko stared towards the looming gates into the village. Lanarii warriors now patrolled the wall.

"Good. It looks like I'm finally starting to do things right."

Neko glanced up at Riken who was still staring straight ahead as they approached the village border.

"Anyone can kill a creature, swaying your hand and showing mercy takes more willpower, I believe."

"You're right."

She glanced around, Arran nowhere to be seen.

"Hey, where did Arran go?"

"I believe he has gone somewhere to lick his wounds."

Neko cracked up at the comment.

"Yeah, I guess I showed him. Somehow, I don't think he's gonna see it that way. He just doesn't like me."

Riken and Neko entered under the stone archway and into the silver village.

"Give him time, Neko. This is a big adjustment for him. Remember, he has thought you dead for many summers. In time, you two will rectify your bond."

"I highly doubt it. He's probably pissed I made him look bad. Even if we are related by blood, we're complete strangers, and I don't even remember him, or any of my real family."

She thought a moment.

"So, I guess this means that I'm a real live Princess?"

"Yes Neko, you are the long-lost Princess Seaonna of the Clan Destayy."

"This is so unbelievable and cool. Me, Neko, a Princess!"

Riken glanced down at her tousled appearance.

"True. Perhaps we should get you cleaned up. Your ordeal in the temple has left you rather dishevelled."

"Yeah, I could really go for a nice hot bath and clean, dry, clothes."

Riken held his arm out for her to take hold.

"If you would follow me, I will see to that immediately."

Neko linked her arm in his, she laughed and together the pair made their way back to the palace.

Once back at the palace, Riken lead Neko to another unknown wing. There he showed her the bathhouse.

"Whoa," Neko stated staring at the large room before her. In the center was a large pool, steam rising from its surface, a familiar glow of the silver crystals illuminating the large area.

"These are the royal baths. It is a natural hot spring that we have molded to suit our needs."

Riken walked over to a nearby wooden cupboard. Pulling forth a large towel, he handed it to Neko.

"Once you have changed from your sodden clothing, leave them here. I will get someone to fetch them and have them laundered for you. I will also have another dress sent up for you, one similar to the other one you were wearing yesterday."

"Thanks. I really appreciate it."

Riken inclined his head to her.

"You are most welcome, Princess. I will see you in the morning. Sleep well."

With that, he made his exit, leaving Neko alone to soak in the healing waters. Neko smiled, and once she was alone, she stripped off her clothing and wrapped the large towel around her. She didn't even bother to try to take the armor off. She walked to the edge of the hot pool, finding that there were steps carved into the pool's side, making it easy to get into the water. Neko gingerly placed her toe into the water, moaning in delight. It was the perfect temperature. She divested her towel and walked into the water, surprised it came up to her hips.

"This is heaven," she whispered, sliding down until only her head was above the water. She swam towards the far end of the pool, the water already warming her cold body. She realized there was a ledge around the pool, the perfect height to sit on and enjoy the relaxing waters. She was just getting comfortable when someone entered the area. Neko wrapped her arms around herself.

"Miss?"

Neko sighed in relief, relaxing as the small girl from the day before stepped forward, in her arms fresh clothing.

"I will set your attire on the shelf here."

She glanced down and then gathered Neko's dirty clothes.

"I will return theses first thing tomorrow miss, before you go to the morning meal."

Neko offered a shy smile.

"Thanks."

The girl nodded and left just as quickly as she had arrived.

Neko decided to swim a little more and then go to bed. She was suddenly exhausted, and she had a feeling it had to do with the warm water that surrounded her. Once she got out of the water, she used the large towel to dry herself, relieved as she discovered the armor she wore dried off a lot better than if it were made of fabric. She smiled. If it could magically shrink to fit someone then having it dry quickly was not such a hard feat. Neko put the dress on, smiling as she realized it was exactly the same style as the other one she had been wearing, save that it was a dark grey instead of pale green.

She slipped on the silver flats that had come with it and placed the now damp towel on the shelf where her dress had been previously sitting. Neko glanced around then pulled the Water Stone from its place in her bra. She held it up, scrutinizing it in the silvery light. It seemed to glow with an inner blue light, mesmerizing her.

"Wow," she stated as she continued to stare into the gemstone for a few moments before shaking her head and replacing the stone to its hiding place. Neko let out a huge yawn and decided it was time to get to bed. A quick glance at her watch told her it was just about 10:00 pm. Neko yawned again and headed back into the main hallway, from there she found her way back to the main entrance foyer and remembered the way back to her room. Once back in her room, Neko was intent on going straight to sleep. This day had been long and tiring. As she lay back in the soft downy pillows of her bed, Neko closed her eyes, and in moments, she was sound asleep.

Troy and Alexander looked up as the Lanarii King himself waltzed into the area where they were being held prisoner, still tied to wooden stakes in the ground. Another Lanarii accompanied him.

"Your highness," one of the guards addressed Riken. The two Lanarii guards then bowed respectfully to their leader.

"At ease," Riken stated. Beside him, Landis stood, a scowl on his face. Riken's gaze met Troy's.

"You may release Prince Troy."

The guard who had spoken earlier did as he was told, cutting Troy free of the bonds that held him prisoner.

"What is this?" Troy asked while rubbing at his raw wrists as he slowly got to his feet. Riken gave him a shrewd stare, fighting the urge to sneer at the Prince.

"I made a promise to Neko that I would release you once she faced and completed the trials."

Riken gestured to Landis.

"There is a stipulation, however. You are to be shadowed at all times while you are in my village. Make no mistake; if you do anything to jeopardize my people, you will be dealt with accordingly. It is only my high regard for the Princess that I even allow you to run free."

"Princess?" he pondered as Riken refused to say anything else.

"You may ask her about that. If she wishes to enlighten you of recent events, that is her decision alone. Now, if you would follow me, we are to meet her for the morning meal."

Troy decided to keep his mouth shut. As he followed the Lanarii King, he glanced over his shoulder. Alexander shot him an angry scowl.

"What about my brother?" Troy enquired as Riken shot the other man a hard stare.

"He will remain as he is."

Riken turned. He was finished talking to the Prince. He had agreed to free him, and he had. That was the extent of his benevolence. As they headed towards the palace, Troy spoke up.

"What about my possessions, my sword?"

Riken's words were ice when he spoke.

"Your things will be returned to you once you have left this village. I will not allow you to have any weapon of any sort within these walls."

Troy felt his temper flare at the haughty leader's rebuff.

"As you wish, Lanarii King," he bit out. Now was not the time to be picking fights, especially when he had just been freed. He needed to show he was harmless. Troy had to admit he was impressed with the village, not that he would voice that aloud. As they approached the palace, the King remained stoic. Soon, they entered the main hallway and down a smaller corridor. There, it opened into a rather nice breakfast nook, complete with a full morning meal and refreshments. Troy felt his mouth water as the smell of freshly prepared food filled his senses. Riken sat down, looking to Troy who remained standing and awaiting an invite.

"Be seated," Riken commanded as Troy hastily sat down, eyeing the delicious food before him.

"The Princess will be arriving momentarily."

Troy was curious, who was this Princess, and how did Neko get into good standing with her enough that they had convinced the Lanarii King to release him into the village? Troy forced himself to pick at the food before him, feigning boredom. He was not about to let the King see him gorge himself on food. He had too much pride to show any weakness before the Lanarii.

Neko was up before her watch alarm went off, which was odd seeing how tired she had been the night before. She felt strangely energized, and she welcomed this new feeling. She walked over to her door as someone gently knocked.

"Come in," Neko stated, smiling brightly at the girl who entered, Neko's clothing cleaned and folded as promised.

"Just on the bed is fine," Neko blurted out, realizing she had yet to ask the girl her name.

"Hey, what's your name? I don't think I properly introduced myself."

The girl did as Neko asked. Turning to face Neko, she returned the smile with a small one of her own.

"My name is Adalynn."

She bowed slightly.

"Nice to meet you. By the way, thank you for helping me out these last few days. I really appreciate it."

"You are welcome, Miss."

Neko grinned as the girl gestured towards the door.

"Are you ready to join Lord Riken for the morning meal?"

"Yeah, I'm starving!"

Adalynn allowed Neko to exit the room first.

Neko needed no guidance as she headed down towards the dining area. She was starting to learn her way around the palace, which was more of a mansion. Neko smiled, at least she could see to find her way there, and it didn't seem so bad after the entire cave fiasco the day before. As she entered the breakfast nook, she paused. There sitting and dining together were Troy and Riken.

"Troy?" Neko asked, a smile lighting her face as the Prince turned towards her when she called his name. Troy stared at Neko. She wore a finely tailored Lanarii dress and slippers.

"I have kept my word, Princess. He is free as you have requested."

Riken watched as Troy gave Neko a screwy look.

"You are the Princess?"

Neko looked a bit uncomfortable.

"Uh, yeah, about that, turns out I'm from this world after all."

Troy looked to Riken who remained silent.

"How is that possible?" Troy questioned as Neko approached him.

"It's a long story. I'll tell you all about it, after breakfast though. I'm starving."

Troy stared at her as Riken moved over, making room for her to sit beside him. She started helping herself to the food before them. When Troy looked up, his eyes met a steely tawny gaze. Riken was scrutinizing his every expression.

"I would like that," Troy sullenly retorted as he averted his gaze. He was not about to get into a pissing match with the Lanarii, even though he wanted nothing better to do than to run the Lanarii through with the bastard's own blade. Neko remained oblivious to their staring contest as she started eating what food she had taken. The food of the Lanarii contained many flavors that were new to her, but she found she enjoyed the foreign cuisine. As she ate, Riken struck up a conversation.

"I have decided to have a celebration in your honor, Princess Seaonna."

Neko blinked, shaking her head vigorously.

"Oh no. You don't have to go to the trouble."

Riken held a hand up.

"I insist and so has your brother. I am making the arrangements to have it tonight after the sun has set. I also have a gift for you. I will have it sent up to your room before the feast."

"A gift, for me?" she echoed as Riken returned the smile with one of his own.

"Yes. I believe it is fitting for you to have this gift, but I will say no more for risk of ruining the surprise."

Troy fought the urge to make gagging sounds. This Lanarii was so noble and just. No one was that selfless. Yet, he had Neko eating it all up.

"With that said, I must go make the arrangements. You will need to excuse me, Princess. Please feel free to explore the village. The rest of the day is yours. I will see you tonight."

Neko stood up to let the King get out from behind the large wooden round table.

"Sounds great," Neko beamed as she returned to her seat as soon as Riken had gotten out from behind the table and to his feet.

"Until then," he softly spoke before he turned and left, not even saying goodbye to Troy.

Neko grinned over at Troy like a fool.

"Isn't this so exciting, a feast just for me."

"I can hardly contain myself," he deadpanned as Neko's face fell.

"You're angry?" she asked as Troy gave her a piercing glare.

"Your damn right I am. That, that creature has been a belligerent cad."

Neko felt her joyous emotions fade.

"What do you mean?"

"He threatened me. He has this other Lanarii watching me like some murderous villain when I have done nothing wrong."

Neko glanced over at Landis who looked rather annoyed at needing to babysit Troy.

"I'm sure he didn't mean it like that. Give it some time. Riken will come to see you mean no harm. Please Troy, for me?" she asked her eyes pleading as Troy yielded to her request. He did not need her to be angry with him.

"I owe you thanks, Neko. You promised to free me, and you did."

"It's good to talk with you again. This whole thing has been like some really messed up dream."

"This Princess business, what happened while I was detained?"

Neko rolled her eyes.

"You would not believe the crap storm that hit once I arrived here with Riken."

Neko regaled him with her adventures, filling Troy in on the details. All the while, the Prince absorbed this new information as he and Neko reconnected.

Chapter Fourteen

When Neko had finished telling her story, Troy could only stare at her in shock.

"You are a Dolphinian then?"

"Yes. That's what I've been saying for the last half hour."

Neko laughed as Troy took a deep breath, his eyes meeting hers.

"Will you stay here now? This is your real home after all."

"This is really cool and all but I have a life back where I'm from. I have parents who are probably worried sick about me—where I've gone."

Neko looked longingly out the glass window to her right.

"Hey, I got an idea. Let's go explore the town. I'm sick of all this depressing talk."

Neko offered a huge grin to Troy who gave her a tight smile in return.

"Whatever you wish, Neko. I am just relieved I am no longer a prisoner."

Troy shot Landis a grudging look.

"Well, for the most part, I suppose."

Neko got to her feet.

"Come on, let's go. It'll be fun," Neko urged as Troy agreed and walked with her into the main foyer, well aware that the Lanarii tasked to follow him gave them only a few feet of privacy.

"Did you have a particular area you wanted to see first?" Troy asked as Neko pointed towards the far side of the village, towards the shore of Lake Tariin.

"I wanted to check that beach out. It looks like some really nice beachfront. Might be nice to go sit and relax there, but I was thinking we could just take in the village and save the beach for last."

Troy concurred. It was better than being shackled to a pole, even if he had Neko chatting his ear off. Troy looked over his shoulder at Landis. The Lanarii did not look impressed. Neko took Troy's silence as his agreement and started walking towards a vendor that caught her eye. Before long, the pair had gotten back into familiar routines.

"This sure is a lot nicer than running from rebels, eh Troy?"

Troy shot her an unamused look.

"Did he ever return your stone to you?"

Neko stopped walking, her eyes serious.

"No, he didn't, but I'm okay with that. He's trustworthy. I know you two don't like each other, but maybe you guys just need to get to know one another. You might even become friends one day."

Troy could hear the teasing tone in her voice as he gave her a playful shove.

"Shut it," he growled as Neko burst out laughing. Troy couldn't help but smile at her jovial mood.

They continued towards the beach, now only a few minutes' walk from the sandy shoreline.

"Oh wow, it's nearly one," Neko stated, glancing down at her watch. Troy gave her a screwy look, not understanding what she was saying.

"What is one?" he questioned as Neko laughed and showed him her watch.

"Where I come from, this tells me the time. One is an hour after midday meal here."

Troy understood somewhat.

"As in a sundial."

"That's what Riken compared it to, and yes, it's exactly like a sundial."

Troy and Neko paused, both taking in the beautiful scene before them.

"Oh, wow, have you ever seen anything so pretty? Look at all that white sand!" Neko yelled as she gave a whoop and charged towards the water, Troy followed at a more leisure pace. Neko couldn't get her slippers off fast enough as she stepped into the refreshing water.

"Oh, that's a little chilly," she stated as she waded in to her ankles, her dress short enough that it didn't hang in the water as she went in a few more inches. Troy gave her a dubious stare.

"Well, are you coming in? It feels great on the feet."

Neko yelled as Troy sighed, but started removing his boots. After a few days of being a prisoner, he was starting to feel a bit unkempt, and he would rather have a cold bath than to smell like a peasant. Neko smirked and as soon as Troy was close enough, she kicked water at him, soaking him with cold droplets. She was surprised as he gave her a devilish grin and then to her delight, he humored her and splashed her back. Neko gave a piercing scream as water hit her collar, making goose bumps rise on her arms. Not to be outdone, she splashed him again. This time it was a bit more, and within seconds, both were soaking wet head to toe but rather refreshed. Troy ran at Neko and went to splash her, but at the last moment, he ducked down and grabbed her around the waist, intent on throwing her into the water to get her good and drenched. He did not count on her hooking her foot around his calf and making him lose his balance. Both went sprawling into the water, getting completely soaked in the process. Troy and Neko both burst out laughing as they sat in the water, only their heads above its surface. Neko grinned and nodded towards the lake.

"Come on. Let's see if fancy pants chases us if we swim out a ways."

Troy smirked, deciding he wanted to see the Lanarii guard flustered.

"All right," he replied as Neko splashed him in the face with a jet of water.

"Race ya!" she hollered as she took off swimming, Troy right on her tail as the two swam some few hundred feet out into the placid lake. Landis cursed as the Princess and his ward swam farther into the lake. He was supposed to be watching the Prince but what could he really harm in the lake? From their interactions, the two were close friends. Landis thought about them perhaps scheming, but they were yelling and screaming so loud that anyone on the shore could hear them. Landis sighed. Where they were, the water was only chest deep, and he did not feel like going in after the duo. Landis slowly removed the bow from his shoulder as he let a devious smirk slip onto his face. If the Prince tried anything, he would find himself with an arrow in his arse before he knew what had hit him.

Riken had left the palace immediately after he excused himself from the morning meal. He had many things to prepare and not much time in which to have everything ready for the night's festivities. He smiled fondly and headed for his first order of business, getting a dress commissioned for Neko. He knew she was happy with the one she currently had, but he wanted to have one fitting for a Princess. He smiled. He had already gotten a seamstress to start making clothing similar to the ones in which Neko had arrived. He had a hunch she would appreciate that more than a wardrobe full of dresses. He approached the vendor. A female Lanarii and her daughter bowed respectfully.

"My lord," the woman addressed Riken. "What can we assist you with today?"

Riken gestured to all the beautiful materials in the shop.

"I would be honored if you would make for me a beautiful dress for the Princess to wear tonight. After all, it is her coronation of sorts."

The little girl beamed.

"I heard she was a Princess. Is it because she faced the trials in the temple?"

The mother shushed her child, shooting Riken an apologetic look.

"It is all right."

Riken gave the girl a fond smile.

"That is true. She is the Princess Seaonna of the Clan Destayy."

"Wow. Is she nice?" the girl badgered Riken who nodded.

"She is very nice," he assured as he looked back to the seamstress.

"My lord, what style of dress do you wish? I do not mean to rush you, but if I am to have the dress ready in time. I must start it right away."

Riken understood and leaned in closer.

"It will be a bit different style, but I have faith you will do just fine. All your dresses are lovely."

The Lanarii woman beamed.

"I thank your kind words, my King. Let us get started, shall we?"

Once Riken had chosen the colors and explained the pattern, the seamstress set out to finish the dress.

"That is a rather complex gift for someone you have just met."

Riken turned as Arran fixed a skeptical gaze on the King. Riken felt slightly annoyed by the obvious expression.

"You disapprove?"

Arran shook his head, waving it off.

"It is your choice. What do I care?"

This time Riken cast Arran the skeptical stare.

"You should care a great deal, this is your younger sister we are discussing, and her best interests should be your top priority."

Arran scoffed and kicked at the dirt.

"She is only related to me by blood. I know next to nothing about her."

Riken offered him a patient look.

"And you are just as much a stranger to her. She is convinced that you hate her. Driving a rift between yourselves will not mend your lost bond. It is a sad thing that you two did not grow up together, but your sister, long thought dead, is alive and you should be grateful for that," Arran cursed the King's intuitive nature.

"I am a rebel. What could I possibly offer her when she is in such good standing with the Lanarii King and the son of King Arwin?"

"Arran, you do not give yourself any credit, which is one similarity between you and your sister."

Riken chuckled again, mirth alighting his amber eyes as he continued.

"You are her only living family. You can teach her about her people, tell her about your parents. She remembers nothing of her time here when she was a young child. Show her that she has your support."

Arran felt nauseous.

"I have been a horse's ass towards her."

Riken began walking, the Prince walking beside him as they headed into the market area.

"She is a forgiving individual. I am sure if you spent some time with her, you would see she is an engaging young lady."

Arran stopped, looking at the Lanarii King.

"You like her?"

"Yes, she is—"

Arran cut him off.

"You *like* her."

Riken realized what the rebel Prince was hinting at.

"Not in that way. There is only one I see that way, and she is no longer here. Even if this were the case, I would not pursue Neko. She has more important endeavors to occupy her time."

Arran felt the tension leave his body as Riken chuckled.

"You feign indifference. Yet, you cannot help being protective of her."

Arran looked skyward letting forth an audible groan as he rubbed his face with his hands.

"You are right. It is my duty to protect her, and I should start acting like her big brother."

Riken gestured to a nearby food vendor.

"Would you care to join me with the planning?"

"Yes, I would. Thank you for including me."

As Riken decided on the main course, Arran glanced towards a jewelry stall.

"Riken, I would like to get a chain for the element stones, so that Neko may wear them. What are your thoughts?"

Arran gestured to the leather cord that held the Wind Stone and Fire Stone around his neck.

"I think a chain of durability would be ideal for Neko," Arran stated as both shared a smirk.

"Yes. She does tend to be a bit accident prone."

Both chuckled at that and Riken gestured to the stall.

"I think it is a great idea and she will appreciate it."

Arran idly touched the two stones.

"They belong to her by birthright, and I must respect that they have chosen her as their guardian. I will help her learn her position as the guardian of the sacred element stones of our people."

Riken approached the vendor, Arran at his side, as the pair began preparations for the evening celebrations.

Neko laughed, overjoyed that Troy had finally let loose and was actually having fun. They stayed in the water a little longer and then decided to head back towards shore. Neko glanced over to see Landis sitting calmly on a fallen log, his bow resting in his lap.

"Come on, let's explore the beach," Neko offered as she and Troy leisurely strolled down the long expanse of sand. They had stopped and sat down in the warm sand, chatting away as Landis looked on from some fifteen feet away. Neko didn't know how long they had stayed at the beach, but it was long enough to know she was starting to get hungry.

"I'm freaking starving. What about you?" she asked as Troy gazed down at her, waiting for her to notice he was staring at her. When she felt eyes on her, she turned, looking into cerulean orbs. There was a strange hunger in his eyes that made her feel a bit nervous.

"Troy?" she asked as he leaned closer and grabbed a small strand of her hair, running it through his fingers.

"It is just that today, with you seemed so, perfect…so right."

Neko blinked rapidly, not sure what to say or do.

"Uhh…" was her intelligent reply as Troy grinned and closed the gap between them. He released her hair and tilted her chin up, so she was eye to eye with him.

"Did you enjoy today?"

Neko dumbly nodded as a rose blush dusted her cheeks.

"Yeah, it was uhh…great," Neko stammered as Troy smirked. Neko could hardly speak, let alone resist his charms. He closed the distance between them, and his lips met hers in a tender kiss. He felt her go rigid as he tried to deepen the kiss. She had no idea what to do and that amused him even more. Troy was somewhat shocked as Neko placed her hand on his chest and gave him a firm push, putting some distance between them.

"What are you doing?" she questioned, confusion evident in her eyes and voice. Troy gave her an arrogant look.

"I think that would be obvious. I am kissing you."

He leaned in to kiss her again, grabbing her by the upper arms only to have her lean farther back as his grip tightened.

"No. You can't just go kissing someone without asking them first."

Troy felt his temper slip.

"Well, you sure as hell took your time deciding."

Neko blinked, seeing the frustration in his eyes.

"I'm just… I've never kissed anyone before okay."

Her blush covering more of her face as Troy gave her an even stare.

"Fine then, Neko. May I kiss you?"

Neko opened her mouth to reply then looked to her left as the sound of a blade being drawn behind them got their attention.

"You may not. Now kindly release my sister before I cut your hands off."

Troy clenched his jaw as he glared up at Arran who stood with his blade drawn, ready to make good on his threat.

"All right," Troy hissed releasing Neko's arms as he and Arran got into a heated glaring contest.

"Neko, I must speak with you, in private," Arran growled, his eyes never leaving Troy's.

"Is there a problem?"

Landis's soft voice defused some of the tension. Arran glanced at the Lanarii.

"There is no problem. I need to speak with my sister is all. Why did you not stop him when he attacked her?"

Landis raised an eyebrow.

"Meaning no disrespect but she was not asking for help. I was watching," Arran growled and offered his hand to Neko who slapped it away and got to her feet.

"I can handle it," she snapped, not so annoyed he had jumped in to save her honor or whatever, but to the fact that he was treating her as if she were a five-year-old child.

"Come with me," Arran clipped as he turned and started walking down the beach. Neko sighed and looked to Troy.

"I'll see you later okay?"

Troy nodded as she turned and ran after the rebel leader. Troy remained sitting in the sand, annoyed to no end that his attempt to court Neko had been interrupted by Arran.

"Of course, he would have to be your brother. Makes sense. Both of you are annoying to no end," Troy snarled to himself, directing his frustrations into a glare he fired at Landis who promptly ignored the irate Prince.

Chapter Fifteen

Neko glared a hole in the back of Arran's head the entire time they headed towards the far end of the beach, well away from Troy.

"You've got your nerve," Neko spat as Arran turned to face her, annoyance in his eyes, but he let her continue her rant.

"You can't say anything nice to me at all. You're rude, and then you come running to my rescue with some misguided notion of protecting my honor or whatever the hell that was back there."

Arran was not expecting her barrage to be that in depth. She really was seething at him.

"Look, before you continue, let me speak."

Neko set her jaw but gestured for him to speak his mind. Arran growled but then decided to apologize to her.

"I am not proud of the way I treated you, but I cannot afford to trust just anyone, especially some girl who has connections to that damn child of the Philistine King."

Neko blinked. Arran certainly didn't come off as refined, but then again, neither did she.

"I already told you—"

"I am not done yet."

Neko felt ready to kick the jerk in the shins but refrained from such a childish act.

"I see now that I was wrong, and since the stones have chosen you as their rightful guardian, I can no longer deny our connection. So, I apologize for my actions and anything I might have said to upset you."

Neko looked up. He had about four inches on her, making her feel even more like a child.

"I'm sorry too, sorry that I kicked you in the face when we first met, but I'm not sorry for punching you. You asked for that."

Arran couldn't help but laugh at her joke. It was funny even if it was at his expense. A funny thing happened then. They were actually agreeing and just like that, they were both laughing, and the past hard feelings were forgotten.

Once the siblings' laughing fit subsided, Neko smiled up at Arran.

"So, you're really my big brother eh? Is that why you got all protective of me back there?"

Neko gestured over her shoulder to where Troy had been sitting. He was long gone, Landis in tow. Arran nodded.

"Yes, I was angry, and it took some words from a wise Lanarii to get me thinking properly."

Arran gave Neko a serious look.

"Being a guardian is difficult enough. I cannot imagine how hard it would be, especially being sent to another word to fulfil your duty."

Neko looked abashed.

"I got this for you, as a welcome home and coronation gift."

Arran held out a beautiful silver chain. The links looked rather durable and on the chain sat the two element stones of Fire and Wind.

"For me?" she asked, afraid to touch them. Arran laughed at her hesitation.

"They are yours to protect now."

He handed her the chain. She put her finger up, signaling him to wait.

"Hold on to that for a moment."

She turned around and fished the Water Stone from her bra. She grinned as she turned back around and held up the blue gemstone.

"There," she stated as she took the chain and placed the third stone on the chain. Arran raised a quizzical eyebrow.

"You had the Water Stone hidden down your front?"

"Looks that way. Hey, I figured that would be the safest place."

Arran shook his head, chuckling.

"Here," He held his hand out. "Let me put it on," he offered as Neko dropped the chain and three stones into his palm, turning her back to him so he could clasp the chain behind her neck. Neko assisted him by holding her hair up and out of the way. Once in place, Neko turned, looking down at the three stones that seemed to ignite with an inner light.

"They seem to recognize you," he offered, also noticing the glow the stones seemed to emit. Neko chuckled.

"It sure seems that way."

Arran gestured towards the palace.

"We should probably be getting back. The feast will not be too long away, and you still need to get ready for tonight."

Neko agreed as she and Arran headed away from the beach and back towards the village and palace beyond that. As they walked, Neko admired her necklace.

"Thank you, Arran."

Arran glanced down at his sister, a smile playing on his lips.

"You are welcome, Seaonna."

Neko paused, a strange look coming across her face.

"Please, just call me Neko. That's my name now."

Arran was confused but nodded. He would ask her about that later. He did not want to ruin the good mood, and there would be a lot of time to get to know his sister and all her quirks.

Neko glanced over at her brother as they strolled towards the palace, the sun starting to descend behind the tall mountains of which Rinnyus seemed to be nestled right in the center.

"So, Arran, what happened to make you and Troy such enemies, cause the way I figure, he would have been too young to harm you personally."

Arran took a deep breath. Once he had realized whom she was, he knew there would come a time when she would ask about him and his life before they met. He thought he would be ready for this conversation, but he had no clue where he should begin. He decided before the war would probably be his best course of action. Neko thought Arran had decided to ignore her and her question, but then he finally spoke, staring straight ahead and refusing to look at her.

"When the war hit, it was Troy's father who attacked our people. He gave the order to storm the palace. Our father, King Trydus, did what he could to give our mother the time she needed to get the element stones away from Arwin's greedy hands. I was just a boy then, fourteen summers old at the most. I was there when Father was killed. I got separated from you and Mother, and before I could get my bearings, I was knocked unconscious by falling debris."

Neko had wanted to ask a question about the stones but decided to ask after Arran finished his story. Pain flickered in his eyes, and he had been kind enough to tell her the story, so she didn't want to be rude by interrupting him.

"That bastard managed to get the Wind Stone, but not before Mother took you and the other stones and fled. She came here to Rinnyus first and gave the Water Stone to Riken."

He paused to collect his thoughts. Neko decided to ask her question.

"Why didn't they just use the stones to fight King Arwin? Surely they could have overpowered him with all four stones."

"I thought you knew Seonn— Neko. The stones had chosen you as their guardian, but you were only a child, seven summers old and too young to fight in the war."

"But who was the guardian before me? Someone must have been old enough to wield them until I was old enough to."

"The last guardian was our grandfather. The stones had lain dormant for years, and our parents were shocked when I was not chosen. Then, when you turned seven, they activated, letting us know beyond a doubt that you were the next guardian. Father would have passed on his knowledge of your responsibilities had he survived."

Neko let this information sink in.

"What happened to you then, after you got knocked out?"

Arran shot his sister a wilting look.

"What I tell you now, please keep it between us. I do not like people to know of my history after the war."

"I won't tell a soul, promise."

Arran sighed and once again stared straight ahead, thankful there were not many people milling around. Most had already headed to the gardens behind the palace.

"When the battle had ended, and I came to, I was taken prisoner by Arwin. With Father dead and you and Mother on the run, I had no one to save me but myself. I was lucky that the King had taken off after Mother and so I posed as a servant, telling the King's soldiers I was a kitchen boy. They assumed Mother had taken us both and ran with the stones. Unfortunately, an orphaned kitchen boy is not worth much, and so I was sent to a slave market and sold."

Neko could feel tears forming in her eyes.

"Arran, I am so sorry that happened to you."

Arran gave her a pointed stare, shocked at the compassion that filled her grey eyes, the eyes of his father.

"Do not be saddened, Neko. It was because of my life after the war that I grew as strong as I did. The world is not fair, and I learnt this by trial and error. No upbringing in a palace could teach me such helpful life lessons."

Neko wiped the tears that threatened to spill from her eyes.

"Did you escape?"

"No, a mercenary saw me and bought me. I suppose he could see something of worth in a scrawny kitchen boy that no one else could."

Arran looked towards the palace. Both siblings staring at the stone steps.

"That is how I stumbled upon the Fire Stone. He had lifted it from some treasure hunter. To make a long story short, the bounty hunter and his men went toe to toe with my master and his men. When the dust settled, only a few from both sides were left alive. I took the stone from my dead master and hid it. No one caught me, and I made myself scarce. I was not about to become someone else's slave or let the stone fall into corrupt hands."

Neko felt her jaw drop.

"So then, how did you become the rebel leader?"

"It was not that difficult. There are many who oppose the King's rule. Once word got around that I was the son of Trydus and had an element stone at my disposal, it was not hard convincing people to join my cause, especially other Dolphinians that had been wronged in the war. You and I were not the only ones who lost family."

"So, you were able to summon the Fire Stone's powers?"

"A little, I was a fool in that I did not realize the Fire Stone had activated a few days before I met you. There are some individuals who can summon a fraction of its powers, but it is nothing like when a guardian uses the powers of the stones. All three stones in Arorus activated when you returned. When you got close enough, they flashed, recognizing you as the true guardian."

Neko shrugged, but then she decided to go back to her first question.

"But why do you hate Troy?"

Arran gave her a hard stare.

"He is the son of the bastard who killed our parents."

Neko felt her temper starting to slip.

"Yes, his father did that, not Troy. Just because he is related to the man does not make him the same. If it weren't for Troy, I wouldn't be here, and I wouldn't know you or who I am or was."

"How can you trust him?"

Neko gave her brother an irritated stare.

"Because he is my friend and he told me himself that his father is not fit to rule."

Arran blinked at this information.

"What else did he say?"

"Not much. He just wanted to help me find the stones so I could get back home. Troy risked everything to help me Arran. He even took the Wind Stone from his father's treasury."

Arran still looked unconvinced.

"I will think about what you have said. For now, we should head in. You need to get dressed. The feast is almost ready to begin."

Neko blushed as her stomach made its demands clear.

"Yeah. I could go for a bite to eat," Neko stated as both smiled at one another and headed into the palace to get ready for the feast. Once they got into the main entranceway, Arran gave Neko a tight smile.

"I will go find your suitor."

Neko gave him a dirty look.

"He is not *that*."

Arran raised an eyebrow.

"Do you even know whom I was referring to?"

Neko blinked, her cheeks heating up. He had a valid point.

"Uh, Troy?" she asked as Arran chuckled.

"Just go get dressed. I am sure Riken has made the Prince look acceptable for the feast."

Neko rolled her eyes and tore up the stairs, excited to go to the feast.

Chapter Sixteen

Neko was panting when she made it to her door. She stood up straight as Adalynn stood beside the door.

"Miss, you are late. We must make haste."

Neko gave her an embarrassed grin.

"Sorry about that. I kinda lost track of time."

Adalynn let a ghost of a smile creep onto her face.

"It is all right. Come. You must see the gift Lord Riken has left for you."

Neko blinked. There was the childish attitude she had been hoping to see in the girl.

"Adalynn?" Neko asked casually. "I was curious, how old are you."

"I am sixteen summers, miss."

"I thought you were near my age. You're the only one, aside from Riken, who will actually crack a smile."

Adalynn gave Neko an amused look.

"Yes. The older Lanarii tend to be a little more reserved."

Both girls shared a conspiring look before giggling like ten-year-olds.

Neko froze as she spotted the items laid out on her bed.

"Holy crap, is that…for me?" she asked in wonder as she stared at the beautiful dress before her.

It had long flowing sleeves, and it was floor length. It was dark, forest green and silver.

"It is in very fine taste," Adalynn chimed in, giving Neko a mysterious grin.

"Lord Riken has doted on you."

Neko felt herself blushing.

"He's just being nice. Stop that, would ya?"

Both girls laughed at this as Neko picked the dress up. The silky sleeves felt like water running through her hands. The dress was a dark green and was a bit heavier than the silken sleeves that were a deep silver.

"If you would undress, I can help you get into this dress."

Neko gave Adalyn a nervous look.

"Okay, but you need to promise not to laugh or tell anyone. I kinda made an oops."

Neko slowly removed her dress revealing the armor she had on, still form fitting as ever.

"Miss that is—"

"I know, the armor of Annalise. I didn't mean for it to happen, I swear. I was just curious to try it on and then it wouldn't come off and yeah."

Adalynn raised an eyebrow.

"Why not just ask Lord Riken to help you with that?"

Neko shook her head vigorously.

"No way. He would so laugh at me and my stupidity. He told me no one could wear it. Why I even tried it on, I'll never know. I'm just a complete dork."

Adalynn did not know what a dork was, but judging by Neko's context, it was along the lines of a fool.

"I am sure the dress will cover the armor, but you should talk to him about it."

Neko agreed and removed the rest of her damp dress, letting it fall to pool around her ankles. She stepped out of the dress and towards Adalynn who held the new dress ready to step into. Once it was on, it took Adalynn only moments to draw the corset strings in the back. Neko noticed the dress was in two separate parts. The first part, the underdress, was made from the silver material and attached to the sleeves. There was a copper collar made from a stiffer material that left her higher chest exposed but her neck covered. It fit over the top of the sleeves. The belt was the last touch and made the entire dress work. It was made of that same stiff material as the collar and was in a V-shape. The center where a belt buckle would be was a circular silver piece the size of Neko's palm. She walked towards the full-length mirror. Slowly, she stepped into view, staring wide-eyed at the stranger staring back at her.

"You look very fetching, miss," Adalynn stated as she produced a brush from her robes. "If you would allow me, I would be happy to style your hair."

Neko nodded her consent as she took a seat on the end of her bed, still shocked at how beautiful the dress was.

Forty-five minutes later, Neko was dressed, hair styled in a loose bun at the top of her head and light makeup applied. She couldn't help staring at the girl in the mirror before her, enamored by the person that was her but wasn't.

"Wow, thank you Adalynn. You made me look good… like really good."

"I am happy you approve. Now, hurry miss. You are late for your own party."

Neko did a gleeful squeal and gathered her skirts, lest she did something embarrassing like a face plant down the stairs. As she descended the stairs, she found that Riken stood waiting for her at the bottom of the stairwell.

"Sorry for keeping you waiting," she announced as Riken glanced up at her, his eyes going wide as Neko offered him a shy smile.

"Thank you for this beautiful gift. I love it," Neko blurted out as she reached the floor, looking to Riken who continued to stare at her but did not say a single word.

"Riken?" Neko asked, her voice shaking slightly as the Lanarii blinked and offered her a charming smile.

"You look striking, Princess."

Neko blushed, her face going beet red.

"Thanks."

Neko felt lightheaded as Riken offered her his arm to take.

"Shall we? The feast is about to commence."

Neko took his offered arm, screaming at herself in her head not to mess this up and pull a classic Neko klutz move. Riken led Neko through a hallway she had never been down before. It was as wide as the main entrance way. Near the end, she could see a stone archway and beyond that what looked to be a huge rock slab veranda with foliage behind that. As they emerged through the arch and onto the terrace, Neko could see they were in a large garden area with trees and plants of every shape, size, and color imaginable. All around the area was a halo of the silver crystals, making the area look all the more magical.

"You did all this for me?"

Neko wondered aloud as Riken patted her arm with his free hand.

"Yes, but one thing Neko—please do remember to breathe."

Neko laughed at the joke meant to settle her nerves, but she still felt rather exposed. Down a few more stone steps sat a large table with all kinds of food and drinks laid out for the extravagant dinner party.

"Attention, attention please."

Neko looked to her left as a Lanarii spoke, his voice booming over the quiet murmur of the guests milling around.

"Presenting his highness, King Riken of the Clan Drumii and Princess Seaonna of the Clan Destayy."

Neko wanted to run as what seemed like thousands of eyes focused on her, when in reality, perhaps it was only a hundred or so. She still felt ill and was thankful she had an empty stomach.

"Remember to breathe," Riken coached as he gently smiled down at her and then began to address his people.

"At long last, the guardian of the sacred element stones has been revealed to us."

He paused a moment before continuing.

"We hold this feast in honor of her return."

Riken led Neko down the stone stairs and towards the head of the long stone table in the front. There, she noticed Arran and Troy sitting together. Neko smiled at Troy's wide-eyed stare. Arran had an equally floored look, both their jaws dropping.

"You two are going to attract flies if you keep that up," Neko teased as both gave her unimpressed looks.

Arran watched as Riken offered Neko a seat, situating her between the Lanarii King and himself. He glanced over to see Troy was not at all happy with the seating arrangements. Arran couldn't help but smirk. He really did not care for the spoiled Prince or his interests in his sister.

Neko was ready to fall asleep. She had eaten more than her fill of food and drank more of the honey mead that she should have. She could feel she was a bit tipsy. Once they had finished eating, everyone had made their way farther back into the gardens where a bonfire burned brightly, which could have been another reason Neko was feeling so sleepy. She smirked over at Troy who sat next to her. Once dinner had been over, he had practically rushed to sit beside her. Neko felt her face flush remembering the kiss they had shared earlier. She giggled aloud, causing Troy to give her a quizzical look.

"What is so amusing?" he asked as he caught her hand in his, giving it a gentle squeeze.

"Sorry. I've just had a little too much wine."

Troy smirked at her, leaning in towards her and she avidly leaned in to him. The sound of someone clearing their throat made Troy stop and glare over his shoulder at Neko's brother, who was giving him the mother of all glares. Troy sighed in frustration as Neko gave his hand a reassuring squeeze.

"Don't worry. He'll quit being so protective once he sees you're not at all like your father."

Troy gave her a tight smile.

"I hope so, because frankly, he is being a tad ridiculous."

Neko giggled and released his hand as a server handed her another goblet of wine. Troy declined another share of the honey wine. He had to keep his wits about him. Troy made a quick scan around the area, his Lanarii nanny nowhere to be seen. He supposed Riken had given Landis the night off as Troy was surrounded by many Lanarii and he would be an idiot to try anything here. Riken stood up, and after a few moments, he managed to gain everyone's attention.

"I would like to take this moment to tell the tale of how the element stones came to be."

Riken waited until everyone settled in comfortably and then he began his tale.

"It is not known just how the sacred element stones were brought into existence. It is safe to say they were here a lot longer than we Lanarii. Some say they were made by a very powerful mage. Others say the gods themselves made the stones, but which is the truth we shall never know. When the stones were discovered, there were said to have been five stones for the five provinces of Arorus.

One stone was cast in shadow, and so the darkness consumed that territory, the ruins of the Shagonaa civilization remain buried in the sands and wastelands of the Sortonn Desert. The guardians hid the Spirit Stone away, fearing its dark nature and hoping to keep the darkness from this world. The remaining stones led our peoples into an age of prosperity. Something peculiar happened then. A single guardian was chosen to protect and control all four stones and, of course, the other remaining nations were displeased. After the last guardian had passed into the next world, the stones did not choose a successor immediately and went dormant. A council was held in Ciinta to decide the next course of action. It was decreed that a temple would be built in the homeland of the previous guardian and an accord made. An accord stating that the nations would not fight over the stones but rather await the next guardian. The stones were contained there to await the day when someone worthy of their powers would appear. Many people from all over Arorus journeyed to that temple on the island of Kiirya to see if the stones would choose them, but alas, the stones remained silent. Many years later, one of the provinces broke the treaty and attacked. Ciinta was razed to rubble in a night, and many died in that senseless attack. That nation's king then set his sights on the Dolphinian royal palace and planned an attack, intent on taking the four stones for his own selfish endeavors. As Ciinta burned to the ground, the stones suddenly activated, choosing their next guardian, a young child, the Princess and daughter of the Dolphinian King and Queen. The attack on the Dolphinian Royals was fierce, but the Dolphinian King Trydus fought back valiantly, giving Queen Novalee the much-needed time to take the stones and their new guardian to safety before King Arwin could get his hands on them. Tragically, the Queen did not escape the King's wrath, and he managed to gain the Wind Stone, taking the queen's life in the process. The Princess seemingly disappeared, the remaining element stone also unaccounted for. King Arwin searched for the child and the remaining stones. Years passed, and the stones remained hidden, awaiting the return of their guardian, but the child was never found...until now," Riken finished his story, looking to Neko who gave him a goofy grin, her wine goblet now empty. Neko blinked and looking around. She realized that Troy was gone.

"Neko?"

Neko turned, noticing Arran giving her a curious look.

"Where is your friend?" he asked, also noticing Troy's absence.

"He probably had to make a pitstop. I'll go find him," Neko offered as she got to her feet, snickering as she fought to gain her balance.

"I'm fine," she growled at her brother who gave her a concerned look.

"Just tell Riken I'll be back in two minutes. Okay?"

Arran watched as Neko headed towards the far end of the garden. As she got closer, she noticed there was a shrubbery archway that seemed to lead from the garden back onto one of the main roads of the village.

"Troy?" she asked, not too sure where to even start looking for him. She let out an exasperated sigh and walked through the archway, cursing her dress. She had to finally grab it by the front and hold it up as to avoid tripping and falling flat on her face. As she walked, she began thinking about when she had met Troy. He had seemed annoyed that he even had to talk to her.

"But then in the treasury."

Neko blinked, feeling a bit of anger flare to life. He only started taking an interest in her after her stone had activated with the Wind Stone and then they had left the next day. She wondered why he would risk his father's wrath to help a stranger he had basically just met.

"Troy!" Neko yelled out, not caring if she was being loud. There was no one around anyways. They were all still at the feast.

"Come on Troy. This isn't funny," she yelled out, her voice echoing off the stone buildings. Neko blinked, wondering if maybe

Troy had gone to chat with his brother, the story Riken had told might have irritated the Prince.

Troy cursed in disdain as the damned Lanarii King started telling the story of the stones, making his father out to be the villain. Without a second glance, Troy got up and left the area, everyone too immersed in the story to notice he was making his leave. He smirked, all the easier to free Alexander now that his nanny was gone. Troy spotted an exit and headed back out onto the vacant streets of the large village. Once he was sure no one was following him, he headed towards the square where his brother was held captive. Troy stuck to the shadows, cursing under his breath as he spotted two Lanarii guards. Of course, Riken would not have been foolish enough to leave Alexander completely unattended. Troy glanced around for anything that might prove useful. The only thing he had was a sharp dining knife that he had taken from the table when they had been eating. It was hardly more than a small dagger and throwing knives were not his specialty. That skill belonged to his older brother. Troy formulated a plan. If he could sneak up behind one of the guards, he could take him out silently then all he had to do was attack the other guard before he alerted anyone else of the escape plan. Troy picked up a nearby rock and threw it into the darkness, well past the Lanarii's field of vision. As he watched, it made a loud clatter when it hit in the darkened alleyway.

"I will investigate," one of the guards stated, leaving his post. As Troy sensed his opportunity, he snuck into the square. Alexander saw him and yelled to the other guard, masking any noise Troy might have made getting himself into position.

"Eh Lanarii, I need to piss."

The Lanarii shot the eldest brother a wilting look.

"And that is my problem how?" he sneered as Troy drew his blade and snuck up behind the unknowing man. Troy quickly grabbed him, one hand in his hair as he reefed the Lanarii's head back, holding his blade to his throat.

"One move or sound and I spill your blood right here."

Troy emphasized this by drawing a small line of blood on the Lanarii who immediately stopped struggling. Troy unsheathed the short sword on the guard's belt. Using the pommel, he hit the Lanarii the back of the head, rendering him unconscious.

"Well played. Now get me the hell out of these ropes," Alexander hissed as Troy used the acquired sword to cut his brother free of the coarse rope.

"Here."

Troy handed Alexander the knife, which the eldest brother flipped in his hand, getting a feel for the weight.

"You best make yourself scarce. I need to get back before I am missed."

Alexander glared at his brother.

"What about our deal—the stones?"

Troy grabbed the fallen guard's tunic and started pulling him towards the shadows.

"Neko has them. All I need do is get them from her."

As he spoke, Neko's voice rang out calling for him.

"I will get the other one. You deal with her. She is going to have the entire guard down here with her yelling like that," Alexander snarled as Troy stood up and went to find Neko, leaving Alexander to deal with the other guard.

Alexander smirked and waited. Seconds later the other guard came into view, and Alexander let his blade fly. So precise was his skill with throwing knives; that even a dinner knife hit its mark, piercing the guard's armor and heart. Alexander wasted no time silencing the fallen guard and taking what he could for weapons.

Chapter Seventeen

Arran paced near the veranda. He thought Neko had been gone too long, and there was no sign of her or Troy. Riken had noticed Arran's frustration and politely excused himself from a conversation to go ask what was bothering the rebel Prince.

"Arran, you seem troubled?"

Arran turned to the King.

"I am worried about Neko. She went off to find Troy, and neither one has returned. I have a bad feeling."

Riken also felt a stirring of disquiet as he took in this information.

"I agree with your unease. Perhaps we ourselves should take a small stroll. I would like to make sure our prisoner is not involved."

That was all the persuading Arran needed to follow the Lanarii King into the quiet streets of Rinnyus in search of Neko and Troy.

Neko turned down a familiar street and ended up back in the old square where she had first found Troy and his brother held captive. As she rounded the corner, a figure blocked her way. Neko let out a startled scream before Troy's face came into view. Neko placed her hand to her chest in an attempt to calm her erratic beating heart.

"Troy," she panted as the Prince shot her an annoyed scowl.

"Quit screaming. It is just me. What are you doing, following me?"

"I wasn't following you, well maybe, but I was just worried about you. Why did you leave? Was it Riken's story?"

"No. I left just after he started. I have heard it all before. My father started the war, blah blah blah. My father saw an opportunity, and he took it."

Neko gave Troy a serious look.

"I wanted to ask you something. I was going over it on my way here. Did you only offer to help me get home because you knew who I really was?"

Troy ran his hand through his hair. He wore a simple mahogany jerkin and matching trousers.

"Neko, I will not lie. I promised you I would not."

Neko let him continue, his eyes meeting hers in a serious gaze as his eyes fixed lower, focusing on the stones hanging from her neck.

"At first, when I saw your stone, I thought maybe you could help me find all the stones. I was thinking you would go back home and then I could use them to become King of my own land, make a name for myself without my father's ego looming over me."

Neko would admit she felt a bit hurt at his admission. Troy gave her a warm smile.

"But that was before I got to know you, Neko. I really do like you."

Neko felt herself smiling, but stopped as he looked over at something just behind her left shoulder

"Troy, what is it?"

She went to turn around to see what had gained his attention when she felt something solid at her back. She found her left arm pinned to her side and held in an iron clad grip. Neko winced as pain ran down her one wrist held in a bruising grip, but she was grateful for the dress collar as someone held a blade to her throat, his or her strong arm across her chest ensuring she would not be getting away anytime soon.

"Make one peep, and I will slit your throat, yeah?"

Neko felt sick as she finally realized just whom it was that held her captive.

"Not just yet," Troy stated as he gave Neko a playful smirk, fear radiating in her eyes as he took a step closer.

"Troy, help me," she pleaded as he laughed at her.

"Why would I do a silly thing like that? We have you right where we want you."

Troy's gaze fell upon Neko's stones. As he reached out and took the stones in his grip, his eyes met Neko's once again.

"I do like you, but I like the freedom and power the element stones offer me a lot more."

Neko felt like crying. Troy had been plotting to steal the stones all along, and she had foolishly refused the warnings both Arran and Riken offered about the Prince.

"Troy, don't do this, please."

Neko tried to struggle, but Alexander's grip tightened and threatened to break her wrist.

"Do what, become King? You are not calling the shots now, little Princess, and no one is here to save you."

Troy and Alexander both chuckled as Neko felt anger replace her fear. She was mostly angry with herself for being so stupid.

"I trusted you, Troy," she snarled as Troy took the stones from around her neck, breaking the chain in the process, laughing in her face.

"You are weak and not fit to control the powers of theses stones. You are just a pathetic little girl."

Troy stuffed the three stones in his pocket as he continued his rant.

"With the stones, I will become King, and together, my brothers and I will rule this entire land. Everyone will bow before our rule, or they will die; it is simple."

Neko glared at Troy.

"Princess, where is the Earth Stone?" Troy growled as Neko continued to glare at him.

"Now Princess!" Troy snarled as he raised his short sword towards her. Neko gave a startled scream as Alexander shook her.

"I don't have it with me if that's what you're hoping. It's still with Riken."

She sneered, wincing as Alexander used his arm to squeeze her, making it harder for her to breath.

"You had best be lying. Give the stone to me!" Troy screamed, grabbing Neko by her throat.

Riken and Arran both took off like shots as they heard the small alarmed scream that had come from where Alexander was held prisoner. Arran saw red as he tore into the area and saw the two brothers manhandling his little sister. Riken was equally enraged, but he had better luck at hiding his emotions.

"Let her go," Arran snarled while drawing his two short swords as Riken drew his weapon.

"Release her, and we shall finish this with our blades," Riken spoke, his voice low and deadly.

"Come on. We have what we came for," Troy hissed as he tore off into the alleyway. Alexander remained holding Neko, using her as a shield.

"Troy has the stones!" Neko screamed before Alexander pressed his blade harder to her throat.

"No closer or I spill her blood," he threatened as Arran looked to Riken.

"Go after him. I will help her."

Arran nodded and took off after Troy, leaving Riken and the eldest Prince in a deadlock.

Riken gave Neko a reassuring look.

"It will be all right, Neko," he stated in an eerily calm tone as his eyes met the ice blue ones of Alexander.

"Release her. She is innocent."

Alexander chuckled darkly.

"Is she? As long as I hold this blade to her throat, you will not do anything to provoke me."

Riken glared at the Prince.

"Now, if you want her to make it through this night, you will drop your weapons at your feet and take twenty paces backwards."

Riken had no choice but to do as Alexander ordered. He would not risk Neko's life.

"All right. I shall do as you say," Riken placated, dropping his katana and a dagger he had at his side. Placing his hands up, palms facing out, he started walking backwards. Neko felt anger bubbling up. How could she just stand there and be used as a shield? She was not a helpless girl, and she was damn sick and tired of being treated as one. Neko kicked her leg backwards, her foot meeting scarcely any resistance as she hit Alexander directly on the side of the knee, catching the larger man by surprise. As he staggered forward hissing in pain, he released her as his leg buckled dropping the arm holding her captive. A split-second decision on her part had Neko whipping her head backwards with devastating velocity as the back of her skull collided with Alexander's face. The sickening crunching sound of cartilage was her indication that she had done some damage to the Prince's face. Neko wasted no time as she stumbled forward, making a run for Riken who looked equally shocked by her actions. Alexander snarled in rage. His knee on fire and his nose broken and bleeding, he raised his arm and threw his knife, the blade hitting Neko in the back, just behind her heart. Neko cried out and fell to the ground. Alexander did not stop to watch her die, instead, he turned and raced into the shadows. His fury was damn near making his blood boil. How had a girl gotten one up on him? Wiping the blood from his broken nose, he cursed and continued on his way to rendezvous with Troy. He needed time to escape the Lanarii and meet back up with Troy near the lake where they could steal a boat and make their way to Numis. Alexander had to hand it to Troy. His plan was a good one. Most would think they would head for the forest to take cover, not the lake. Once the Lanarii discovered where the brothers had gone, they would have a considerable lead on the Lanarii and the rebels.

Neko blinked. Her entire body hurt, especially her wrist where that giant had nearly snapped it.

"Neko!"

Neko groaned as someone turned her onto her back, causing her to wince as a dull throb in her shoulder blade made her come fully awake.

"Princess?"

Riken looked shocked.

"How are you alive? I saw that blade hit you."

Neko was in no mood for being civilized at the moment. Her head ached something fierce.

"You'd rather I wasn't?" she snapped as Riken's eyes showed remorse.

"Of course not," he returned as Neko realized that she was lying on her back and her head was currently in the King's lap as their eyes met.

"Did anybody get the license plate of that bus that just hit me?" Neko wondered as Riken surveyed the damage.

"I'm sorry. I ruined your dress," Neko stated, annoyance in her eyes as she attempted to sit up, Riken helped her into a sitting position where Neko remained. She was not about to get up anytime soon.

Neko watched as Riken's eyes found the ripped sleeve of her dress and the armor showing underneath.

"You are wearing the armor of Annalise," he stated in wonder as Neko rubbed the back of her head, her hair wild and probably sticking out in a gravity defying mess.

"Yeah, sorry. I was going to tell you. I just wanted to try it on and then it wouldn't come off."

Riken silently thanked Annalise for her foresight. Neko would not have survived if not for the armor.

"I am not angry, Neko. That armor will only fit one. It was meant for you."

"But you said only one—"

"It was made for only one. It will not fit any other."

Neko let that tidbit sink in.

"Oh…well, I guess that's a good thing, but how do I get it off?"

"Perhaps we should get you looked over by a healer," he offered as they heard a curse and then Arran appeared from the darkened alleyway.

"I lost him. They are surely headed into the forest, the cowards. We need to track them immediately."

"They may have gone towards the lake, by the time we rally the men and set out, they will have too much of a head start. We must protect this village. The brother tried to kill Neko."

Arran went pale as Riken's words sunk in.

"Pardon me?" he spat while Neko waved her hands, groaning as the movement sent pain shooting up her arm.

"I'm okay. I'm fine. Please, can we just get out of here? I hurt all over."

Riken got to his feet, gently helping Neko to hers.

"I shall carry you. We do not know the extent of your injuries."

Neko protested, but the look that Riken gave her left no room for negotiation.

"Fine," she mumbled as the Lanarii King scooped her up into his arms as if she weighed nothing.

"Thank you," she whispered as she leaned her head against his neck and allowed him to carry her back to the safety of the palace. Arran followed a few paces behind, vehemence blazing in his turquoise eyes.

Neko was shocked as Riken brought her into his study, catching Sornna's attention immediately.

"Go fetch the healer. Have her make haste," Riken ordered, his commanding tone leaving no room for questions. Gently, he set Neko on the one-armed couch, noticing her wince at the slightest jostle. He noticed the large bruise on her wrist. He cursed the brute that did this to her.

"Try not to move around until we make sure you have not broken anything."

Neko agreed and glanced around.

"Where's Arran?"

Riken shook his head. The Dolphinian had refused to go into the study. He had mentioned something about securing the village, but Riken knew better. Arran was worried. Riken did not have much time to ponder Arran's emotions as the healer whisked into the room.

"I will take good care of her, Lord Riken."

Riken took the hint and gave the healer the privacy she needed to tend Neko. He would need to rally his men and put extra guards on duty just in case the two brothers were stupid enough to return.

"Princess, I will return later. Please rest and let the healer do her job."

Neko nodded and watched as Riken vacated the room, leaving Neko alone with the healer who looked irked about being summoned so suddenly for such minor wounds.

"I'm sorry. He overreacted. I'm not hurt that bad."

The healer had long midnight hair, which was odd seeing as all the Lanarii Neko had seen had light blonde to medium brown hair. In addition, her eyes were crimson.

"The King does not overreact Princess."

Neko gave the Lanarii a flat look. She was in no mood for the favored haughty attitude the Lanarii seemed to have towards her or anyone not of their blood.

"Let me see your wounds. Please remove your dress."

Neko did as she was asked, slightly smirking as the healer took in the armor Neko wore.

"You are lucky your armor protected you. It is odd to see it worn when for so long it has sat."

Neko watched the woman's eyes fill with sadness.

"Did you know the person who made it?" Neko enquired. The Lanarii nodded.

"Yes, Annalise was my sister, we came from a Lanarii clan on the other side of the Talla Mountains. It was her union with King Riken that was to unite our two peoples."

Neko blinked.

"But then the war happened?"

"Yes. The war took Annalise's life but not before she forged the armor. She told me one day someone would arrive, and the armor was made for that person, but she would not tell me nor King Riken any more than that."

"Why not?"

The Lanarii gently took Neko's arm, checking her wrist.

"I do not know."

Neko winced as the touch made her cringe.

"Your wrist is badly bruised. I can heal most of it, but you must rest it for a few days at the very least."

Neko watched in a daze as the Lanarii held her palm above Neko's wrist and a faint white glow filled her hand. Neko stared in dumbfounded shock as her bruise slowly vanished from her wrist, along with most of the pain, replacing it with a slightly warm feeling, as if she had exposed her hand to sunlight.

"Holy crap." Neko's face lit up. "That's really cool. Thank you, uh…"

The Lanarii cracked a faint smile.

"My name is Tetriiuna."

"Tet-tree-onna? That's a really pretty name."

The woman inclined her head.

"Thank you, Princess."

"Neko is just fine. Neko is good."

Tetriiuna gave her a quizzical look.

"You do not like your title?"

Neko looked to the floor.

"Well, it's just really weird is all. I mean, until a few days ago I didn't even know I was a Princess."

Tetriiuna understood this.

"Yes. I see. Then it would be rather awkward I imagine. You will grow accustomed to your role. Be proud of your heritage child."

Neko felt her cheeks flush.

"I will. It's just gonna take me a little bit to get my head wrapped around the whole idea."

Tetriiuna gave a slight chuckle.

"Yes. Come now. Let me take a look at your back."

Neko complied and let the healer help her out of her now ruined dress.

"I'm not one for dresses, but I really loved this one."

Tetriiuna ran her hand down the armor.

"Do you know how to remove the armor?"

"No. Do you?" she asked hopefully as the Lanarii moved her hand around to the side.

"Yes, I do. There is a tiny clasp that will let the armor go slack and disengage the magical enhancements so that it may be removed."

Neko tried to see, but she could not twist that way.

"Here."

Tetriiuna grabbed Neko's hand and guided her, showing her the tiny clasp that felt more like a flaw in the metal than a clasp.

"Now, pull it."

Neko did, using just her finger, gasping as the armor went loose. She tried to remove it over her head but hissed as pain ran through both her shoulder blades.

"One moment please, Princess," Tetriiuna said as she placed her hand in the center of Neko's back, using her other hand to lift the loose armor.

"Your back is extensively bruised."

Once again, Neko felt that warming sensation and then her back felt a lot better.

"That should do," Tetriiuna indicated as she dropped the armor and walked around to look at Neko.

"Do you require more healing?"

Neko could see the Lanarii looked rather ill.

"Your healing drains you?"

Tetriiuna waved it off.

"It is a side effect of healing. I will regain my energy by sunrise, this is my job, Princess. I am only happy that I could help you."

Neko offered her a warm smile.

"Thank you for your help. I feel way better now."

"You are most welcome. I must now go rest. I will inform King Riken that you are healed."

Neko waved as the Lanarii let herself out. She was taken aback as Adalynn came racing into the room once the door had been open.

"Are you all right? I just heard about the attack!"

Tetriiuna chuckled at the girl's excitement. It was not hard to see the two girls had become fast friends. She let herself out, and once the doors closed behind her, she leaned against the wall, fighting off the wave of vertigo that hit her.

Chapter Eighteen

Neko groaned. She was relaxed now that she had bathed and put her regular clothing on. Neko then glanced down at the armor that sat on her bed, smiling at it.

"I didn't know you, but thank you, Annalise. You saved my life," Neko whispered as she looked down at her wrist that looked as if it had never been hurt at all. Neko glanced up as someone knocked on her door.

"It's open," she called out expecting Adalynn but shocked to see Arran, who looked ready to start a brawl.

"Arran?" Neko asked as he shot his smoldering glare at her.

"What the hell were you thinking?"

Neko cringed at the harshness of his voice.

"What do you mean?" she asked as Arran snarled at her.

"Did you even try to fend them off?"

Neko felt her jaw drop.

"I didn't think—"

"You are right. You did not think. You let them take the stones and almost kill you as well!"

Neko felt her cheeks blaze in mortification.

"Arran—"

"The stones are your responsibility I would not have given them to you if I had known you were going to just hand them over to Troy and his brother."

Neko felt her temper get the better of her.

"So, what now? You still think I'm on Troy's side? I was alone, and I didn't know Troy was plotting against me until his brother snuck up behind me and grabbed me."

Arran clenched his jaw, trying to reign in his temper.

"I warned you about that little bastard, but you assured me he was trustworthy. Now, because of your poor judgment, they have three of the stones! Many people are going to suffer for your inability to do your duty. No one else can do this but you, and now we are at a serious disadvantage."

Neko felt the tears pooling in her eyes but blinked them back, her temper getting the better of her.

"Well, I'm sorry if I'm not perfect. You don't have to be such an asshole about it. Don't you think I feel bad enough without having you throwing it in my face?"

Neko was screaming now, anger flashing in her eyes and her face turning red as Arran stood where he was, shocked that he had provoked such a reaction from her. Arran took a deep breath. She was not one of his men that he could reprimand, and he was annoyed with himself for making her this upset. Arran watched as Neko crossed her arms and shot him a glare, her eyes blazing with irritation.

"Neko?"

His tone was softer as he sighed and ran his hand through his hair, unnerved by her stony glare.

"I apologize for upsetting you. I just do not think you realize how important the stones are."

Neko remained silent, that steely gaze still in place.

"I should not have been so harsh. You have had a lot to deal with these past few days. Please Neko, say something."

Neko took a shaky breath, her eyes meeting her brother's. Her eyes were full of loathing, but at least she had spoken again.

"I'm not a violent person. I've barely learnt how to fight, let alone fend off two experienced fighters. If I tried anything that bastard had a blade to my throat and I thought they were going to kill me. I mean I couldn't even use the stones to aid me. Maybe I'm not supposed to be the guardian, and maybe it's a mistake. Obviously, you seem to think you could do a better job than I can."

Neko gave a frustrated growl and slid down the bed to sit on the floor, massaging the bridge of her nose to alleviate the headache that was throbbing painfully behind her eyes.

Arran felt all his earlier anger and fear melt away. He took a seat beside Neko, giving her a reassuring pat on the leg.

"For a nonviolent person, you sure can throw a punch."

Neko laughed at the joke. It was meant to cheer her up, and it was working.

"Still sore about that one?" she teased as Arran gave her shoulder a nudge with his.

"Of course I am. Lord Riken thought it was highly amusing. You even got him to smile."

Arran took a deep breath and continued.

"I find it hard to believe that you cannot fight. I will personally show you how to fight. I have faith you will learn quickly and as for the stones, Neko, Riken told me what you did with the Glodiirii. That itself is amazing." Arran leaned closer, whispering, "But you know why I was so angry. It was mainly because I almost lost you, again. That was what got to me, Neko."

"But I'm just a tart," she stated as Arran shook his head.

"No, you are a little shit."

Both burst out laughing as Arran pounced on Neko and started to tickle her relentlessly. It was at this moment that Riken decided to check in on the Princess only to see her and Arran rolling around on the floor like children. Riken hated to ruin the moment of bonding, but as he stared down at the last element stone in his hand, he knew

Neko needed to have the last stone with her so she could learn how to call upon it at any given moment.

"Forgive my intrusion," Riken announced his presence. Both siblings froze and looked at him as he offered a polite smile.

"I thought you would need this."

Riken held his hand out, offering Neko the Earth Stone. Neko slowly got to her feet and stepped towards him, closing the gap between her and Riken.

"Thanks," Neko whispered as she took the stone from his open palm, looking at the gemstone that lit with an inner fire as soon as it fell into her awaiting hand. Riken glanced over to Arran who had also gotten to his feet. Neko wasn't quick enough to stop the yawn that overcame her. She was beat and wanted nothing more than to curl up in the nice comfortable bed and sleep for three days straight.

"It is getting late. Perhaps we should all get some rest, and then we can meet in the morning to discuss our next course of action over morning meal."

Neko nodded, letting out another large yawn.

"Excuse me," she stated politely as the other two shared a look.

"All right, tomorrow morning it is. Good night," Arran stated as he vacated the room, Riken right behind him.

"Sleep well, Princess."

Riken bowed slightly before he exited the room.

"Goodnight," Neko called to both of them as her door shut behind them leaving Neko to her own devices. Neko gazed down at the emerald. Even now, it amazed her, and she found it strange that such a tiny stone could have such power within it.

"I will make this right again," Neko vowed with determination in her voice as she fastened the chain around her neck, securing the stone around her throat. Finally, the events of the entire day had gotten to her, and she was ready for sleep. Apart from being stiff and sore, she felt a lot better than she had only hours before. Stifling another massive yawn, she pulled the covers back and slinked into the bed, grinning like a fool as she nestled into the heavenly mattress. She snuggled into the pillows and cocooned herself in the comforter. Within minutes, she was sound asleep.

The next day, Neko's watch once again tore her from her dreams.

"Gotta remember to shut that damn alarm off," she grumbled, her eyes bleary after the deep sleep from which she had just awakened. She yawned, stretched and then froze. She felt fantastic. She was sure she would have some sort of aches and pains. Neko shrugged and got out of her bed, feeling bad that she never made it, but when she returned in the evenings, it was always made. She located the brush Adalynn had given to her and brushed her hair, letting it hang free for the day. She did not plan to do anything that required any more physical exertion than shoveling food into her mouth. As her thoughts drifted to food, she realized just how hungry she was. Her stomach seconded that by gurgling loudly.

"Yeah, yeah, yeah, I'm going," she griped as she glanced down at her watch that read 7:55 am. Annoyed that she didn't get to sleep in, she made her way down the steps and into the breakfast nook, the smell of fresh food slamming into her like a brick wall. Neko's mouth began watering as she made a b-line towards the table where Riken sat, already eating his breakfast. He glanced up when she entered the room, offering her a smile as he gestured to the table.

"Good morning, Neko. I trust you are well rested?"

Neko took a seat and nodded as she started helping herself to food.

"I was a little concerned when you did not arrive for morning meal yesterday, but Tetriiuna advised me you might need a full day's rest to recuperate and to let you awaken on your own."

Neko stopped mid-chew.

"What? I slept for an entire day?"

She was shocked, and Riken chuckled at her stunned look.

"You went through a rather trying ordeal Neko."

Neko swallowed her bite of food.

"Well, I do feel a lot better, considering everything."

Riken chuckled and smiled at Neko as she glanced around.

"Where is Arran?"

Riken continued watching her.

"He is most likely with his men. The two that accompanied him are leaving to send word to the rest of the rebels of what has transpired. He has asked them all to meet him in Larrow the next full moon."

Neko suddenly wasn't hungry anymore.

"I shouldn't have gone looking for Troy alone."

Neko felt an overwhelming sense of guilt fill her mind as Riken reached across the table and placed his hand on hers.

"Do not be so hard on yourself, Neko. You are alive, and that is what is most important. The stones are meant to be with you. You will get them back."

Neko gave him a hopeful look.

"You know I was thinking that same thing last night, or rather the night before last."

Neko paused a moment, gathering her thoughts.

"Hey, I have a favor to ask you."

Riken's eyes met hers.

"Yes?" he asked as Neko looked longingly over at the spread on the table.

"Well, after the other night, I don't want to be caught with my pants down again, so I was thinking that maybe I could learn some sort of blade combat or something like that?"

Riken gave Neko a disarming smile, his eyes alight.

"Funny you mention this. Your brother and I were discussing this very thing last night. We would like to train you in basic combat and swordsmanship, so that the next time you face Troy, you will be better matched."

Neko felt a smile spreading across her face.

"Great minds."

"It was actually Arran's idea. He believes you will be a very quick study."

Not long after Neko and Riken had finished their meal, Arran entered the breakfast nook, smiling at his sister.

"Look who finally decided to grace us with her presence," he teased as she stuck out her tongue, laughing as he gave her a cheeky grin.

"I was just telling the Princess about our chat from yesterday about her training."

Arran looked from Riken to Neko.

"You agree?" he asked her as she gave a fervent nod.

"Yes. I think it's a good idea."

Arran gestured for Neko to move over so he could sit at the table.

"I also have another suggestion."

Riken spoke first.

"We do not know what Troy and his brother are planning. They may try to reclaim the last stone. As far as they know, they have dealt with Neko, which is one advantage we have."

Riken looked from one sibling to the other.

"It would be wise if you two stayed here in Rinnyus. You would be protected and have a safe place in which to commence with your training, Neko."

Neko looked over to her brother.

"It is a very wise idea. We thank you, King Riken, for your generosity."

Riken waved off the formalities.

"Our peoples were once allies long ago Arran. Perhaps reforming that alliance would benefit both the Dolphinians and the Lanarii."

"So, who would be training me?" Neko spoke up as Riken looked to Arran.

"We both would."

Arran answered immediately, "We are both well-trained fighters and with both of us training you, we will have you fighting fit in no time."

Neko bit her bottom lip.

"Something tells me that's a nice way of saying you're both going to kick the crap out of me until I can learn to kick the crap outta you two."

Riken and Arran both chuckled at her candid interpretation.

"You are correct, Neko, but if you encounter Troy again, he will not go easy on you, so neither will we."

Neko gave her brother a lopsided grin.

"All right, I'll do it. I need all the help I can get."

The next few weeks passed by quickly. Most of the day, Neko was taught how to fight by her brother and the Lanarii King. Arran taught her mostly hand-to-hand combat, as he was well versed in it. Riken took over the swordsmanship training, as he had many years of practice with the blade. Together, the two hounded Neko relentlessly, and after the first week, Neko had the bumps and bruises to prove it. Near the end of the second week of incessant training, Neko had started to learn a few tricks and used them to her advantage when facing her two trainers. In the evenings, she would head into the palace gardens and work by herself, training with the Earth Stone. Every day, she grew stronger and every day that passed left her feeling more confident in her abilities.

"Neko, guard your left side," Arran berated as he managed a hit, knocking her back a few feet while receiving the mother of all glares from his sister who was tired and wanted to go have a bath and a meal after a hard day of training.

"Arran, I'm tired," Neko grumbled as she lowered her guard, refusing to train anymore.

"Giving up so soon?"

Neko glanced towards the voice. Riken stood in the doorway that led to the sparring hall, a wooden blade in each hand.

"You still have blade practice with me."

Neko groaned and flopped down on the wooden floor.

"No more torture," Neko mock-wailed as Arran and Riken looked at each other.

"I kinda sorta went overkill practicing with the Earth Stone last night, and I'm so tired."

Riken gave her a no-nonsense look.

"So that is what happened to my gardens last night. The gardener is not impressed."

Neko snickered.

"Sorry," she apologized half-heartedly, causing the Lanarii King to look skyward.

"If you put as much effort into hand-to-hand combat as you did playing with that damn element stone, you would be kicking my arse all over this village," Arran stated, slightly annoyed. Neko only offered him a childish grin.

"But then you would never want to fight with me if a girl handed your ass to you all the time."

Arran sighed and offered Neko his hand, helping her to her feet.

"You best keep practicing while I am in Larrow. When I get back, I will not go easy on you."

"Why can't I go too?"

Arran looked to Riken for help, but the other male wisely kept his nose out if it.

"Neko, we have already had this conversation. You are not safe outside theses walls, and I will not risk your safety. You can be angry with me all you like. I will not change my mind."

"I got it, geez. You really do have that big brother complex down to a tea."

Riken chuckled at her disgusted look as Arran smiled affectionately at his younger sibling.

"That is my job," he offered. Neko laughed and pushed his hand away as he tussled her hair, making it look like she had gotten into a fight with a dust devil and lost.

"You better be careful too. Okay?"

Arran smiled and looked her in the eyes.

"I will return as soon as I am able. Keep up your practicing, all right?"

"Okay, I promise. Maybe I can beat Riken at hand-to-hand." she shot a hopeful look over to the Lanarii who raised his eyebrow.

"You wish to spar with me?" he asked as Neko felt her cheeks heating up.

"Only if you want. It's not a big deal if you don't," she blurted out quickly as she looked down at the floor. Arran rolled his eyes. His sister's fondness for the Lanarii King was all too obvious. Riken graciously pretended not to notice, and Neko fought to banish the blush dusting her cheeks.

"Well, with that, I am leaving. Care to see me off, Neko?"

Neko nodded. Anything to get her away from the Lanarii who seemed to have a knack for making her flustered with hardly any effort on his part.

"A safe journey to you, son of Trydus."

Riken and Arran clasped hands in a farewell as Neko fidgeted in the background.

"Thank you. I will return with my men. We shall bring as many supplies as we can carry."

"Thank you for that consideration. We shall see you soon. Good luck."

Riken looked to Neko.

"Once you have said farewell, I expect you to return here and be ready for your lessons," Neko growled but nodded.

"All right, ya damn tyrant," she snickered as she walked with her brother out into the main hallway of the palace and to the entranceway. Landis stood with a cloak and a leather pack filled with supplies.

"Are you sure you'll be okay by yourself?" Neko questioned as Arran shot her a look.

"Neko, I have been on my own my entire life. I will manage. Your concern is not justified."

"Just be careful, okay Arran?"

The rebel leader smiled down at his sister.

"I promise. Now remember your training and get that damn Lanarii to spar with you."

Arran winked at Neko as he fastened his cloak and secured his pack. They headed down the road and towards the main gate. It was a silent stroll. They stopped at the gate some ten minutes later.

"All right, I need to go now. Be good," Arran smiled, giving Neko a pat on her shoulder. Neko shook her head.

"Oh no, that is not how you say goodbye."

Neko grinned and lunged, gripping onto her brother in a giant bear hug, causing her stunned sibling to stagger back a few paces.

"All right, I will miss you as well, crazed woman."

Arran chuckled as Neko removed herself from him. He turned and gave a wave over his shoulder. He did not look back as he headed down the road towards Larrow.

Chapter Nineteen

Around the same time that Arran started his trek to Larrow, Troy and Alexander had finally made it back to the palace of their father. As they traveled, they had also been training themselves with the element stones. Troy had claimed the Fire Stone as his, and Alexander had chosen the Wind Stone, leaving the Water Stone for their other sibling, Traven.

"Do you think we can convince Traven to side with us?" Troy pondered, as the pair sat under a tree just outside of Feeno, a small village near the palace.

"He would be a fool not to join us. Besides, of the three of us, he dislikes Father the most," Alexander stated in boredom, inspecting his fingernails as Troy stood up and started pacing.

"What exactly is our method of attack? I suppose our first task will be to find Traven and gain his assistance in dealing with Father, perhaps as a way to prove himself."

Alexander also got to his feet, observing his younger brother formulating their plan.

"I was thinking." Alexander voiced his opinion, "Doing what Father had sent me to do and that is to capture you, I will bring you back as he wanted. Unfortunately, when the Lanarii caught you, they took the element stone you had, and we barely escaped the barbarians with our lives."

Troy smirked, impressed with his brother's scheme.

"Good. Then Father will still trust you. You can then offer to put me in the dungeon because that is what Father will do. We will then be free to find Traven and get him to join our cause. Together, the three of us will kill Father and take the crown for ourselves, one-third of the kingdom for each of us."

Alexander chuckled darkly.

"It is a sound plan."

Troy gazed down at his Fire Stone fastened around his neck. Beside it sat the Water Stone. He took the stones off and handed them to Alexander.

"You best hold onto them until our meeting with Father is over."

Alexander took the stones, tethering then to his neck as he hid all three stones under the collar of his tunic.

"All right. I suppose we should bind your hands to make it look more convincing. I will give you a boot dagger just in case we get separated. That way, at least you can escape your bindings."

Troy gave his brother a flat look.

"Do not look so pleased with yourself."

Alexander chuckled loudly.

"We need to have Father convinced that I really have captured you and returned you for punishment."

Troy sighed and held out his hands as Alexander grabbed a small piece of coarse rope from his pack, making sure to bind Troy securely.

"All right you little rat. You are going back to Father for judgment."

Alexander made his voice rough, but his eyes filled with mirth at the unimpressed look his brother shot him.

"You are having entirely too much enjoyment with this scenario Alexander," Troy deadpanned as both brothers shared a smirk.

"Yes. I am enjoying this Troy, but it will be even more worthwhile to see father's face when we dethrone the old fossil."

"And when he sees we have obtained three element stones, he will be all the more livid. He has been searching for the stones for years with naught to show for it."

Alexander gestured to the road.

"Shall we be on our way then? This is a show I do not want to miss."

Traven made his way down the dark, abandoned corridor. Ever since the war, the east wing of the castle was all but abandoned. Not that he minded. It was a great area to read his books unhindered by servants, guards, and his father. Traven had to admit he liked it that way, besides there was nothing else to do. After Troy had stolen the prized element stone, and his father sent Alexander after him, the castle was rather calm. Another reason Traven had to be disgusted with his father, no one had even bothered to ask if he wanted to go find Troy. With Troy and Alexander gone, his father still refused to give him a second glance. It infuriated him to no end, and now he had to hide out in the east wing just to get away from hearing his father go on and on about the element stone and how Troy was ungrateful for taking that strange girl and disappearing into the wilds. Traven rolled his eyes. Even thinking about the entire situation was bothersome.

"He could have sent me with Alexander," Traven muttered as he came to a screeching halt, voices from down the hallway catching his attention. Slowly, he made his way closer, careful to avoid making any sounds that would alert the people talking that he was there. He might not have had brute strength like Alexander or a natural charisma as Troy did, but he was a master of stealth. Anything going on in the castle he knew about. He knew he had talent. If his father could not see that, then the King was an idiot. He stopped when he could hear the entire conversation. Traven recognized his father's royal advisor immediately, there was no mistaking that annoying voice. He did not know the other man, but judging from his eccentric wardrobe and the ridiculous hat upon his head, he was an outsider, someone brought in for his area of expertise.

"King Arwin wants any information about this hidden element stone, the dark stone hidden away in Arorus, your contacts are needed."

Traven furrowed his brow. He had never heard of this dark element stone before now.

"Dark stone, sir? I beg your pardon, but that is just a myth. There is no proof that I have found that would indicate this rare element stone even exists."

Traven smirked. That was not the right answer, and a loud echo of skin on skin verified his notion.

"Do not demean my intelligence. You are getting paid very well to find this information. The King is getting impatient with your dawdling, so you best get me that information or have your head rendered from your body. Do you understand me, you wretched charlatan?"

Traven listened as he heard a confirmation and then the two men left the area, their footsteps fading, as they got farther away. Once he was sure they had gone, Traven stepped out from the shadows, a calculating look in his indigo eyes.

"Another element stone?"

He pondered this new information as he let out a long breath and continued on his way to his chambers. He decided he would need to look into this mysterious stone. What game was his father playing at now? Traven received another surprise as he entered the main hall and a commotion caught his attention. He watched as servants raced around like fools.

"Hey, you, what is going on?" Traven hissed while grabbing a serving girl by the arm. Her eyes went wide, and she paused, catching her breath.

"My lord, your brother has returned with your other brother in custody."

Traven released the girl who tore off, wanting nothing to do with the moody Prince.

"Of course," he hissed as he decided to head to the library. He was not in the mood to be a part of the drama that would now unfold.

"I suppose it cannot be helped."

He decided to make himself scarce. He had no time for family politics, especially when his father had a fit and punished Troy. Traven thought Troy was a fool for letting himself get caught.

Alexander gave Troy a hard shove. Troy cursed under his breath and fell to his knees before his father. If he did not know any better, he would have though he had been his brother's prisoner.

"As you asked, Father, I brought the little thief back for his just rewards."

The King remained seated on his throne, a look of contempt cast down on Troy who refused to look up at his father.

"Look at me you little shit," King Arwin screamed as Troy complied, his eyes full of scorn. He could not wait to dethrone this false pretender.

"You dare steal from me. Did you actually think you would get away with it?"

Troy offered a cocky grin.

"That is why I did it."

The King glanced to Alexander.

"Where is the girl?"

Alexander looked to his father.

"She is dead. There was an unexpected delay when I found Troy."

The King focused on the eldest Prince.

"Delay?" he questioned as Alexander ran his hand through his short hair.

"When I found Troy, he and the girl had been captured by the Lanarii. I just managed to escape them with my life and with Troy. The girl and the element stone were lost to the damn Lanarii."

Arwin glared back at Troy.

"This is entirely your fault. You knew how important that stone was. I should have you hanged for your insolence."

Troy remained silent as Alexander chuckled.

"That would be doing him a service, Father. Why not make him suffer a while, perhaps put him in the dungeons?"

The King directed his glare towards the eldest brother.

"And what are you gloating about you great daft ox? Did I not give you specific instructions to retrieve Troy, the girl, and the element stone? It was not that difficult a task."

Alexander's smirk dropped, replaced with an enraged scowl.

"What could I do against an army of Lanarii? I only had four men with me, all of whom were slaughtered. I was lucky even to have escaped."

The King was in a foul mood and did not sympathize with his eldest son.

"My orders to you were clear, get your brother and the girl and bring me back my stone. You are incompetent. I should put you in the dungeon with Troy. You have greatly disappointed me, Alexander."

Troy did not need to see Alexander's face to know his brother was very close to losing his temper and exposing their plot in the process. Troy decided to alleviate the situation.

"Perhaps we are incompetent because of who raised us, Father."

The King scowled at Troy, his face going red with rage.

"That is enough. Take him to the dungeon, and get the hell out of my sight!" the King screamed as Alexander hefted Troy to his feet and dragged him out of the throne room.

As soon as they arrived at the dungeon, Alexander exploded, driving his fist into the face of the only guard in the area.

"Who the hell does that son of a jackal think he is?"

Troy sighed and held out his hands. Alexander shot him a wilting look but used his dagger to free Troy.

"Calm yourself, Alexander. You will have your revenge, but for now we need to keep level heads," Alexander growled and gave the fallen guard a kick in the ribs. The man did not move. He was out cold.

"Yes, the plan, I know."

Alexander took out the element stones, handing Troy the Fire Stone and Water Stone.

"Let us get this plan into motion. I am ready to deal with that frail old man."

Troy smirked and placed the Fire Stone around his neck. He pocketed the Water Stone and looked to Alexander.

"All right, the first order is to find Traven and gain his alliance."

The two brothers shared a conniving grin.

"Shall we?" Troy invited as the two headed back up to the main floor to find their youngest brother.

Traven glanced up as he heard the library doors open. He was shocked to see Alexander and Troy.

"I heard you two made it back, but I did not think Father would let you go so easily, Troy."

Traven slowly stood up from the chair he sat in, staring across the room at the two brothers, realization dawning on him.

"Of course, Father has no clue you two have banded together," Traven spoke with certainty as Troy smirked and Alexander spoke.

"Sharp as ever Traven, we have a deal for you."

Traven relaxed his stance, gesturing for them to continue.

"The deal is this," Troy spoke, revealing the Water Stone. He held it up for the youngest brother to see.

"Is that what I think it is? "Traven asked as Alexander nodded.

"It is yours, along with one-third of this kingdom if you agree to help us kill Father."

Traven grinned.

"I am appalled that you would even think I would refuse."

Troy grinned and tossed the stone at his younger brother who deftly caught the tiny gemstone.

"When do we plan to overthrow Father?"

Troy shared a look with the eldest brother.

"Immediately."

Troy chuckled darkly.

"The quicker we get rid of the old badger, the better."

Traven held up his hand.

"What about the other two stones? Who gets them?" He gave Troy an expectant look as Troy shook his head.

"The other one is with the Lanarii, and there are only four."

Traven waggled his finger with a knowing look in his eyes.

"That is not as I understand it. Apparently, there is one more stone to be located, the dark element stone. I overheard Father's advisor going on about it this very afternoon."

Troy answered his younger brother's earlier question.

"We will need to share the remaining stones. I meant it when I said that we all get equal parts. We cannot be at each other's throats if we are to rule theses peasants with an iron fist."

Traven agreed with his brother's wise words.

"You are correct, Troy. Perhaps we should deal with Father first and then discuss obtaining the two remaining stones, which I assume will be a high priority."

Alexander chuckled and faced Traven.

"Always so clever little brother. I like that plan. Troy?"

Troy grinned as he brushed his fingers over his stone.

"It is the perfect course of action. Let us become kings this day my brothers."

They shared triumphant grins, and together the three brothers made their way towards the throne room and their future kingship.

After a quick stop at the armory, the three brothers stopped just outside the throne room.

"Here is the plan. Alexander, you and I will use the stones to create a diversion. You use the Wind Stone to knock the guards back, and I will use the Fire Stone to hold them at bay," Traven interjected.

"Would it be better if you at least offered to let him give up the throne? If he does, he will look even more unfit to rule, perhaps even making those faithful to him turn on him."

"I like the way your mind works, Traven. What say you, Alexander?"

The eldest brother sneered darkly.

"After father's rebuff this afternoon, I would like nothing better than to see him with a little humility."

Troy looked towards his two brothers.

"All right. Then this will be our plan. We walk in, demand the throne and kill anyone that gets in our way. With the three element stones, we will be unstoppable. Perhaps, Traven, you might want to stick to the blade. You have not had any training with the Water Stone yet."

Traven shrugged and patted the short sword tethered to his hip in a leather scabbard.

"Whatever you wish."

Troy grinned at his younger brother's impatience. It was well-known that Traven had a dislike for the King ever since their mother had been murdered, the killer still at large and it was no secret Traven blamed the King. Troy squared his shoulders and looked to Alexander who gave a curt nod. The two eldest brothers kicked the wooden doors open, making them crash against the walls while destroying the silence of the throne room. The King shot out of his seat, glaring at those who dared disturb his privacy.

"What is the meaning of this?" the King cried out as his sights were set on his three sons strolling into the room.

"Sit your arse down, old man," Alexander spat, pointing his ever-sharp throwing knife towards his father.

Traven glanced at the half a dozen armed guards in the room who came to full attention as they sensed the impending threat to their King.

"At ease," Troy barked out as he took a step towards the King.

"Can we not talk like civilized adults, Father. We have a very interesting offer that you might want to hear," the eldest brother stated as the King glared towards him.

"I should have known you would not condemn your brother so easily."

The King looked back to Troy and gave his consent.

"Very well, you have a moment before I have the three of you thrown into the dungeons."

The King returned to his seat, deciding he was in no danger, Traven scoffed at his complete lack of self-preservation. The King was an idiot to lower his guard so quickly. Troy grinned triumphantly as he addressed his father.

"It seems, Father, that we have all come to the same conclusion. You are no longer fit to rule, and you are nothing but a weak, foolish coward."

Rage filled the King's cerulean eyes.

"How dare you—"

Troy cut him off.

"You are only angry because you fear the truth I speak. Now, this is our final offer. Step down from your title and relinquish the kingdom to us. Do this, and we might spare your pathetic life."

King Arwin once again got to his feet.

"Guards."

The words had barely left his lips when Alexander laughed and raised his palm. Four of the six guards went flying backwards as an invisible force threw them against the far wall with bone jarring impact. Troy laughed, and fire blazed around him, trapping the King and Troy in a deadly ring of flames.

"Deal with the guards," Troy ordered his brothers as he drew his blade and faced his father who wore a look of shock.

"How…how did you do that?" he asked, dreading the answer as he spotted the ruby around his son's throat.

"I think you know very well, Father. I accomplished in weeks what you could not in years, the element stones are ours, and you have no power anymore."

Troy grinned maliciously as his father drew his own blade.

"You are a little fool if you think I will go down without a fight!"

"Look around you, Father. You are the fool. You cannot even accept defeat when it is staring you in the eyes."

Troy lunged as the flames around them dimmed, giving Alexander and Traven a clear view of the duel between their brother and father. The ring of metal on metal echoed off the throne room walls, the only audience the remaining two brothers and two guards who had yielded to their attacks, both semi-unconscious on the stone floor. Troy and his father exchanged several parries before the King saw an opening and struck, his blade biting into the exposed skin on Troy's upper arm. Troy lost muscle control and dropped his blade as blood seeped into the sleeve of his tan tunic. The King gave a triumphant chuckle, pointing the tip of his blade at Troy's throat. Suddenly, shock filled Arwin's face as Troy's eyes bled from blue into crimson. The King yelped in fear and pain as his blade turned red hot and he had no choice but to drop the blade, his palm stinging.

Troy glanced down at his arm, it was bleeding, but it was not fatal. They stood glaring at one another. The King watched as the wall of flames dispersed, leaving a black soot mark on the polished floor. Troy smirked, his eyes still that eerie shade of blood.

"Goodbye, Father."

Troy raised his hand, expelling fire from his palm that engulfed the King. Arwin screamed in terror as the flames bit into his skin, melting his jewels and clothing to his body as he fell to the floor, writhing in agony. Troy looked to Traven as his younger brother summoned the Water Stone, dousing the flames that covered the King. Troy used his uninjured arm to pick up his father's blade and stood above the once proud King who was now a blubbering mess.

"Please, spare me. I am you father. I can help you with the stones. There is a guardian that can activate their true powers."

Troy sneered, "She has been taken care of. Alexander made sure of it."

The King laughed, rasping as he coughed up blood.

"The guardian is not dead. If that were so, the stones would cease to work. The guardian must live if you want to use the stones. I implore you, please spare me."

There was hysteria in the King's voice, and Troy thought it was thrilling to incite this reaction from such a strong-willed man, a man he had once feared. Troy chuckled darkly as he raised his father's blade.

"Begging does not suit you, Father."

With that, Troy plunged the blade into Arwin's chest and through his heart.

Alexander chuckled, and Troy looked back to his brothers, his gaze falling on Traven.

"Traven, may I commend you on quickly gaining control of your stone's power."

Troy looked to Alexander.

"Is it true what Father said, that the guardian must be alive if the stones are to remain active?"

Traven cut in.

"Why would he lie? He was trying to save his pathetic carcass. This guardian, you two have met him. Where is he?"

Troy glanced towards Alexander.

"She is back in Rinnyus. Is your aim not as good as it used to be Alexander?"

Alexander shot his brother a dark look.

"My aim was true. Obviously, something protected her, which is a good thing seeing as we have discovered we need the little shit alive," Troy growled in annoyance.

"She will be safe with the Lanarii for now. I am certain they will protect her with their lives. All the same, we need to find her and extend her an invitation to the royal dungeon. We cannot have her up and dying on us. These stones give us power, and I will not let that go to waste."

Alexander cleared his throat.

"I have an idea. There is a contact of mine who can find and bring the girl back to us, for a modest fee, of course. That way, we can continue our conquest, and he can deliver her to us."

Troy nodded.

"That is a sound idea, Alexander. Now, let us make haste. We have our coronation to plan and a kingdom to conquer!" Troy exclaimed as both his brothers yelled in victory, raising their blades to their success.

Chapter Twenty

Neko panted as she wiped the sweat from her brow. Riken stood poised as ever, awaiting her next attack that most likely would be blocked and result in her falling on her arse for the hundredth time that day.

"Come on Riken," she yelled.

"Can't you let me win one round?"

Riken gave her a stern gaze, motioning for her to come at him again. Neko muttered a few choice words under her breath before she lunged, her blade raised as she tried to use sheer force to catch the Lanarii off guard. He easily deflected it and sent her staggering towards the ground. Neko knew it was childish, but she gave in to her anger and let forth an enraged scream, throwing her blade some ten feet to her left. She turned to Riken, her face bright red as her eyes alighted with an inner rage that made him rethink his actions in getting her so angry.

"You are such a tool," she screamed as she turned and left the area, fighting the urge to summon the Earth Stone and hang the smug Lanarii from his ankles with a rather large vine. Riken blinked as he watched Neko stalk off, her wooden blade left where she had thrown it. Riken felt a bit remorseful as he walked over and picked up the sword. He had been working her hard all morning. He was impressed with her swordsmanship. It had improved vastly in the previous few weeks, but she just could not let go of the frustration that overtook her once she could not land a blow, and then her skill became non-existent when she got into a fit about it.

"What was that all about?"

Riken turned as he recognized the baritone. He smiled and greeted the rebel Prince.

"Arran, you have returned safely. When did you arrive?"

"A little while ago. My men were tired, so I gave them the day to get settled in."

Arran looked towards Neko's retreating form.

"Why was she so vexed? I was certain she was going to come at you swinging."

Riken sighed deeply.

"She does not like to lose, but I refuse to go easy on her for the sake of her feelings. She needs to reign in that vile temper of hers, or I fear she will never be able to keep her wits in a real battle."

Arran snickered. He now had a partial beard growing, and he looked ready for a nice long relaxing soak.

"She is probably upset for looking bad in front of you."

Riken looked skyward.

"She tries too hard to learn in a moon cycle what takes most people many summers," Riken speculated as Arran grinned at the other man.

"Perhaps I can talk to her, see what is going on in that hard head of hers."

Riken gestured in the direction Neko had stormed off. He offered Arran the practice blade.

"Can you please return this to her then?"

Arran accepted the blade and chuckled.

"Of course."

Mirth radiated from his eyes as he walked past the Lanarii King and into the bustling village center, confident he would have no problems locating his irate sister.

Neko was still fuming when she made it into the village plaza. Riken seemed to enjoy humiliating her. Neko stifled her internal rant as she spotted a familiar face sticking out in the crowd of Lanarii. As Neko approached, it was indeed who she thought it had been—tall, dark hair and deep green eyes.

"Logan?" she asked. At hearing his name, the brunette turned and smiled down at Neko.

"Why hello little Princess."

Neko glared up at the six-foot giant.

"I told you to call me Neko. When did you get back? Is my brother with you?"

Logan chuckled.

"One question at a time please."

Neko laughed, and her aggravation at Riken was gone. After their brief introduction in the pub, Neko had wanted nothing to do with the man who had threatened to stab her. He had approached her in the palace, looking ashamed as he handed her a familiar black cloak. He had apologized to her for being such a scoundrel that day, and then he gave her the kicked puppy look, and she caved. Since then, they had become fast friends.

"Where is Arran?"

Logan scoffed.

"He is around here somewhere, undoubtedly looking for you. How is your training coming along?"

Neko growled, "Not so good. That damn ass Riken likes to make me look like a moron."

"Would you rather he let you win just to appease you?"

Neko shook her head.

"No! I just wish I was half as good as he is."

Logan laughed loudly.

"Give it some time, Neko. You have only been training for a moon cycle. It takes many years to become an adept fighter. King Riken has many years of training on you, and I doubt even I could hold my own if I dueled him."

Neko did feel a little better, but only slightly.

"Well, I guess you are kinda old," she teased as Logan mock glared at her.

"Watch it now. Besides, I am only a few years older than you are."

Both shared a grin.

"I'm glad you made it back okay. How many men came with you guys?" Neko enquired as Logan gestured to the village square. Many rebels milled around the area.

"About a hundred or so. There are more who will arrive once word reaches them. There is also a rumor that Troy and his brothers have taken over their father's kingdom."

Neko felt her heart drop.

"That's not good.... Wait. You said brothers. Are both of them helping him?"

Logan nodded.

"Yes, Troy, Alexander and Traven."

Neko felt sick, bile rising in her throat as Logan gave her a worried stare.

"Princess, are you feeling well? Your face has gone deathly pale."

Neko shook herself out of the apprehension she was feeling.

"No. I'm fine really. I'm just a bit tired from training is all."

She did not sound convincing at all to Logan, who gave her an intense stare.

"Neko!"

Arran's voice cut through the crowd as Neko glanced up, grinning at her brother.

"I should get settled. Will I see you later?" Logan asked as Neko offered him a quick smile.

"You betchya," she giggled as she tore off towards her brother. Leaping at him, she gave him a huge bear hug, almost knocking him over in the process.

"I'm glad you're back. It's been so boring here."

Arran chuckled, returning the hug with one arm.

"I missed you too."

He laughed as Neko gave him back his personal space.

"This is yours, I believe."

He handed her the blade. Neko blinked but took the blade back.

"You saw that, didn't you?" she looked embarrassed as Arran chuckled.

"Is he mad at me?" she asked causing her brother to raise an eyebrow.

"Neko?" he asked as she looked up, their eyes meeting.

"Do you like King Riken?"

Neko felt her face heating up.

"Well, he's okay, I guess."

Arran raised a sceptical eyebrow.

"That is not what I mean, and you know it."

Neko looked to the ground.

"Yeah, maybe a little bit," she admitted as Arran smiled down at his sister.

"It is not such a bad thing. He is a respectable individual and a King as well."

Neko glared at her brother.

"That's not why I like him. Okay? He's just so easygoing, and he never holds a grudge even when I'm being an idiot."

Arran watched as his sister grew flustered.

"It's just he's been so nice to me since the day we met, even when he thought I was in league with Troy. He believed in me even when I didn't believe in myself. That's why I like him. Okay?"

Her tone meant she was done with the conversation. Arran accepted that and grinned. He could not resist teasing her.

"Well, Neko, I never thought you would go for an old man."

Neko glared at her brother and gave him a solid shot in the arm.

"That's what you get, smart ass," she hissed, tearing off and giggling like mad as her brother gave chase, intent on catching the little brat and throwing her into the lake for her mischievous behavior.

Neko sat in the sand beside Arran as they watched the sun setting over Lake Tariin.

"I love this place. It's my favorite spot to sit and watch the sunset," Neko mused as Arran listened to the calming noise of the waves washing up on shore. There was a slight breeze blowing across the lake cooling them.

"So were you ever angry that I returned. I mean the stones would go to you if I never came back to Arorus."

Arran smiled slightly.

"No Neko. You are the true guardian of the stones. They chose you, and I do not resent you in the least. I only wish we had met under better circumstances."

Neko laughed.

"Yeah. I guess 'hey I'm your long-lost sister and I'm gonna kick you in the face' is kinda a bad first impression."

Arran grinned as he reminisced about their first encounter.

"I was so mad that day, but I was impressed that a slip of a girl like you stood up to me."

Neko grinned and found a flat stone. Throwing it across the lake's smooth surface, she made it skip three times before the stone disappeared into the water.

"I was so scared that day. I thought I was going to die. I wish I had known that Troy was such a pecker head then. It would have saved us a whole lot of bickering."

Arran gave her a loose hug.

"Everything happens for a reason, Neko. The important thing is that we finally know the truth and now we can work on fixing things."

"Arran, we need to get the other stones back from Troy and his brothers."

Arran looked down at Neko.

"You said his brothers. You know about the third one?"

"Yes. Actually, Troy told me a few days after I met him he had two brothers and Logan told me today that they took over their father's kingdom."

Arran looked over the lake once again.

"Troy, Alexander, and Traven, they each possess an element stone. A spy reported this to me not long ago. They are wasting no time."

Neko looked to her brother.

"How do we stop them?"

Arran was at a loss for words.

"I do not know. I only know that the stones need to be returned to their resting place within the temple on Kiirya Island."

Neko looked out over the lake once again. A warm orange glow covered the area as twilight encroached on the land.

"The only way we can possibly get the element stones back would be to sneak up on the brothers, and that will be difficult. They will be very guarded about every aspect of their lives now."

Neko nodded but spoke slowly.

"They think I'm dead, right? Maybe I could disguise myself as a servant girl and—"

Arran stopped her before she could finish her thoughts.

"Absolutely not! Neko, having them think you are dead is our greatest advantage. If they capture you, they get the last stone and then we will be completely lost. It is too much of a risk."

"We need to do something. We can't just sit around here with our thumbs up our asses."

Arran turned to his sister.

"When did you get so vulgar, little sister?"

Neko snorted.

"Since always."

Arran rolled his eyes.

"Do not be so impatient. Before we go running into battle you need to be able to hold your own with a sword, something you have yet to do."

Neko glared at her brother.

"Not you too, Arran. I'm trying my hardest but let's face it, I suck at swords, as you probably saw today."

Arran nodded, but he did not fully agree.

"Perhaps it is not your skills, but in the weapon you are using," Neko jeered at the comment.

"It's a piece of glorified wood, Arran. I haven't even graduated to a metal blade yet."

Arran grinned at her expression.

"Yes, precisely. Maybe you need to be using a real blade."

Neko felt her jaw drop.

"Yes. That's it, and then Riken can hack off my arm," Her voice laced with sarcasm as her brother shot her an annoyed scowl.

"I know it is hard for you to believe, but just maybe if the training seemed a little more realistic, it might inspire you to fight as if your life depended on it," Neko groaned and fell backwards, lying in the sand, her gaze finding the few stars that were out and she focused on them.

"Let's face it, Arran. I suck at fighting."

Arran chuckled.

"That is not correct. You do amazingly well in hand-to-hand."

Neko looked over to her brother who was giving her a doting look. "Arran, have you ever beaten Riken in blades?"

Arran chuckled.

"No, Neko. I have not. He has had many years using a blade, and it is your temper that is hindering your progress. Perhaps if you treated swordplay like a dance rather than a slashing contest, you could develop a technique and keep your temper in check."

Neko blinked a few times.

"So, your saying, use a real blade and dance instead of fight?"

"Exactly."

Neko sat back up and grinned.

"Well, I'll give it a try, 'cause what I'm doing now isn't getting me anywhere, obviously."

"Shall we head in. It should be nearing evening meal and I for one, am starving."

Neko laughed and got to her feet. Offering her hand to Arran, she helped pull him to his feet as well.

"I second that," she stated as the pair headed back into the village and towards the glowing palace.

Alexander stood outside the palace walls, awaiting his contact. He did not wait long before a person stepped out of the shadows, Alexander's stone flashing as the other person caught him off guard, his stealth uncanny.

"My lord," the man purred as he stepped closer, his frame hidden by a cloak as dark as night.

"Darius, I have a job for you."

Alexander threw a rather large pouch of gold at the other man, who deftly caught it in his hands, pocketing it.

"This fee is steep, even for you."

Alexander chuckled.

"This job is very important. I have someone I need you to retrieve, alive and unharmed. I will give you the other half after this package is delivered to me."

The other man smirked, his white teeth flashing in the dark.

"Who is the target?"

Alexander handed Darius a scroll.

"All the information is here, I do not need to remind you what will happen should you fail in your task. My brothers and I will not accept failure."

Darius bowed slightly.

"As you wish my lord. I will return when the job is complete."

Alexander turned and headed back into the castle, a smirk in place, everything was going as planned.

Chapter Twenty-One

Neko stood in the training hall, her metal blade ready to duel Riken. She tried to mask her excitement. It would do her no good to give away the surprise from the get-go. She had risen early, intent on being in the training hall before the Lanarii. She snickered to herself. She had been secretly trying out her new moves with the metal blade in the privacy of her room, and her bedposts had the proof of her blade strikes where she had put too much power into a swing. Since Arran's suggestion a few weeks past, Neko had been getting better at curbing her temper, pretending Riken was on mute and ignoring his taunts. She realized he was only doing it to distract her. She gave him credit. It was a rather ingenious teaching method. Neko smirked at the surprised look Riken gave her when he entered the training hall.

"You are up early," he observed as Neko brought her blade into a fighting position, wasting no time with pleasantries. If Riken wanted to play mind games, she would also try to throw him off guard. Neko could see his annoyance at her rudeness. Perhaps she could get the better of him today. Neko ran at him, and as he went to block her forceful swing that never landed, she dodged at the last moment and did a complete turn quicker than Riken could follow. Neko was behind him, her blade tip on the back of his neck.

"Neko?"

Riken turned to face her as she wore a pleased grin.

"I believe that's one for me," she stated in a singsong voice as Riken gave her a glare.

"That was underhanded."

"Just admit it. You're mad because I actually managed to get a hit on you," Riken growled, a sign she was getting under his skin, so Neko continued.

"Ready to go again or do you need a moment to unbunch your panties?"

Riken snarled and lunged, expecting Neko to try to dance away. He prepared for the dancing but was rudely disrupted when Neko went for him and with the flat of her blade, hit him solidly in the ribs. Had she been fighting in battle, he would have been nearly cleaved in half, such was the strength of her attack. Riken was starting to get annoyed. How had she suddenly seen through his defenses and how could he not sense her attacks. It was rather off-putting, to say the least.

"Seriously?" she asked as Riken went after her again. The same as before, she could sense his moves before he even knew them and she countered them with ease. Neko managed another hit on him. This time, it was a painful blade slap across his shoulder blades. It did not help as he suddenly realized Arran and a few more people, Lanarii and rebels alike, had entered the room to watch their sparring. He felt something he had not felt in a long while. He felt meek, and it was because of this girl before him. He tried to banish the anger, but it was fruitless. He was annoyed that she had managed to fight his fire with fire all her own that was bigger and brighter, and it irritated him to no end. Before he could stop himself, he gave a battle cry and went after Neko, determined to win this bout and save face. Neko felt the energy shift and using the Earth Stone's powers she saw Riken's energy flux from a light blue to grey, not a big difference but enough to know Riken was not playing now. By some fluke, Neko had learnt that her element stone could pick up on people's moods, specifically by colors. If she concentrated enough on one person, she could see their colors. She had been secretly training with Arran, seeing what emotions caused what colors. Light blue was stable, grey or red-tinged meant anger, and anything else was probably not a good thing. She had also discovered that in sensing people's auras, she could see their reactions before they even made them, giving her a second or so opportunity to make an attack of her own. The only downfall was that using this aura-reading thing drained her energy very quickly and so she had only a few minutes in which to use this power continually before she needed to stop to regain her manna. Neko felt a spark of anger herself as she realized Riken wanted to win at any cost. The way he held his blade meant she had to be very careful of her next few moves. Riken brought his blade down, and Neko blocked the blow meant to break her collarbone.

"Hey!" she heard Arran yell in protest and saw him come rushing towards her, ready to attack Riken. Riken turned on the rebel Prince.

"You will not interrupt." His voice was stone cold, and he turned back to face Neko, his Lanarii guards holding Arran back from disrupting the fight. Something strange came over Neko then. Her stone pulsed and she felt her energies renewed as if she had just awakened from a long sleep. She felt the warmth and the power from the Earth Stone spread into her body, and she knew she could do this. She was meant to do this. Riken lunged at her. Using his foot, he gave her a solid kick in the stomach, knocking her onto her back but she managed to keep a solid grip on her blade. He went in for the kill, and as he brought his blade down, Neko did a full roll, causing his blade to crash into the wooden floor right where her face had been seconds before. Riken managed to get his blade stuck for a fraction of a second, but it was all the time Neko needed to counter. Neko used her right foot to deliver a sidekick to the stunned male's face. She did not hold back as she used her momentum to get back to her feet and put a safe distance between herself and the Lanarii. She held her blade up, ready for the next attack that was sure to follow. Riken pulled his blade free and glared at Neko, his lip split, and he could taste blood. This only managed to enrage him more. Neko watched his aura tinge pink, then go bright red. There was no doubt that he was pissed off. After that cheap shot though, Neko was not entirely happy either. Riken came at her again. Neko blocked, swinging her blade in a circular motion. She used a strength she did not know she possessed and used her blade to jerk the King's blade from his grip, sending it smashing into a shelf of spare weapons some ten feet away. It was at this moment Riken realized he had lost the fight and his temper. He knew he had gone too far. His gaze met Neko's, and he was sure he would see a triumphant grin. Instead, he was faced with a mask of hostility, rage pooling just behind her eyes that were now a vibrant shade of emerald. There was a power behind those eyes that frightened the Lanarii King. This strange warrior could not be the same Neko from mere moments ago. Riken's eyes went saucer-wide as the entire room trembled and the floor all around him splintered, sending broken pieces of floor everywhere. Vines shot up from the ground, caging the spectators and keeping them away from the brawling Lanarii and Dolphinian. Neko extended her hand and Riken could not avoid the sudden onslaught of vines surrounding him, wrapping around him, then lifting him into the air as they constricted his torso while he struggled to escape. He was helpless. Both he and Neko knew it.

"Neko!"

He tried to reason with her, but there was nothing familiar in those emerald depths.

"We are done here."

Neko's voice was regal and slightly deeper, but there was no doubting the power behind those words. She lowered her hand, and the vines released Riken, dropping him several feet to the floor where he landed in an unceremonious heap. He stayed as he was, watching Neko return her blade to the sheath on her side. Without another word, the remaining vines retreated, and Neko stalked out of the room, leaving some very astonished individuals in her wake.

Arran glared at Riken as the Lanarii picked himself up, looking into the eyes of the irate Prince.

"Arran, I—"

He did not get to apologize as Arran took a swing at him, hitting him across the jaw and splitting the Lanarii's lip even more. Arran wanted nothing better than to hit the man repeatedly, but after Neko's display, he had more important things to deal with.

"What in the seven circles of hell was that?" Arran screamed while Riken glanced up at the angry rebel and wiped blood from his split and swollen lip.

"You were trying to hurt her, not train her. What would possess you to do that?" Arran snarled as Riken shook his head, unsure himself.

"I do not know what came over me," he defended as Arran swiped his hand across his chest in agitation.

"You liar. I damn well know what happened. You who are so proud, you who are so noble, could not stand the fact that someone might best you in a duel."

Arran shook his head, looking at Riken as if he were the biggest piece of garbage in the world.

"You promised to protect us, to protect her, but how can you protect us from yourself, Lanarii King?"

Arran looked to his men who stood in the decimated hall.

"Get your things together men. Tell the others we leave for the base as soon as we are packed."

Arran glared at Riken as the Lanarii opened his mouth in an attempt to protest the rash decision.

"Shut your filthy mouth. You will never see her again," he growled as he walked past Riken, jarring the Lanarii's shoulder with his as he walked past. Riken remained where he was, shocked as Arran's words sunk in. He felt sick to his stomach, and for once in his life, he did not have any sage advice for himself, except that he was a complete fool.

Arran raced from the destroyed training room. He glanced around frantically, trying to locate Neko. She had just left this area only moments earlier. Arran glanced towards the large staircase, affirming that she had most likely gone to her chambers. He tore off up the stairs, taking two at a time as he raced down the hallway and came to a screeching halt before her closed door.

"Neko?" he inquired, lightly knocking on her door, he could hear her moving around in the next room.

"It is Arran. Please open the door Neko."

He heard the lock slide open and Neko let him in, turning her back to him, her shoulders slumping in dejection.

"Neko?" he asked as she turned, a haunting look on her face.

"I'm so sorry for the trouble I caused. I didn't mean for it to go so far."

Arran shook his head.

"Do not apologize, especially to him. This was not your fault Neko. That damn arse had no right attacking you like he did."

"You're not mad at me?"

Neko's voice wavered as Arran shook his head.

"Of course not. I am just thankful that you held him off. What you did back there was remarkable. Neko, how did you do that?"

Neko sniffled, her eyes meeting her brother's. They were now back to their calm grey color.

"I just…did. I'm not even sure how I called upon the Earth Stone, but it granted me its power. It was like I was in a dream."

Arran gave her a kind smile.

"I am sure you can tell me all about it on our travels."

Neko blinked, confusion on her face.

"Travels?"

"Yes. After that incident, we are getting as far away from the Lanarii as we can."

Neko gave him an apprehensive look as she sat down on the end of her bed.

"We're leaving this place, is that a wise idea?"

Arran looked at her as if she were a small child.

"Neko, do you not understand? Riken almost killed you today. Thank the gods you were able to hold your own. We are no longer safe here, and it is my job to protect you. We are leaving this very afternoon, so get your things packed now."

Arran headed for the door.

"I am going to pack my things as well. Once I have finished, I will meet with you back here. Do you understand? Please lock the door behind me and do not leave this room until I come to get you."

Neko nodded, in a stupor of sorts, comprehension dawning on her that Riken had, in fact, really tried to kill her. The sound of her door shutting made her snap out of her daze as she stared blankly at the closed door. Her brother had been telling her something but damned if she could remember what he had just said to her. Neko shook her head and started gathering her things. The first thing she noticed was the armor from Annalise. She debated leaving it, but it had been made for her and would not fit anyone else. She only had a few belongings to take with her. Getting them prepared took no time at all. She felt drained as she paced her room, awaiting her brother's return. Neko's door opened slowly, and she glanced over, expecting Arran. Instead, Riken was the one to enter the room.

In his hands, he held a sword in a sheath. Neko froze, her heart hammering in her chest as she stared fearfully at the Lanarii King, whose expression fell as they made eye contact. Riken did not know what to expect when he went to see Neko. He had wanted to fall to the ground and beg for her forgiveness, even if she started screaming at him. As their eyes met, there was no anger. Only fear filled her eyes. She feared the very sight of him, and this made his chest constrict painfully. He could not stand that he had done this to her.

"Neko…I…have failed you. This is for you. Please be safe."

He gently set the blade down on the nearby dresser. Riken had made the blade for her, deciding once she had passed his training it would be his gift to her. Now he would be fortunate if she even took it with her. He could not stand seeing that fearful look in her eyes. He took the cowards' way out and vacated the room without a backwards glance. There was nothing more he could say or do to reassure her.

Once she was sure Riken had left, she released the breath she had been holding. She remained where she was standing, staring wide-eyed at the blade he had given to her. What was she supposed to do with that? Slowly, she started to approach the blade, reaching her hand out to brush the tips of her fingers against the scabbard that was made of an ebony wood, decorated with golden filigree vines. Neko jumped and screamed as Arran burst into her room, a full leather pack slung over his shoulder and another empty one in his hand.

"Neko?" he asked as his sister gave him a haunting look. "Are you ready?"

She nodded as he looked down at the sword.

"What is that?"

Neko gave him a placid stare.

"It's a sword," she stated as Arran rolled his eyes and let out a frustrated sigh.

"All right, get it and your things and let us be gone."

He handed her the empty leather bag.

"Take only what you can carry. Leave the dresses behind. You will not need them in the wilds."

So, with her pack filled and new blade at her side, Neko left the palace with Arran, there destination, the rebels' hidden base.

Arran's men were given their orders and awaited the siblings in the forest on the outskirts of the Lanarii village, near the Katrii waterfalls.

"Ready?" Arran asked looking down at Neko, who nodded.

"Come along. My men are waiting for us, and there is nothing else left for us here."

He turned and headed into the forest, Neko turned back, staring at the silver village. For a moment, she thought she might be able to see Riken watching them leave from the balcony of his study. She shook her head, and the image faded. He had never been standing there to begin with. She turned and followed her brother into the dense forest, unaware of the solitary being who stood in the shadows of a large pine tree. Sadness etched in the King's face as he watched her disappear into the dark forest.

Chapter Twenty-Two

The trek to Larrow was uneventful. Even the Glodiirii seemed to keep their distance as the large group of rebels marched through the thick forest and finally reached the city on the lake. Neko stared across the open expanse of the large body of water. It was not nearly as beautiful as Lake Tariin. Arran glanced down at his sister as he ordered his men to split into smaller and less obvious groups, especially with Troy and his brothers now in command of the vast kingdom. Come the morning they would disperse, some of his men he sent to inform the other rebels to avoid the Lanarii domain and instead return home to their hidden encampment at the base of the Talla mountain range near the far side of Lake Ladorius. It had been a grand total of three days since Neko and Arran had left Rinnyus.

"I know you are upset about what happened, Neko, but we must do what is best for us. We need to keep ourselves protected, you especially."

Neko understood. She just hated how things had been left. Neko absent-mindedly brushed invisible dust particles from her blade. Once they had stopped to rest for the night, Neko had finally taken her first good look at the sword Riken had left for her. It was a narrow blade with a duel edge and about the length of her forearm. She knew undoubtedly great effort had been put into making this exquisite blade. Arran gave a frustrated groan as his sister continued to stare at the blade, completely ignoring his attempt at a conversation.

"Perhaps we could take a detour on our way back to the encampment."

Arran noticed he had Neko's full attention as she gave him a questioning stare.

"Detour?"

"Yes. I was thinking once we set sail instead of going across the lake and straight to camp, we will head down the Rizenna River to the very end where it lets out near Numis. From there, we go to Kiiyas and make our way to Kiirya Island. Then I can show you our homeland."

Neko felt excitement welling in her stomach as a smile lit her face.

"Really? You'd take me to see the palace?"

Arran smiled ruefully.

"It is the least I can do. It is important for you to see your real home and make new memories to replace the ones you have forgotten."

Neko stayed silent as Arran gave her a concerned look.

"Are you feeling well?"

"Just a bit tired. We walked pretty far today."

Arran agreed. They had made very good time. He would continue to be nervous until they had all returned to the safety of the rebel encampment. Before Arran had even been born, there had been a grand castle, now abandoned and falling apart. He wondered what had happened to the previous owners to make them abandon everything. Lucky for him it was now where his rebels called home.

"Arran?"

Neko pulled him from his musing, "Why are we going off on our own? What about your men, shouldn't you stay with them?"

"My men can handle things on their own. We are strong and hidden near the wastelands. Not many are brave enough to venture that close to the desert."

Their conversation ended when Logan and Skylar approached the siblings.

"Sir, you sent for us?" Logan asked, flashing Neko a friendly smile.

"Yes. I have instructions for you two. I have decided to take Neko to see the palace. In my absence, you two will take charge. I want you to make certain that you are not followed. If you are, you know what to do."

Skylar and Logan both nodded.

"Yes. Disband and take different routes back to base," Skylar recited as Logan looked to his leader.

"Should some of the men accompany you and the Princess?"

Logan looked hopeful as Arran shot him a cynical stare.

"If you are hoping to come along, then the answer is no. I need you and Skylar to look after things while I am gone," Arran stated in a matter-of-fact tone.

"We can travel faster and hide ourselves easier if it is just the two of us. We shall not be gone long, a moon cycle at the most to get there and arrive back at base."

Neko once again was lost in her own thoughts as the men conversed. She sat staring at her blade, wondering what Riken was doing this very moment. Neko knew she should be furious or at least upset, but the truth was she missed the Lanarii. She missed talking with him and getting him to smile at her odd behaviors. It just felt wrong without him.

"Neko?"

She shook her head looking up at her brother who had called her.

"There you are, off in your own little world again."

"What? do you want?" she asked, in no mood for joking around.

"I said we will leave with the others at dawn. Halfway down the lake, the river Rizenna branches off. We will be taking a smaller paddleboat while the other groups continue down the lake."

Arran looked down at his sister. She looked ready to fall asleep where she was sitting.

"Go on, get some rest. I will fetch you in the morning."

Neko offered him a meager smile and got to her feet, heading to her sleeping roll. They were camped on the outskirts of Larrow to avoid suspicion had they all stayed in town for the night. Arran had sent a few men in for supplies. That way, they could bypass the city and onlookers with big mouths. Arran had already sent half his men down the lake hours before knowing that their large numbers would alert someone they were on the move.

True to his word, Arran was up at the break of day. He lightly shook Neko rousing her from her slumber. Neko groaned in protest, but the threat of a cold bucket of water over her head changed her mind quickly. Neko shot her brother a death glare as she rolled up her bedding and packed her things for their journey. As they headed down towards the boats, Neko noticed everyone looking a little unnerved.

"What's going on?" Neko wondered as she looked to Arran who also looked a bit frazzled.

"Rumors are that Troy and his brothers are heading this way. I do not know how close or if it is even true, but I will not take that risk. It could be they are heading back to Rinnyus to claim the Earth Stone."

Neko glanced around at the rebels.

"Come along Neko. The sooner we get onto the lake, the sooner we can get down the river."

Neko followed her brother silently as they walked for the better part of an hour. Soon, she could see the lake through the trees. She listened to the murmurs of the rebels. They had to walk single file down the narrow dirt path. Once they got to the water's edge, they had about ten feet of beach area in which to load and launch their boats. The boats were quite small compared to the barge she had been on with Troy. Arran approached a boat that was the smallest one Neko could see, maybe twice the size of a canoe and upon closer inspection, it was made of hide rather than wood like the other boats.

"That's our ride?" Neko inquired, apprehension evident in her tone. Arran chuckled as he threw his pack into the boat. There were two seats, one in the front, the other in the rear, leaving the middle for packs and food. The entire rig was about fifteen feet long end to end and about five feet across in the middle where it was the thickest. Neko decided it really was a canoe, just huge compared to any she had seen back home.

"It is very well built, I can assure you," Arran stated, picking up two wooden oars.

"Come on. Get your things in and sit down. I will cast us off, and we can be on our way."

Neko saw no other option, and she really didn't feel like arguing with Arran. Perhaps a scenic boat ride down the lake would be a nice change of pace as opposed to hiking all damn day. Neko got into the boat. Surprised at how stable it was, she took a seat in the rear and placed her things at her feet. Once settled, she took the paddle Arran handed her. He placed his paddle inside the hull of the boat and started to push off. He did rather well and only managed to get his boots wet. Neko had secretly been hoping to see him take a dive into the icy waters. Arran gave her a cheeky grin.

"You were not thinking about pushing me in now, were you Neko?"

Neko laughed. Apparently, her poker face was not a very convincing one.

"No. I was thinking I wouldn't have to, that you would just fall in all on your own."

Arran snorted and turned his back to her, getting his paddle out.

"All right, just do as I do. This boat is very light and takes hardly anything to get it moving."

Neko rolled her eyes as she started paddling. She did know how to operate a canoe.

Neko enjoyed the lake, but once they had arrived at the river mouth, she felt relieved to be off the massive body of water. They had paddled all day, taking only a few small breaks. Once they reached the river, Neko knew they would be camping for the evening. She was thankful the boat was so large. It offered them the perfect place to sleep and Arran had brought along a water-resistant tarp. So, in the event of it raining, they had a shelter that took only moments to set up, making it pretty much a floating tent. As they built a small campfire on the shores of the lake and went about getting their dinner prepared, Neko found herself once again thinking of a certain Lanarii. She banished the thought and forced herself to look for dry bits of firewood. Riken should have been the last thing on her mind.

"Do not stray far."

Neko shot her brother a sly grin.

"Why? You scared I might get lost?"

"No, but we should show a degree of caution, just in case," Neko continued her search, keeping Arran's words in mind. She did not stray from the sight of the fire. Her head snapped up as the sound of a small twig snapping alerted her to another presence. She glanced over her shoulder and looked back towards where she had heard the sound.

"Hello?" she asked as she wrapped her right hand around the handle of her blade, just in case she had to draw it. Silence replied as she glanced around, looking for any clue about what had made the noise. It most likely was wildlife. Neko concentrated and used her heightened senses to see if there were any nearby auras. The fact that there was nothing in the area had her on edge.

"Neko?" Arran called to her as she took one last look around before she turned and headed back towards their camp.

"Coming."

Riken released the breath he had been holding. How he had evaded her was beyond him. He had been tailing them for a few days now. He had noticed the rest of the rebels were heading down the lake, but Neko and Arran had made camp near the river mouth, suggesting they were going to continue down the river. This had baffled him until it dawned on him that Numis sat at the end of the river. That town must have been their destination. He decided to return to Rinnyus and enlist a few more Lanarii to help follow the siblings. They might not have been on speaking terms with him, but he was going to do what he could to ensure they were safe. It was the least he could do after the way they had parted. Riken watched as Neko finally left the area, and he nimbly jumped down from the tree branch on which he was standing. Once on the ground, he decided to make for Rinnyus. With luck, he would arrive in good time. He knew Neko and Arran were constrained by the slow pace of the river and that gave him plenty of time to make arrangements.

As the Lanarii King headed back into the forest, another shadow slipped out from behind a tree. The man smirked as he realized his job had become all the easier. Stupidly, the rebel leader had decided to take a long way back and had refused any extra men. Now it was the two of them all alone in the wilds, and he could bide his time getting the girl. Darius smirked. With Troy and his brothers due any day in Numis, he would not have far to go to deliver the girl to the three brothers. Darius silently crept closer to the sibling's camp. He was not about to lose his mark, not when he was about to make the easiest gold of his life. As he crept closer, the girl stopped talking, her head whipped up.

"Neko? What is it?"

Darius silently cursed as she stood up, hand on her blade as she glanced around.

"Something is out there. I can sense it," Arran growled and stood up. Darius decided to play the lost man as he staggered into their camp.

"Hold on now. I mean no harm. I saw your fire. Can you help me? I am afraid I am a little bit lost."

Arran narrowed his eyes, taking the man in. He was tall but built. His skin was a bronzed caramel, and his eyes were a light brown, making them look almost red. He was wearing a dark cloak and had a wicked looking blade at his side. Recognition dawned on Arran as he took in the stranger.

"You're a Shagonna."

Darius offered a friendly smile.

"Yes, my friend, I surely am. Impressive, not many of my kind left in this world."

Neko slowly lowered her hand, but her grey eyes bore into the mercenary, watching his every move. He would need to tread very carefully.

"My name is Darius, and I am trying to find my way to Kiiyas."

Arran nodded.

"You are on the right track, keep following the river. You will come to Numis. From there, it is an easy few days' journey."

Darius blinked.

"Forgive my flagrancy, but are you two perhaps headed that direction?"

Arran shook his head, as Neko wisely remained silent.

"Sorry, my friend. We are headed up the river, heading for Larrow I am afraid. Otherwise, we would offer to take you."

Darius nodded, knowing fully well the rebel leader was lying to his face.

"That is too bad. Would you two mind terribly if I shared your fire tonight. I will be no bother, and I have gold. I can ease your minds. I am no robber."

Darius hobbled forward, extending a small bag of gold as the two siblings stood side by side, making them the perfect targets. Darius chuckled, opened the bag, and then threw the powder within at the two shocked siblings. The powder worked almost instantaneously as both fell to the forest floor coughing and gagging as the potent substance sent them into darkness.

Chapter Twenty-Three

Neko groaned as sunlight assaulted her senses. Her eyes slowly opened to reveal the forest floor. She attempted to sit up only to find her hands bound as she noticed she was leaning with her back against a tree. Upon further inspection, she realized that her feet were tied together with coarse rope as well.

"Ah, good morning to you, Princess."

Neko glanced to her left, glaring at the stranger from the night before.

"What's going on here. Where is my brother?"

The man grinned as he cut a slice of apple with his boot dagger, casually leaning against a tree some ten feet from Neko.

"He is alive if that is what you are asking."

Neko tried her restraints, finding them secure.

"As for what I am doing here, I was sent to find you and return you to the new Kings."

Neko felt her heart start to race.

"You can't. Please just let us go."

Darius smirked.

"Sorry, Princess. That is not how this works. I am here to deliver you. Your brother is not part of the deal."

Neko sighed. She could feel the power of the Earth Stone around her neck. Obviously, the idiot had failed to find it, which was a good thing. She had to get free and find Arran.

"Where is Arran?" she asked, glancing around their camp.

"He is right behind you, tethered to the other side of the tree, not that it will help you any. Soon, we shall head down the river, and he will stay behind to await whatever fate has in store for him," Neko snorted, giving the Shagonaa a disgusted glare.

"You think you can get away with this? There are rebels only hours behind us—"

"Do not try to bluff me, little girl. I have been following you two since you left the others on Lake Ladorius. I know the both of you are alone."

Neko glared at the tall man as he sauntered closer, cutting a piece of apple as he knelt, so he was eye level with Neko. He offered the piece of food.

"Would you like some?" he asked, blinking as the girl smirked wickedly.

"Yeah. I'm up for some revenge."

Darius was about to ask what she was talking about when a vine shot from the ground at his feet, moving too quickly to dodge. It wrapped around him like a serpent, binding his arms to his sides as the thing constricted, effectively trapping him. He stared at Neko, a green light blazing from beneath her shirt as her eyes shone the same brilliant emerald, that haughty smirk still plastered on her face.

"I'm guessing the brothers left a few key things out about me."

Darius stared in shock.

"You possess an element stone."

Neko grinned.

"Bingo."

She tried her bindings, smirking as she twisted her body and managed to wiggle out so that her hands were now bound in front of her.

"I forget just how stupid you guys are, always thinking that girls can't do anything for themselves. News flash buddy, I don't need rescuing. I do fine just by myself."

Darius growled, trying to free himself as Neko freed her legs and then walked over to the downed mercenary. She scooped up his dagger and used it to cut her hands free, appraising the blade as she smirked and slipped it into the boots she wore.

Darius felt rage bubbling up as she stole his favorite blade.

"When I escape, you are—"

This time Neko cut him off.

"You're not escaping, asshole. So deal with it."

Neko went around the tree and cut her brother loose. She gave him a groggy grin.

"I trained you well."

Neko rolled her eyes and helped her brother to his feet.

"What do we do with jerk face?" Neko asked as the two siblings stared down at their captive.

Arran sighed, drawing his sword.

"Probably should kill him."

Neko shook her head.

"I got a better idea. He said he was going to leave you tied to the tree to await your fate. Maybe we should do the same to him."

Arran raised an eyebrow at his sister.

"When did you get so evil?"

Neko snorted.

"Hey, an eye for an eye. He pissed me off."

Arran chuckled and uncoiled some rope.

"Well, I cannot argue with her. She has a good point, my friend."

Darius glared at the two siblings as they prepared their boat to travel down the river.

"Come on. You cannot leave me here," Darius yelled as the two ignored him. They had stolen everything he had save for the clothing on his back.

"Release me. I give my word I will not pursue you."

Neko looked towards Arran who shot the desert man a disgusted sneer.

"Let fate decide your path, dishonorable sell sword."

With that, the two settled in their boat and paddled down the river, leaving Darius tied to a tree so that he could meet his fate.

Neko and Arran made it to Numis within the week. Arran stated it had been the quickest trip down the Rizenna he had ever taken. Numis was almost as big as Larrow but positioned on a large bay. The town was full of merchant ships, all sailing to and from Numis, Kiiyas, and Port Ednus. Neko had learned all this from a map Arran carried with him.

"So, when we get to Kiiyas, we're going on a ship to the island?" Neko enquired as Arran continued to walk through the crowded streets, keeping close to Neko as he searched for pickpockets or any other potential threats to her.

"For now, that is our plan. Ideally, a small fishing boat would be the safest way to get to the island, and with enough gold, thanks to our mercenary friend, the captain will turn a blind eye to us."

Arran glanced down at Neko and gestured to the cloak she had draped over the strap of her pack.

"Perhaps you should put your cloak and hood on."

Neko did as he asked, thinking he was just a tiny bit paranoid until they saw the people gathered before them in the town square.

"Neko!"

Arran hissed grabbing her by the upper arm. He gestured to the town square and she followed his gaze. She shivered as three imposing figures stood upon the raised stone platform. Arran slowly pulled his hood over his head, and Neko felt panic welling in her stomach.

"We need to get out of here," she frantically whispered as Arran shook his head.

"We must go through the square to get to the road that leads to Kiiyas."

"Can't we come back later, we can't stay here!"

"Neko stop. Keep yourself and the stone hidden. Just act normal."

"Easy for you to say. How can you be this calm right now?"

"Because I need to be, for both our sakes. Quickly now, let us go."

Neko allowed him to guide her through the crowd. She heard him curse as they found themselves boxed in with the villagers by the royal guards, made to listen to whatever address the brothers were going to give.

"Citizens of Numis."

Neko stared as Troy's commanding voice echoed across the area.

"We come here today to announce our kingship."

There was a pause, and then the townsfolk started to talk amongst themselves.

"There was no announcement of the King's decision!"

A man standing ten feet from Neko yelled as she glanced up fearfully, Troy's eyes fell upon the crowd.

"Who said that?" he snarled, his eyes flashing with fury.

"You are no King of mine."

The same man spat as Troy raised his hand and a stream of fire slammed into the man, sending him into bystanders too slow to get out of the way.

"Anyone else have something to say about our kingship?" he yelled as Alexander stepped forward.

"He was unfit to rule, weak and spineless. We are the new rulers. Bow to us or meet the same fate as the late King and this peasant."

Neko wanted to bolt. Only Arran's ironclad grip on her arm rooted her to that spot.

"We must not draw attention to ourselves. They are simply demonstrating their position as the new rulers."

Neko glared at her brother.

"Until they see us. Then what genius?"

"We are well hidden. From up there it is just a sea of faces, and they are not looking for us, so we are fine. Let them finish their announcement, and then we can get out of here."

Neko grudgingly accepted his suggestion and prayed they weren't recognized.

Troy chuckled as the people stared up fearfully at him and his brothers.

"Now, peasants, go about your business. We are done here."

Troy sneered as the three brothers disappeared from the platform, people giving them a wide berth as they headed towards a local inn. The guards left their posts and allowed the people to continue with their day. Arran pulled Neko from the crowd and towards a small alleyway. They ducked into the darkened passageway and stared at each other.

"That was too close," Arran hissed. Looking back to make sure they were alone.

"You think? What are they doing here?"

"I am not sure."

"We're not safe here."

"Then I suggest we leave now and be out of the city by nightfall."

"The sooner, the better."

Neko was a nervous wreck. Once they left the alleyway, they headed towards the west end of the city, slipping out just before the gates closed for the night.

"Calm down, Neko. We are safe."

Arran could see his sister looked ready to lose her dinner.

"How are we supposed to face them and get the stones now. Did you see all the guards they have?"

"Neko, you need to calm yourself. We are not completely helpless."

"If it was us and them then maybe we stood a chance, but with all their men, we will never get a chance at getting the stones back!"

"Then perhaps now is not the time for us to acquire the stones."

Neko shot him a pleading stare.

"I need them to get back home! We can't just let Troy and his brothers use the stones to make people obey them!"

Arran gave his sister an irritated look.

"We cannot go running in blindly either."

"So, then what can we do?"

"All we can do is wait. We can tail them, but that is a dangerous game if they discover us. We cannot allow them to get the last stone."

Neko growled and kicked the dirt at her feet.

"This is so stupid."

Arran offered her an apologetic smile.

"Perhaps we should head back to base. It will give us time to figure out another way to reclaim the stones."

"No. We came this far already. Let's just go to the palace. I want to see it."

"Are you certain?"

"Yes. Like you said, they are just stoking their egos, bragging about their kingship to people."

"That was more than bragging back there. They were sending a message."

Neko sighed deeply and gestured to the dim road.

"Should we camp out or keep going?"

"Let us head into the trees and make camp. No one will see us and then we can start out early in the morning."

"All right, let's get going before it's too dark to see."

Troy glared down at the man who had been his father's informant. He was rather drunk and swayed in his seat as he finished another pint of ale.

"Is this him?"

Troy looked over to Traven who nodded, eyeing the drunk man in disgust.

"Yes. He was the one Father's advisor was talking to about the stone."

The drunk man hiccupped and grinned at Troy.

"Ah yes, the Spirit Stone, it was hidden away some time ago. Only the Lanarii know of its location."

Troy smirked, and fire lit up his palm, his eyes turning that deep red once again as the man instantly sobered, fear filling his eyes as Troy grabbed hold of his tunic and threw the man to the dirty pub floor.

"Or for a handsome fee, I could perhaps give you my notes."

Alexander drew a throwing dagger.

"Or for the price of your pathetic life, you give us your notes."

The man's willpower caved, and he dug around in his cloak, thrusting the sparse notes in their direction. Traven snatched the papers while sneering down at the blubbering man on the floor.

"Well, is it worth sparing his life?" Alexander impatiently asked as Traven skimmed the notes.

"Only guesses at best, according to some book he found. It makes mention that the last known guardian of the stone hid it deep in the wastelands." Traven chuckled, "but that is incorrect, is it not?" he stared down at the man who trembled under the indigo stare.

"Tis all I know. I have nothing else to offer."

Alexander heard enough as his foot connected with the side of the man's face, causing his face to collide with the unrelenting floor some feet away where he remained immobile.

"How do you know he was lying?" Troy asked as Traven spoke.

"Because the stone was hidden just after the four element stones chose a single Dolphinian to guard them. The Spirit Stone would have been hidden when the people of the Sortonn Desert died out. If I had to guess it would be right around the time that the temple for the element stones was built. The stone caused that race to die, alerting the guardian of the stone's darker nature," Traven growled in annoyance.

"Perhaps the guardian himself knew about the Spirit stone, but all the other guardians are gone now."

"Well, that is just wonderful," Alexander spat as Troy looked thoughtful.

"Maybe the old drunkard was right. I know Father mentioned that after the war, the ruins of the Dolphinian palace had caverns running underneath it, which is how the Queen escaped him. He chased her through those very caves."

Traven cut in, "The palace is nothing but rubble. Those caves would be inaccessible now."

Troy looked to his siblings.

"We have the element stones to aid us. What can it hurt to go look at the ruins? It is only at most, a week's travel from here to the island."

Alexander also spoke up.

"Troy has a point, if we got the Spirit stone, think of all the power we would have, no one, not even those damn Lanarii, could contend with us."

As they conversed, the idea to travel to the abandoned palace seemed even more appealing.

"All right," Traven admitted, "in the case that this quack is not telling the truth, I think it is worth a quick look."

Troy grinned.

"Then it is settled. We leave for Kiiyas at first light."

Neko yawned as she quickly dressed, pulling on her armor before Arran returned from gathering water for their long trek to Kiiyas. She made sure her blade was strapped securely to her left side, her pack draped over her other shoulder. Within it, she had her bundled up cloak and meager rations. Arran returned moments later, two canteens filled with spring water.

"Ready to head out?"

"You betchya."

Neko grinned, taking the water pouch from Arran and placing it within her pack. After a few minutes of walking, they were nearly out of the forest. Neko could see the main road that would bring them to Kiiyas.

"Hold on. Listen."

Arran grabbed her arm, stopping her in mid-step as a faint rumbling caught their attention. The two remained where they were some ten feet from the road.

"Horses?" Neko pondered as Arran strained to listen.

"Maybe two or three coming up fast."

They waited half a minute before three horses went thundering past them, the riders a blur as the horses kicked up a cloud of dust.

"Wow, where's the fire?"

Neko coughed and attempted to wave away the dust particles as they stepped out onto the road and watched the riders fade into the horizon. Neko felt an odd sensation course through her body, but it vanished before she had even registered what could have caused it.

"We have ground to cover. Let us be gone," Arran barked out, causing Neko to huff indignantly at his bossy attitude.

Neko followed her brother, the pair walking side by side as the sun rose behind their backs.

As they walked, Neko noticed that there were very few mountains there, only an open plateau of grassland and farms, countless farms. They did not see many people and any that they did see were rather edgy and did not want anything to do with strangers.

"Is it just me or do people around here not like us?"

Arran shot her an even look.

"Usually, Arorians are friendly, something has them spooked."

"Like what exactly?"

"Hard to say. Bandits most likely."

"What about a dragon?"

"A dragon? Doubtful, the fields would be soot and the people would be gone. Dragons do devastating damage."

Neko stuck her tongue out at her brother.

"How much farther?" she asked as her back popped when she straightened up.

"I wish we had horses."

Arran agreed. Having horses would cut their traveling time by half.

"I will make sure we have two sturdy steeds for our journey back."

Neko smiled as they continued on their way. Very soon, she would get to see the palace where she was born.

Chapter Twenty-Four

Neko could not contain the wide grin she had plastered to her face. She and Arran had just boarded a small fishing boat that morning and were on their way to Kiira Island. If she squinted and stood on her tiptoes, she could just make out a tiny speck in the distance. She had badgered Arran all morning about how long it would take them to reach the island. He had patiently told her each time she asked that it was a good two days' trip, providing the wind was in their favor. Arran chuckled at his sister's enthusiasm. She acted like a child that had indulged in too many sweets. He watched her bounce from one end of the ship to the other, pleased that he had made the decision to bring her to her homeland. It would at least give her some closure to her unknown past.

The wind was favorable for them, and they arrived on the shores of the island nearing 3:00 pm the next day according to Neko's watch. Neko stood on shaky legs as she took in the splendor of the mysterious island. They had landed in a cove of sorts. To the left was sheer cliffs the ocean rushing against them relentlessly. The beach they were standing on was about a mile long with beautiful white sand and, to the right, another ridge gradually sloped to higher ground. The crumbled remains of a watchtower silently greeted them.

"Welcome to Kiirya Island."

Arran held his arms out wide, the area just as he remembered it. Neko stared at the looming landscape. The island was a bit bigger than she had first imagined it to be.

"This way."

Arran took her hand as he led her away from the beach and up the remains of a cobblestone road, now grown in with grass. As they crested a small hill, the palace came into view. It was located on a slightly elevated knoll. Crumbled rock spread outwards from where a once grand tower stood. Neko could almost picture what the palace had looked like before it had been demolished. Green moss grew on everything, emphasizing that this place had been abandoned for a while.

"Oh, my…this place is something else."

"This is nothing. You should have seen it when our parents ruled. I wish you could remember it."

"I can at least picture it now. Maybe one day my memories will return."

Arran stared down at her, amazed at how she kept herself so optimistic.

"What?" she asked as her gaze turned to the castle.

"It is nothing. You really impress me. After all that has happened, you still manage to keep going."

Neko offered him a kind smile.

"Setbacks are a part of growing up. There is nothing else to do but get over them and move forward."

"Look at you, little miss philosopher. When did you get so wise?"

"Well, I do have a really cool big brother to teach me."

"Now you are just mocking me."

"I'm serious. You have been such a big help to me, and I wouldn't know anything about my family without you."

Arran gave her shoulder an affectionate squeeze.

"Let us go exploring."

Neko's face lit up as she scrambled towards the ruins, Arran hot on her heels as the pair stopped before the remains of two large wooden doors.

"This was the main entrance way," Arran announced as Neko smirked and stepped closer. The once grand door already opened a few feet, just wide enough for a single person to go through and into the hall. Once inside, Arran placed his hand on her shoulder and made a sweeping gesture with the other hand.

"Picture this hall lit with golden lights, the floor a polished wood and full of our people dressed in lavish attire, musicians playing a waltz in the background."

Neko blinked, imagery flashing before her as she pictured the hall as it might have been. She was stunned as she saw something else in the rear of the room. She could see, sitting in thrones, the King and the Queen. Neko stared as their faces came into focus. Her father looked a great deal like Arran, only broader across the shoulders and darker hair, but the facial features were similar. She then looked to her mother. Shock filling her eyes. She realized she looked just like her mother, save where her eyes were grey, her mothers were a deep emerald. The images faded, replaced by the ruins as Arran gave her a shake, concern on his face.

"Where did you go?"

Neko smiled apologetically

"I saw them Arran. I remember Mother and Father sitting on their thrones. The night of the party, that's when Arwin attacked the palace."

"You have regained your memories?"

"Just from the party, a fleeting image, nothing more."

"It is a start."

Neko smiled. He was right.

"This place is a damned mess."

Neko and Arran froze as a harsh voice echoed off the walls.

"Quickly get down," Arran whispered and pulled Neko behind a crumbled pillar as both sat with their backs to the pillar, the voices growing louder.

"Traven might be having better luck at the other ruins."

Neko felt ill as Troy's voice cut through the area.

"Let us keep searching. That entrance has to be here somewhere."

Arran turned to Neko whispering, "This is not good. We need to get out of here."

"Not to bust your bubble but we're kinda trapped here unless you want them to see us."

"Of course not, but we cannot remain where we are."

Arran chanced a quick glance around the stones, cursing. The brothers were a mere twenty feet away.

"It is just the two of them. I do not know where the third one is. Looks like they are alone, and I see no soldiers."

Neko bit her bottom lip and felt her hand slipping. The small sound of rocks scraping against the floor might as well have been an air horn going off in the silent room. Arran shot her a dark look as both Alexander and Troy paused.

"What was that?" Alexander hissed drawing his blade. Troy followed suit.

"Traven?"

Neko and Arran remained silent, scarcely breathing. Arran grabbed a pebble and tossed it across the room. It made a satisfying echo as it hit. Troy and Alexander had focused in on the pillar. As they approached, another rock hit off the far wall. Alexander placed his finger to his lips and pointed to the pillar. He had heard the first stone and knew better than to fall for the distraction. He was not disappointed as two figures bolted towards the doors. Alexander summoned the Wind Stone and used it to slam the wooden doors closed, trapping the two.

"Nice try."

He sneered as the two turned. He could not hide the annoyance as he recognized the two siblings.

"I thought I had killed you. My aim was true. How did you survive?" he snarled at Neko, whose hand dropped to her blade.

"You thought wrong, and it's called armor. Look it up," Neko returned, as Arran drew his blade and stood before Neko, shielding her.

"Why would you two follow us here?" Troy stared at the siblings.

"No matter. You two have made our job all the easier. Hand over Neko and the Earth Stone, and we will let you go free rebel scum."

Both brothers had their blades drawn ready to attack. Troy watched, slightly confused as Neko pulled forth a short sword, taking a fighter's stance beside her brother as he spoke.

"I cannot do that, Troy. The element stones are not toys to be played with. They are dangerous."

Troy and Alexander shared a smirk.

"What do you two plan to do exactly, take them from us?"

Alexander chuckled as he eyed Arran.

"Leave the brother to me," Alexander stated as he approached Arran. Troy's gaze caught Neko's.

"I will only say this once more. Hand over the stone Neko or have me pry it from your hands."

To prove his point, he approached Neko as she kept her fighter's stance. She realized Arran was leading the other brother away from her.

"I grow tired of this. Give me the stone!"

Troy raised his hand, fire pooling in his palm as Neko stared. Troy launched the fireball and Neko raised her blade to protect herself, blinking as the fire went streaking past her. She realized why when she found herself separated from Arran by a ten-foot high wall of fire.

"Come here, little Princess."

Troy lunged, his blade ready to sever Neko's arm from her shoulder, but he was stunned as she blocked his blade and with a strength he did not know she possessed. She pushed him back, making him stagger a few feet before he glared at her. As their eyes met, her fear now replaced with a determination he never thought she could be capable of.

"I see that Lanarii filth has been training you," he taunted, trying to get a reaction. All he received was a focused gaze.

Neko allowed him to make the first move. He had used a lot of energy summoning that fire. She wondered if he had discovered the stone drained manna quicker with flashy displays. Troy gave a yell and ran at her, anger flashing in his eyes as she blocked the strike meant to remove her arm. She had to smirk when she blocked him and sent him stumbling backwards a few steps. He had underestimated her. She focused on calling her stone to her aid as they clashed again. Neko could hear Arran and Alexander fighting, but she could not be distracted. She had to believe her brother could handle himself. Troy landed a glancing blow to her ribs. It hurt, but thanks to her armor, he did not draw blood. Neko once again felt that stirring and she willed the power to obey her. Feeling the warming sensation filling her, she shook the ground. Large dirt spears shot up and startled Troy as one nearly impaled him. He stared at Neko. Realization dawning on him that she was a considerably better fighter than he ever expected her to be.

"It looks as if I have underestimated your fighting prowess."

Neko held her blade, ready to attack even though Troy had lowered his weapon.

"Think about it, Neko. You could join us, live like a Queen, have all your heart's desire."

Neko could not believe she had liked this individual at one point. How could she not have seen through his evident façade?

"So, you can kill me the first chance you get? Not happening."

Troy's fake smile fell, replaced with an ugly scowl.

"This could have been easily avoided, believe me. I would have killed you quickly, but for me to keep my powers, you cannot die. Family and friends of yours, however, are expendable pawns."

Neko refused to lose her temper to the likes of the spoiled Prince. She took a deep breath, letting the power of her stone calm her. When she did not react, Troy found himself getting angrier. How had her abilities improved so dramatically in a few short moon cycles?

"You are nothing but a tyrant who uses fear to control people. You are weak minded."

She noticed his face contort as rage clouded his judgment. Just like with Riken, if she could get him off his game she had a chance to defeat him. He laughed as a pained cry caught Neko's attention. She stared towards her brother, dread filling her as Arran faced off against Alexander and the last brother, he was outnumbered, and it didn't look good for him.

"Looks like the tables have turned, Princess."

Troy laughed in her face.

"Capture him," he yelled as he took Neko's moment of distraction and lunged at her. She turned to block his hit, but he managed to cut her forearm, and the impact sent her blade flying across the floor towards the large wooden doors. He smirked, pointing his blade at her as she finally lost her temper and glared at him, her eyes radiating with fury.

"Accept defeat Princess, or do I need to make an example?" he gestured towards Arran as Neko's gaze followed his. Arran sat on the floor panting, blood from his split lip and bleeding nose stained the front of his tunic. Alexander had his blade to the rebel's throat, daring Neko to try something.

"You have lost, although your efforts were valiant."

He walked forward, the tip of his blade resting on her chest, just above her heart.

"Now, give the stone to me before Alexander splits your brother, throat to navel."

Neko looked to Arran. She didn't know what to do. She knew she could not give the last stone to Troy and his brothers, but she could not let them kill her brother either.

"Now Princess!" Troy demanded as Alexander pressed his blade into Arran's neck, drawing a thin line of red across his throat.

"STOP! I'll give it to you. Just let him go—please."

Neko grasped her stone, holding in her hand a moment before ripping it from her neck, her eyes meeting Troy's.

"First, let him go," she tried to bargain. Troy only smirked at her and then nodded to Alexander.

"Release him."

Alexander smirked and backhanded Arran, sending him careening to the cold floor.

"Arran!"

Neko attempted to run to her brother, but Troy caught her by the wrist.

"Give me the stone."

Neko glared at him and then tossed the stone some ten feet away, as Troy raced after it and his brothers rushed Neko. As the four element stones converged, a sudden humming filled Neko's senses, and she glanced around wildly looking for the source of the power. Neko noticed the three brothers were also looking around for the same thing.

"What is that?"

Troy screamed at Neko as the four stones started glowing. Neko and the others watched, awestruck as all four element stones levitated into the air and suddenly went hurtling into one another. Blue, red, yellow and green lights filled the room as a fierce wind tore at Neko's hair and clothing, the others having the same issues. A blinding white light made Neko duck and cover her eyes with her uninjured arm. When the wind suddenly stopped, she chanced a look, staring slack-jawed. Before her up in the air about twenty feet, floated a single stone.

Chapter Twenty-Five

Neko was just as mesmerized as Troy and his brothers as the stone slowly descended, looking like a diamond the size of a golf ball. As the stone stopped at eye level only a foot from her, Neko could see flashes of colors swirling within the stone, as if it were alive.

"Get it."

Troy's voice broke the trance as he lunged. Neko snatched the gem and ran towards the far end of the room. She did not get very far into the next room before Troy grabbed at her and managed to snag her by the back of the belt. She stumbled, and the stone slipped from her grasp, rolling across the dusty floor. Troy made a grab for it, but Neko managed to get a firm grip on his tunic. She used her good arm to reel him back, managing to make him fall onto his rear. Neko grabbed at the stone and lost her footing when Troy seized her by the ankle, crawling over her. Neko screamed in frustration as he sat across her back and grabbed a fist full of her hair, pinning her to the ground as he pried the stone from her hand.

"Did you think you actually stood a chance against me?" he chuckled and pulled back on her hair causing her to wince. Slightly bending, he leaned down and whispered in her ear.

"I will enjoy slowly torturing you and killing your brother with the very stones that you were supposed to guard," Neko growled in anger, hating that he had her pinned down and she was helpless to do anything. He gave her hair a rather hard tug, and she decided to play dirty. With one quick backwards move, the back of her head collided with the side of Troy's face. There was a loud sound of flesh hitting flesh, and Neko found her hair released. She turned onto her back as Troy cupped his cheek while she grabbed at the element stone. Troy pushed her down, wrapping his free hand around her throat. Neko felt her heart quicken as he applied pressure, cutting off most of her air. Neko tried to pry his hand from her throat but his grip was sure, and he was looking down at her, a psychotic grin on his face. Neko tried to grab for anything to aid her, but as black spots danced across her vision, she started to realize she was in serious trouble. Her hand found something hard, and she grabbed it, smashing it into the injured side of Troy's face. He fell like a ton of bricks, his entire weight bearing down on her. Neko gasped for air as she looked to his hand. The stone was gone.

"Neko, get it!" Arran yelled as Neko glanced up, seeing her brother grappling with Traven. Alexander was rushing towards her and Troy. Neko frantically searched the dirty floor, seeing the stone only feet from her. She gave Troy a shove and managed to slide out from under his semi-conscious form. She lunged and grabbed the stone, only to have Troy latch onto her foot, rage in his eyes as Alexander was almost upon her. Neko cursed and grabbed the rock she had used to attack Troy. In a split-second decision, she smashed the rock onto the gem. It made a high-pitched pinging sound before shattering into hundreds of shards.

Neko screamed as a huge pulse of pure energy spread outwards. Pain engulfed her entire chest as she went flying backwards, a blinding white light the last thing she saw before her world went black.

⁂

Riken and half a dozen Lanarii had just landed on the beach and were in the process of unloading their gear when an energy pulse caught their attention. Riken cursed as he glanced around, trying to locate the source of the power. Minutes passed, and nothing stirred. He was about to brush it off and give the order to move out when another, stronger energy pulse hit them. Riken staggered as a bright flash lit the entire hillside. His gut twisted as he raced towards the light knowing something horrible had just happened. They crested a hill and before them lay the ruins of the once proud Dolphinian castle, the area silent and the energy now gone.

"Sir?" Landis asked as Riken motioned for them to approach the main doors cautiously. As he stepped through the open door, he felt his chest constrict. There, only feet from the door, lay the sword he had given Neko. He quickly picked it up and stuffed it into his leather belt, glancing around for any sign of the two Dolphinians.

"Split up. We need to find them," he ordered as he picked his way through the debris.

⁂

Neko's vision fogged as she slowly opened her eyes. She was lying on her back staring up at a ceiling that had bits of sky showing through the porous roof. Neko gingerly tested her limbs, wincing as pain ran down her left hip. She slowly rolled onto her right side and looked down at her hip, groaning as a deep cut oozed blood.

She sat up slowly, noticing the room eerily silent. She felt her heart start as she spotted Troy and his brothers. All three were out cold and looked just as beat up as she felt. To her right, she spotted Arran. Relief flooded her as he groaned and opened his eyes.

Arran, we need to go," Neko whispered as she shuffled over towards her brother, wincing as her side protested the movement.

"You are hurt."

Alarm was evident in his tone as she shook it off.

"Come on. We gotta get out of here like five minutes ago."

A groan from Troy justified her urgency. Neko attempted to stand up, only to have her leg refuse to obey her.

"No!"

Neko glanced over as Troy hovered on his knees above the remains of the element stone, grabbing at the shards as they fell through his hands like sand.

"What have you done?"

Troy turned to look at Neko, his eyes smoldering with barely contained rage. A nasty cut on his left cheek oozed blood down the side of his neck. It was his voice that got to her. It was calm but had an unhinged quality to it that made the hair on the back of her neck stand on end.

"You little idiot, how could you destroy it?" He got to his feet, glaring at Neko his blade in hand, as he approached her and Arran.

"All that power was mine for the taking, but then you had to interfere."

He raised his blade, ready to stab Neko. Neko screamed and attempted to shield herself with her arm as she made an attempt to grasp the dagger handle in her boot. She felt a shadow over her, and she found herself pushed to the ground. Neko opened her eyes. They widened in shock as Arran kneeled above her, his hands splayed out to either side of her head. He gave her a pained grimace as blood dripped onto her stomach. She glanced at his torso, and she felt her fear spike. Through his stomach was a blade, a blade meant for her.

"ARRAN!" she screamed, hysteria taking over as the blade was removed, and Troy kicked Arran to the floor, laughing gleefully.

Neko hovered over him, her hand on the wound, trying to slow the bleeding.

"Oh, my God, Arran, what do I do?"

She was sobbing, tears cascading down her ashen cheeks as Arran coughed, blood trickling out the corners of his mouth. By now, Traven and Alexander had regained consciousness and were flanking Troy as the three looked down on the two siblings.

"Look what you made me do, Neko. Now you will have to watch your brother bleed to death before I end you."

Troy and his brothers chuckled as Neko ignored them and fearfully looked to her brother.

"This is all my fault. Why did you do that?"

"B…because…it was my… choice."

Neko's hand rested on his wound, feeling her entire palm warming. Neko glanced up to Troy who looked down at her with contempt.

"You are just a weak and pathetic little girl."

Neko stared at his blade, the end stained bright crimson as he admired his handiwork.

"Do not be saddened. You will soon be joining him after what you have done," Alexander pointed out as he drew a dagger. Neko blankly stared at them. She had failed, and her brother was about to die for her mistakes.

"Arran, I'm so sorry."

She looked back to her brother, whose eyes were now unfocused, his breathing labored. A deep rumbling made the group look around as the entire area trembled.

"The whole area is unstable," Traven pointed out as Troy glared down at Neko.

"No. I will be the one to end her!"

Alexander gestured towards Neko.

"Then get it done before this place comes down on top of us."

Troy lifted his blade and screamed in pain as an arrow embedded itself in his right shoulder.

"Get your filth away from her."

Troy stared in shock as Riken stood some twenty feet away, his bow taut and another arrow notched.

"The second one shall hit true," he threatened, his amber eyes blazing with animosity. Another tremor had bits of dust and small rocks falling from the roof.

"We need to get out of here!" Traven yelled, the rumbling increasing as five or six more Lanarii appeared, all had bows drawn and aimed at the three brothers.

"Troy, leave her. We need to go."

Alexander grabbed Troy by the tunic, the three running farther into the ruins, searching for another escape route. Riken was at Neko's side in a moment.

"Neko, we must go."

Neko shook him off her arm.

"Not without Arran."

Riken's men were by his side, helping to gather Arran.

"We must go now," Riken urged as he collected Neko's arm around the back of his neck, half dragging her towards the main doors.

There was a rumbling as they made their escape. The building starting to collapse on itself as they rushed to get to the exit.

Troy cursed as they found their way blocked. They had to leave the way they had arrived.

"Come on," Alexander yelled as they backtracked into the room where the Lanarii had been. The room was empty, but the building was coming down. Traven screamed in terror as a large piece of mortar fell beside him, the floor beneath him giving way to a bottomless pit. His screams faded as he disappeared into the inky abyss.

"Move Troy!"

Alexander pulled his brother along, survival overriding bonds of brotherhood as the pair raced for the doors now in sight. Another tremor shook the area, and a huge slab of rock fell before them cutting off their escape. Just like with Traven, the floor buckled and disappeared from under their feet. Troy managed to catch hold of a piece of stable floor, grasping for his brother as their fingers brushed and Alexander slid past, falling to his death.

Neko glanced back as a large piece of ceiling fell, smashing into the palace floor. She heard a terrified scream and stared into the crumbling ruins. Through the open doors, she caught a glimpse of Troy dangling above a large hole. Neko's eyes met Troy's for a brief instant. She saw a wide array of emotions in that moment that spanned from fear to hatred. Seconds later, he lost his grip, and he too vanished into the pit, his scream fading as he descended into shadows.

Neko returned to the crisis at hand.

"Arran!" she gasped as she looked down at her brother. Some of the colour had returned to his face, and he coughed, his eyes wide and alert. Neko looked to Riken.

"You healed him?"

Riken shook his head.

"No Princess. There is no need. He is not wounded."

Neko stared down at Arran, silently asking him if he knew how he had been healed from a mortal wound. He shook his head he was just as confused as she was.

"What the hell?"

Neko kneeled, inspecting Arran's stomach. Dried blood was everywhere, but there was no gaping wound, just a large violet bruise. Neko felt an overwhelming fatigue and wanted nothing but to lay down and sleep where she sat.

"Neko, your side," Arran stated. Neko glanced down. Her cut was still very fresh and stung now that she was able to get her first good look at it.

"That's sick," she groaned turning her head away as Riken raised an eyebrow.

"If you allow it, I can tend to your wounds."

Neko sighed but decided to let him help. They would have plenty of time to discuss their falling out after she wasn't bleeding all over the place.

"Thanks."

"You are most welcome."

"How did you find us?"

Riken helped her get to her feet as he gestured towards the water.

"The ocean water will cleanse your cuts of any infections."

Neko grunted in pain but allowed the Lanarii to lead her towards the water. She refused to let him carry her.

"You never answered my question."

"Remind me again?"

"How did you find us?"

"I have been tailing you since Larrow. Once you two made it to the river mouth, I turned back to get reinforcements."

Riken looked sheepish.

"After the way we parted, I could not bring myself to just let you two leave without some form of protection."

"So, you stalked us all the way here?"

"The night I gave you that sword, I wanted to apologize for my despicable behavior."

Neko laughed.

"But you chickened out?"

"I suppose my nerves got the better of me. I was not prepared for you to be able to summon your powers so readily. I was embarrassed."

Neko tensed and then cursed.

"My sword, it's in the castle."

Her face fell, and Riken couldn't help but chuckle.

"It is only a blade. There are many more."

"But that was my blade, and I really liked it."

"Then it is a good thing I rescued it."

"You have it?"

Neko beamed as Riken gestured to his side.

"It is on my belt as we speak."

Neko sighed in relief and then winced as she twisted wrong, her side aching.

"Come on. Let us get your wound tended to," Neko agreed and slowly followed Riken into the cool water.

The small group of Lanarii made camp at the base of the watchtower, lighting a small campfire to keep Neko warm. Apart from minor cuts and bruises, Arran was fine. Neko however, had a rather large cut on her side and her forearm, and it would take a while for them to heal. Riken took a seat beside her and offered her a piece of dried venison, which she devoured greedily. Arran glared across the fire at the Lanarii King, now that they were out of danger. He was not going to forgive so easily.

"You saved our lives, and we are indebted, but do not think you are forgiven," Arran declared as Riken gave him an even stare.

"I understand. Perhaps we could start anew. I apologize for what I did," Arran scoffed at the Lanarii.

"Stop it. I am sick and tired of fighting, okay?" Neko spat, stopping the ensuing dispute.

"I forgive you Riken. I know you never meant to get so carried away. Besides, we have other things to discuss."

Riken gave her a pointed look.

"Indeed. Shall I start by asking what happened before we arrived?"

Neko sighed and looked to the stars.

"I had no choice after the stones merged—"

"The element stones?"

"Yes. They formed into one single stone."

"How is that possible?"

Neko shared a look with her brother before she answered Riken.

"You got me. All I know is that when Troy came after me, I had no choice but to destroy it or risk him getting it."

Riken stared wide-eyed at Neko.

"That was the energy pulse and light we saw," Landis exclaimed, and Neko nodded.

"Yes. You guys know the rest."

Riken was confused.

"I have never heard of this happening to the element stones."

Neko looked to Arran. He looked just as confused as the Lanarii.

"Anyways, it's gone now and any chance I had at getting back home."

Riken noted the sadness in her voice as she gazed into the crackling fire.

"Not to be rude, but I need to sleep."

Neko's voice hitched as she lay on her uninjured side, her back to the fire. Riken placed her cloak over her and stood up, his eyes catching Arran's in a "we need to talk" expression.

Chapter Twenty-Six

Once Riken and Arran had walked down to the moonlit beach, Riken turned towards the Prince.

"What is going on?"

Arran placed a hand over his bruised torso, shaking his head.

"I am not entirely sure myself. That bastard ran me through. I should be dead, not talking to you."

"What are you saying?"

"I think somehow Neko was able to heal me without the aid of the element stones."

"That seems unlikely. A healer must train many years to even heal minor wounds, let alone a life-threatening one. The amount of manna needed for that would be enormous."

Arran gazed out over the calm sea.

"I thought that too, but when we were safely outside the ruins I was healed and she looked ready to fall asleep standing. There might be a chance she could be gifted in the healing arts."

"I do not know what has happened. The fact that the stones merged is another mystery, I suppose that is a moot point."

"Yes, seeing as it is gone, Neko will never be able to return to her other life."

"It is most unfortunate, but think about if that stone and its powers had fallen into Troy's hands. Neko knew this, and still, she did the right thing, even if it meant she would never return home."

Arran faced the Lanarii King.

"I wish to ask you for a truce, Arran, as your father asked me many moons ago. Together, we can unite our people and repair this land."

Arran felt his previous anger melt. Riken was correct, and holding a grudge would never fix anything.

"All right, I will agree to a truce. It benefits both our peoples and right now we need all the help we can get."

Riken held out his hand, which Arran firmly grasped sealing their deal and renewing the treaty between the Lanarii and Dolphinians.

Neko stirred from her slumber as the smell of cooking food made her stomach demand to be fed. Slowly she sat up, groaning as every muscle in her body felt sore, especially her left side. She chanced a look. The bandages were hardly stained, which she took this as a good sign.

"Good morning."

Neko glanced over at her brother who squatted beside her and handed her a plate full of food.

"You look hungry."

"Starving."

She practically inhaled her food as the rest of the group looked on in mild amusement at her hearty appetite.

"Are you feeling well enough for travel?" Arran asked as Neko gave him a raised eyebrow.

"Travel where?"

"Since we are here, I thought you might want to see the temple."

"Is it the temple they built for the stones?"

"Yes. It is the same one."

Neko glanced over to Riken.

"Will you be joining us? I could go for a small walk to stretch my legs."

Riken offered her a kind smile as she stood up with help from Arran. She left her belongings on her cloak. She wore only her jeans and hoodie she had arrived in Arorus with. It had been simpler to clean her wound without having to pull a skirt up and disturb the tender skin. As a precaution, she made sure her boot dagger was still tucked safely away in her leather boots Arran had given her for their travels. The other Lanarii remained at the tower as the trio made their way across a small open field and towards another stone structure that sat on a raised knoll, reminding Neko of walking across the back of a large saddle. Their trek took longer than expected because Neko had to rest every so often, her energy levels still depleted.

"Perhaps," began Riken," there might be something in the temple that would help you return home without the element stones."

Neko appreciated his kind words, but she knew better than to give in to a false hope.

"I doubt it. I think you're stuck with me, guys. Speaking of which, when we go back I wanted to ask if I could live in Rinnyus for a little bit."

She gave Arran a hopeful look.

"I mean, there is so much for me to learn and I really like it there."

Arran shot Riken a knowing look as he sighed and relented to his sister's wishes.

"If that is what you want then I see no problem. Perhaps it would be a good way to strengthen the truce. What say you, King Riken?"

Riken chuckled.

"I would like nothing better, but please note that all the rebels are welcome in my village."

Arran gave him an appreciative look.

"Thank you, Riken. I will take you up on that offer."

Neko grinned, glad that they had finally gotten over their falling out.

"That's great news. I think in time I will be okay with living here. After all, it is my true home, right?" she sounded like she was trying to convince herself as Riken and Arran shared a look.

"It will take some time Neko, but remember you always have us here to help you."

Arran gave her a quick one-armed hug as they walked, stopping before a large stone archway.

"This way."

Arran took the lead, passing under the archway, Neko and Riken following him in.

Neko gazed in wonder as they entered the grand hall. It reminded her of a cathedral. The roof was completely gone, but the floor showed no sign of debris, so she assumed there had never been a roof to begin with. Shafts of sunlight filtered into the room, causing dust particles to dance across the area. Neko was lost for words as she took in the beautiful scenery. The floor was made of stone that now had grass and small white flowers growing everywhere, only adding to the splendor. Arran grinned at his sister's awe-inspired silence as she wandered farther into the main hall. Near the back of the room was another entranceway.

"Through there is the chamber of the element stones," he informed his companions as Neko walked towards the next room. Riken stopped and stared at the spot where ancient glyphs were inscribed into the wall.

"Arran, what does this say?"

The rebel stepped closer, reading the texts.

"Four stones of light; Earth, Wind, Water and Fire. One stone of Shadow with powers dire."

Riken glanced around, noticing Neko was gone.

"Where has Neko gone?"

"Into the element chamber."

Arran gestured to the adjoining hall as the pair followed Neko.

As Arran and Riken stopped to look at the writing on the wall, Neko ventured into the next room. This room was just as breathtaking as the first. There was a circular hole in the roof maybe ten feet in diameter, letting light pour down upon a raised dais in the center of the room. Upon it sat a large rock slab, set up in a half circle. Across the top of the eight-foot wall were four identical indents where the element stones would have sat. Below this were more glyphs she did not understand. She slowly stepped up to the plaque and ran her hand over the cold rock as she spoke.

"Mom, Dad, I'm sorry you gave your lives to protect the stone that I destroyed, but I had to destroy it. It was the only way I could stop him. Forgive me. I know how important being the guardian of the element stones was to our people."

She knew it was silly to pray to her parents or ancestors, but she felt like she had to do it. Besides, what harm would it do? She was not too proud to speak what was in her heart. She felt awful for her actions but what else could she have done? Her eyes widened as the glyphs under her hand suddenly lit up with a white light. Soon, all the glyphs flared to life, and Neko was surrounded by a warming light. As it spread through her entire body, filling her with a renewed vigor, her vision faded to pure white, as if she were standing in a dense fog. She heard Arran and Riken's faded voices calling to her.

"I'm over here," she stated in a trance-like state.

"Get a load of this glowing stone," she added as she dropped her hand and turned, the odd fog obscuring her vision. She could see nothing else. She thought she should be panicking about it, but she felt safe and was unconcerned that she could not see anything. She felt herself become drowsy and decided she could go for a little nap. Riken and Arran would ensure she was safe. So, she closed her eyes and gave in to the powerful slumber.

Riken and Arran entered the element chamber just as the stone before Neko's hand lit up and a white haze surrounded her. She laughed.

"Get a load of—"

Is all they heard before the white fog wrapped around her, muting the rest of her sentence. Arran and Riken called out her name as they raced to find her, but as the fog dissipated, they saw her fade within it. Neko had vanished. Arran felt a calming sensation, and he just knew that she had returned to her world. Somehow, she had figured out how to get back home. He smiled and spoke.

"Goodbye."

Riken and Arran remained staring at the wall until the glowing glyphs faded and left the rock as it once was. Riken was the first to speak.

"How did she manage that?"

"I assure you, I have not the slightest inkling, but Neko seems to be able to accomplish the impossible."

Riken let out a hearty chuckle.

"You are certainly correct, Arran."

Arran shook his head, a smirk in place.

"Well, I suppose we should be on our way. We have many things needing to be done."

The rebel Prince and the Lanarii King turned, making their way back into the open field.

As Arran and Riken prepared to leave the island, they were unaware of the situation taking place far below the halls of the Dolphinian palace. Amongst the dust and rocks, the falling debris had breached a secret chamber. Three prone bodies lay broken amongst the wreckage. Near one of them a small black stone pulsed to life, glowing a faint violet. The hand beside it twitched ever so slightly, knocking the stone from its perch, causing it to roll down and stop an inch from the finger. Again, the hand twitched, and the stone's eerie light grew brighter. Tendrils of violet vapor swirled around the stone as if searching for something. The tendrils found the hand and slowly wrapped around it as the hand suddenly balled into a fist. The fog rapidly spread from the hand, blanketing the surrounding area in a haze.

"Goodbye."

Neko's eyes flew open, her brother's voice echoing in her head as she stared up at a cloudless blue sky. She could hear birds and realized that she had been moved out into the open field. Bolting up, she looked around.

"Arran, Riken?"

She froze. A familiar white house stood not more than thirty feet away.

Neko felt an intense itching on her inner right arm. She glanced down and gasped as a faint line of glyphs glowed a pale white against her tanned skin. Neko stared in wonder as the words formed before her eyes.

"Guardian," she whispered as the glow faded, replaced by a light gold tattoo. Neko had doubted her entire ordeal until that moment. A huge smile graced her face.

"It was real. That just happened!"

Neko got to her feet, dusting her hands on the sides of her pant legs.

Neko headed towards the front door, stopping halfway to the house. She turned back and gazed up into the azure sky, her grin still plastered on her face.

"Goodbye," she spoke, scarcely above a whisper.

The sound of a vehicle approaching made her turn to the left, spotting the family's black pickup. As the vehicle pulled up to the garage door and turned off, Neko's mother stepped out from the driver's side, giving Neko a screwy look.

"Where have you been?"

Her tone was exasperated as Neko blinked stupidly at her mother who raced towards her daughter, tears streaming down her face.

"Mom?"

Her mother raced forward, joy in hazel eyes as she hugged Neko, her grip rather tight for such a small woman. Neko cringed. She had been in Arorus for almost four months, months away from her home and her parents.

"Well, you know that green stone in your jewelry box?"

Her mother pulled away, her eyes meeting Neko's in a fearful stare.

"What about it?"

Neko felt like a moron trying to explain her bizarre adventure to her mother.

"Well, I kinda sorta saw it glowing, and when I touched it, it took me away."

Her mother gave her an aggravated look.

"Neko, that's not funny."

Neko sighed and hugged her mother, taking in the scent that was only her mother's.

"I'm sorry I was gone so long Mom, that I worried you and Dad."

Neko's mother hugged her daughter closer, vowing never to let her out of her sight again.

"I'm just glad you're back. Come on. We need to have a nice long chat."

Neko sighed and released her mother, wiping the tears that she had spilled. She was happy to finally be back home. As they walked into the house, Neko thought about all the friends she had made. She would never forget them or her enchanting journey to Arorus.

Epilogue

Shadows covered half his face as he smirked and leaned back in his throne, violet tendrils of a smoke-like substance hovered around him as he idly toyed with it in his hand.

"Bring him in," the dark lord growled as a caramel-skinned man was unceremoniously dumped at the feet of the King.

"Ah yes, the Shagonaa. You were given a task, a task that you failed."

Darius glared up at the King, his eyes meeting a cold violet gaze.

"I did all I could. Your brother failed to mention the girl would have an element stone to aid her. Had I known, I could have prepared," Troy scoffed at the other man.

"I have heard enough. You did not complete the task you were paid to do, and you shall rot in my dungeon for your failure."

Troy gestured to his guards.

"Make sure he is shown to the darkest pits of this castle."

Troy chuckled as the prisoner screamed to be released.

"Foolish mortals, soon all will fear me."

Troy's voice took on a sinister baritone as his eyes glowed. Once the rebellion was destroyed, no one would stand in his way of ruling all five provinces of Arorus.

Darius growled in anger and kicked the bars of his cell. He had escaped being tethered to a tree only to get picked up by Troy's men. Truthfully, when he had heard about Alexander's demise, he had thought no one would seek him for failing to retrieve the girl. Darius growled. It was her damn fault he was in this mess.

"Stupid little guardian," he hissed, then started as the shadows in the back of the cell shifted.

"What was that you said, boy?"

The man spoke as he stood up. He was wrapped in a tattered cloak, but there was a fierceness in his grey eyes. They reminded Darius of the Princess who had outsmarted him.

"Nothing. It makes no matter now, seeing as we are down here and she has gone into hiding."

The man gave him a pointed stare.

"So, then the guardian lives?"

Darius gave the man a scrutinizing gaze.

"Just how long have you been down here?"

The man looked frazzled.

"Far too long to count the years, but that is about to change. Tell me, boy, do you wish to get free from this dismal place? If you help me find this guardian, then I will help you escape. What say you?"

Darius gave the man a calculating stare.

"Why is this guardian so important for you to find?"

The man chuckled as his eyes lit up.

"Because it means my daughter is still alive and I must find her."

Darius's eyebrows raised at hearing this interesting new tidbit.

"You are King Trydus, but rumor has it you were killed many years ago."

The late King narrowed his eyes at the mercenary.

"Doubt who I am or not. What say you? Will you help me find the guardian?"

Darius inclined his head.

"If you can get me out of this dungeon, then I will help you. We have a deal. Your kingship."

Darius held out his hand. He was not expecting the firm handshake. The King oozed charisma. This was one person Darius did not want to cross but would make an excellent ally for the days to come. The King smirked and released Darius's hand.

"Good. Let us begin."

About the Author

K.M. Lapointe makes her debut with Awakening Arorus, the first in the series, The Clan Destayy chronicles. K.M. is a stay-at-home mom living with her husband, daughter and menagerie of animals in a small town nestled in the Okanagan Valley, in British Columbia, Canada. When not immersed in writing magical adventures, K.M. enjoys the at home scene, whether it's cooking up delicious Keto meals for her family or slaying dragons as the Dragonborn. She likes taking scenic photos, wherever she is, you can bet a camera is not far behind. She can also be found living it up in the wilds of Sugar Lake where she and her family go camping, hiking, biking and paddle boarding during the summer months. To learn more about K.M. find her on Facebook under K.M. Lapointe or visit her web page www.clandestayy.com